I0552018

COTABATO GIRL
Filipina Lisa's Story

J.S. RAYNOR

Beaten Track
www.beatentrackpublishing.com

Cotabato Girl: Filipina Lisa's Story

Published 2022 by Beaten Track Publishing
Previous edition published 2005 as *A Comfortable Death*
Copyright © 2022 J. S. Raynor

Paperback ISBN: 978 1 78645 568 0
eBook ISBN: 978 1 78645 569 7

Cover design: Debbie McGowan

Beaten Track Publishing,
Burscough, Lancashire.
www.beatentrackpublishing.com

Dedication

This book is dedicated to my wife, Aleth, as this story could not have been written without her assistance. She grew up under very difficult circumstances in the Philippines and has provided much of the factual information on which to base this story. We married in 1993, and the difficulties we encountered in getting her into Britain are described in a separate autobiographical work, titled *Who wants to be British?*

Aleth is a wonderful wife and a dedicated mother to our children, James and Kimberley, and I am eternally grateful for the circumstances which brought us together.

Glossary of Filipino Words

It is not essential to remember these Filipino words to follow the story, yet it may be of interest to the reader to know a few words of this unusual language.

Nanay: mother

Tatay: father

Lola: grandmother

Lolo: grandfather

Inunlan: placenta

Pusod: umbilical cord

Otin: penis

Regla: period of menstrual bleeding

Prologue
The Birth of an Asian

LISA WAS A surprisingly tiny baby, weighing just four and a half pounds at birth. She was more fragile than any of her five sisters or two brothers. Her large, innocent, black eyes, black silky hair and delicate, angelic features emphasised her natural beauty, attracting many favourable comments from friends, relatives and even neighbours.

When her aunt Floriza saw Lisa for the first time, she said to her younger sister, "Dolly, that child will cause you more anguish than all your other children put together."

"What a terrible thing to say about such a tiny, innocent child, Flor. Why do you say such hurtful things?"

The older woman frowned as if trying to choose her words carefully.

"It is in her destiny. I can see many troubles surrounding her. You'll lose everything you have—land and possessions—all as a result of her actions before she reaches the age of twenty."

Floriza had always claimed to have clairvoyant powers, but Dolores did not believe that anyone could see what the future held.

"You know I don't believe in such things, Flor. Only God knows what our future destiny will be."

Floriza was a large woman and, in a gesture of indignation, raised her considerable bosom in an effort to enhance her air of authority, ready to lecture her younger sister.

"It matters not whether you believe what I've told you. I tell you now, she will be trouble. So much so that, in time, you will regret having given her life."

1

Dolores was deeply hurt by her sister's insensitive comments and felt tears starting to form. "I don't want to listen to any more of this. I've got work to do."

Ignoring her sister's plea, Dolores continued, "Just look at the day she was born, Dolly. The thirtieth of December 1965. The very same day that Ferdinand Edralin Marcos became president of the Philippines. Now there is a man who I do not trust at all. He puts on a face of caring, but it is a false one. He cares for nobody but himself. He even spent time in prison after killing Nalundasan, his father's opponent, in the presidential election of 1935. He managed to get an acquittal four years later, only with the help of his father and the corrupt Judge Chua. It was only through force, bribery and corruption that he ever managed to become president of the Philippines."

Dolores became visibly agitated by these dangerous, insensitive words, however true they may be. "You'll get us all in trouble if anyone hears you saying such things. Now, please, Flor, I don't want to hear any more."

With that, she picked up a large bundle of wet clothes and disappeared outside to hang them, hoping that her crying had not been noticed. The laundry would all be dry in a few hours thanks to the intense power of the sun. It was a relief to escape from those hurtful, caustic comments.

It did worry her that Floriza was, usually, correct with all her prophecies, and her predictions about Lisa were upsetting. Dolores did not want her sister to see the many tears running down her cheeks. She loved the tiny, frail Lisa as much, if not more, than her other children, yet she feared that the worrying predictions may, one day, come true. Whatever happened, she could never regret giving life to Lisa, her youngest daughter.

Chapter One
Another Mouth to Feed,
Another Child with Needs

DOLORES TIGUELO HAD not expected to give birth for a few more weeks, but now the infant lay in her cradling arms, only minutes into her new life. Thin and fragile legs kicked the air, free at last from the confines of the womb. Big, beautiful, but as yet uncoordinated eyes looked, as though in wonderment, at the strange sights surrounding the wriggling bundle. The short, staccato cries of a newly born baby were a familiar sound to Dolores, as it was her eighth delivery.

This had been the easiest pregnancy yet, without any sickness or much fatigue. Dolores had continued working as normal, still hand-washing heavy loads of clothes hours before her labour started. It had taken only two and a half hours from the first contraction to the emergence of a new life in the family.

Nelia, the closest midwife in the town of Marbel in the Philippine province of Cotabato, was due to help, yet the baby chose not to wait for her. There were no telephones in this poor remote community, which meant that Pedro, Dolores' husband, would have no choice but to run the mile and a half to get Nelia's assistance.

It was nearly midnight when Dolores, realising the baby was on its way, had pleaded with Pedro to seek the midwife's help. Grumbling, he had started his journey down the narrow, twisting dirt paths through the forest and was soon exhausted from the sweltering heat and the effort of running. It was frustratingly difficult for him as he picked his way through the coconut trees, heavy rain turning the uneven ground into a quagmire and slowing his progress. He reached a clearing where the rain pounded noisily on the roofs of the few timber-built houses in the area.

Finding the right house, Pedro hammered frantically on Nelia's door and was relieved when the midwife appeared. If she had been attending another delivery, there would have been nobody else to help his wife.

"Nelia, please come quickly." Pedro had to pause for breath. "It's Dolores. She's in labour."

"I didn't think she was due yet, Pedro." The woman knew him, as she knew most people in the village, having delivered all his other children.

"Dolores was surprised herself, but she is certain the baby will soon be born."

Nelia peered through the dismal darkness of the wet night. It was December, and the rainy season was living up to its name. "It is very late. I'm certain she will be all right without me."

"But what if something goes wrong?" Pedro asked, remembering the difficulties Dolores had encountered during the birth of their twins only three years earlier.

"I've no transport, and the ground is very bad," Nelia said, searching for an excuse to return to her bed.

Pedro became even more agitated, fearing the worst. Rain dripped from his matted, thick, black hair and trickled lazily down the crinkles in his cheeks. He had been quite good-looking in his youth, but years of neglect and tobacco addiction had taken their toll. Prolonged exposure to the damaging rays of the sun had further roughened his skin, made to look even worse by several days of beard growth.

"Listen, Nelia, if it will make any difference, I'll try and borrow a caribou and trailer to get you there. Please help Dolores."

Seeing the anxiety in his face, she relented. "Okay, Pedro. You don't need to get the caribou. We'll walk. Just let me get my umbrella and bag, and then we'll go."

He breathed a heavy sigh of relief. "Thank you so much, Nelia. Thank you."

Nelia was a big woman and puffed noisily as she tried to keep up with the slimmer, younger Pedro. "Now, don't you run out of my sight, Pedro. I'm not as fit as you, and it is not safe for a woman to be on her own, at this time of night."

"Sorry, Nelia. I wasn't thinking." Pedro skilfully picked his way back along the muddy path, trying to avoid deep troughs of water and looking out for poisonous snakes. A momentary lapse in concentration could prove fatal in this area. The rain was easing, yet large drops of water fell steadily from the canopy, and they were accompanied by the incessant, rhythmic click of crickets from the depths of the jungle.

When Pedro reached his Nipa hut, he rushed into the room where Dolores lay with his new child.

"We have another daughter, Pedro." Dolores lifted the sleeping baby to show her exhausted husband.

He smiled and tried to catch his breath. "Are you okay, Dolly?"

"Yes, I'm fine. That was the easiest, shortest labour of any of the children." Dolores smiled and looked down at the infant with pride. Even though they already had two sons and five daughters, she would love them all the same. She was a woman of inner calmness, not beautiful yet attractive through her character. Years of poverty and hard work had made the twenty-nine-year-old woman look several years older, and her once-long hair had been cut shorter for the sake of practicality, yet she was still thankful to God for giving her a family to be proud of.

Dolores assured both Pedro and the midwife that she was comfortable. Nelia checked delivery of the afterbirth, then took hold of the baby and attended to the umbilical cord. The infant cried loudly at this most intimate intrusion.

When Nelia was satisfied that everything was in order, she offered the tiny wriggling bundle to Pedro. He cautiously took hold of his daughter as if she was a delicate piece of China and made gentle noises to soothe the disturbed child.

"I'll be going now, Pedro. That will be fifty pesos, please."

Pedro was a poor man, and since the baby had come early, he had not had time to save enough money but managed to gather fifty pesos together with a mixture of notes and coins. Nelia knew it was probably all they had but did not offer to reduce the burden. She, like everybody else in the Philippines, had difficulty making ends meet. Stuffing the money into her pocket, she said her farewells and disappeared into the wet night.

Pedro changed into dry clothes, wrapped himself in his blanket and settled down to sleep. Beds for their family were mats comprised of hundreds of small, interwoven leaves, laid out on the rough, wooden floor for comfort and to reduce the draughts from below. Since all the family slept, fully dressed, in the one room—mother, father, seven children and the new baby—none of them had much rest that night.

The Tiguelo family home was one of around fifteen or so small timber shed-like buildings called Nipa huts. These primitive dwellings huddled together in a narrow clearing in the thick forest vegetation. Some of the more fortunate families had electricity, but Pedro, with his large family and small income, could only afford bottled gas canisters for lighting.

The hut had a food preparation area using sticks of wood within a rough stone shell for cooking. When the burning wood was wet from the heavy rain, clouds of choking, acrid smoke would fill the tiny house, permeating everyone's hair and clothes. There was just one other room, which Pedro had furnished with rudimentary benches made from thin tree trunks. This was their living room, where the family had all their meals, sitting at a simple table.

Next morning, Pedro dug a small hole in the ground close to the wall outside his home, into which he placed a small parcel containing the placenta before he brushed the soil back over the top. This was following an ancient superstition that was supposed to ensure good luck for the family. He performed his ritual without ceremony, although it was against the doctrine of the Catholic Church, to which Pedro, his family and most people in the Philippines belonged. Early pagan superstitions and Christianity lived, uncomfortably, side by side.

Dolores was feeding the baby when Pedro walked back into the house. "I've buried the *inunlan*, Dolly. When the baby's *pusod* falls off, I'll put it in the roof." Another superstition was to wrap the umbilical cord in a triangular piece of material and place it in the spaces between the timbers of the roof. There were already seven little packages in the roof of the Tiguelos' shanty residence.

Pedro was a farmer with several pigs, goats and numerous chickens on the small plot of land adjacent to their house. The year had been difficult, with very little earned from selling the livestock he had reared. He could only afford to send his two boys, Antonio aged ten and Enrico, nine, to school, while the older girls helped their mother care for the smaller children and assisted Pedro with the animals.

Chapter Two

APART FROM BEING very small, Lisa was not much of a problem to them. She slept soundly at night and only cried during the day when hungry for her mother's milk. The whole family accepted Lisa and showed special care for the new infant.

Dolores was a devout Catholic and insisted that the whole family attend Mass regularly at their local church. She was looking forward to the baptism, yet it took six months before Pedro could raise enough money for this essential celebration.

The small, always overcrowded, neighbourhood church was a basic, timber building and did not have the facilities for a full baptism, making it necessary for family and relatives to travel to another church three miles away in an outlying area of Marbel.

Dolores' mother, Gloria, made the journey from her home in Balamban, a tiny province of Cebu city, to be at the baptism. It took her twenty-four hours by ferry and a rough journey by bus, yet Gloria insisted that she would attend as it would be her first chance to see her new grandchild.

A small fleet of tricycle taxis carried the family members, including Lisa's brothers, sisters and Pedro's father, Allan, to the ancient church.

Dolores was closer to Floriza than either of her other sisters, Rita and Lucia, even though she did not like her premonitions. Floriza was pleased that Dolores had asked her and her husband, Alfredo, to be godparents: despite her feelings of future trouble for Lisa, she had a great affection for her new niece. Floriza's

8

voice was as big as her bulk, and she spoke with a much deeper, slightly more nasal tone than Dolores.

With difficulty, she squeezed herself into the limited space of the tricycle taxi, leaving little room for her much slimmer husband. The Philippine tricycle is a bicycle with a lightweight, metal sidecar attached to the frame and was the cheapest form of transport in the country.

The driver watched on anxiously and was relieved when Floriza and her husband managed to take their places without upsetting the balance of the vehicle. It took considerable effort to get the pedals moving, but once he had built up momentum, he rode with relative ease along the fairly level road to the church.

Floriza sat proudly, like a queen surveying her loyal subjects from beneath the brightly coloured canopy that provided some shelter from the blistering midday sun. By the time they had reached their destination, the driver had earned every one of his twenty pesos.

The group entered the impressive, ancient stone-built church and made their way to an ante-room, where an elderly nun greeted them. Her duty was to hold a short seminar for the parents and godparents, instructing them in their obligations to the child. Then the family joined other worshippers for Mass, after which Dolores, Pedro, Lisa and the godparents went to the front of the church for the baptism.

Lisa did not think much of having water and oil sprinkled on her head and expressed her feelings loudly. Floriza was holding the infant and, with her broad, rough hands, caressed Lisa's head in an effort to calm her. It took only a few minutes for the ritual to be performed, yet it held great significance for the parents. Floriza brought some candles, which she lit to celebrate the baptism before saying a quiet prayer for Lisa.

The journey back was, again, by tricycle taxi, and Floriza's driver, unsurprisingly, was nowhere to be seen. Her husband, Alfredo, in his usual quiet way, organised alternative transport back for him and his sizeable wife.

It did not take long for the collection of vehicles to return home where everyone was greeted by the mouth-watering smell of roasted pig. Jasmine, Pedro's cousin, had helped prepare for the celebrations and was slowly turning the bamboo spit over a charcoal fire. At first light that morning, Pedro had killed and halved a three-month-old pig from head to foot with his machete. Pedro and Jasmine had filled the stomach with onions and spices before stitching the two halves together again, with the spit in place. The slow-spit-roast method of cooking the pig produced tender, succulent meat, which everyone enjoyed. Lisa's baptism was a fine excuse for a feast, and before long, many relatives and friends had arrived for the celebrations.

Dolores' three older girls handed portions of hot pig and boiled rice to each guest. There was just enough crisp, dark brown crackling to go round. The women chatted together while the men sat in a separate group, smoking and drinking tuba in great quantities. Tuba, the strong local wine, was made from the fermented juice from young buds of the fruit of coconut trees.

Allan, Pedro's father, showed a special interest in the newly baptised infant. For some reason, he felt a closer affinity with his new granddaughter than with any of the others. Allan was an energetic fifty-two-year-old and a widower who owned a mango plantation about three miles from Pedro's house. A very dignified man, renowned for his politeness, he was admired by many of the women, who tried their best to become close, some even proposing marriage, yet he remained faithful to his dead wife.

"May I hold her for a few minutes, Dolly?"

"Of course, you can, Tatay."

Dolores lifted the baby and carefully placed her into Allan's welcoming arms.

He sat down and gently rocked backwards and forwards, caressing Lisa's head with his long, slender fingers. To Dolores' surprise, the often-restless Lisa appeared comfortable in his care and made happy, satisfied noises. Her big, innocent eyes looked into Allan's, and she seemed to listen intently to his every word.

"Now you just have a good sleep, my beauty. My, you are tiny, aren't you? I don't think I have ever seen such a tiny baby, but God sometimes puts the best gifts into the smallest parcels. I know there is something very special about you, and I am certain we will have some good times together over the coming years."

Dolores smiled as she listened to her father-in-law's lengthy conversation with the unusually quiet and content child. He kept hold of her until it was time for her feed and then, gently, handed her back to Dolores.

"I'll be going home now, Dolly."

"So soon? Are you not going to stay a while longer? You know you are always welcome here for as long as you want."

As he stood and faced Dolores, she noticed a slight moistening of his eyes. She could not remember seeing him openly show his emotions before and wondered why. This change worried her.

"Are you okay, Tatay?"

"Yes. Yes, I'm fine, Dolly. Just feeling a little tired. I'll be off home, now, if you will excuse me."

"Of course. Thanks so much for coming today. Take care, please."

She gave him a reassuring hug and watched as Allan's tall, slender frame disappeared into the jungle. She sensed sadness in his demeanour, which puzzled her, since he always smiled and joked with everyone. Perhaps the family gathering had reminded

11

him how much he missed his wife. Pedro had only vague memories of his mother, so Dolly decided not to say anything to him about his father's apparent sadness.

After Allan departed, Dolores' mother, Gloria, held the sleeping infant for a long time, her expression showing great satisfaction with her new granddaughter. Lisa was the picture of innocence in her long, flowing white baptism gown. Everyone who saw her admired her delicate features and agreed that she would be a beauty as she matured.

Dolores had inherited her looks and calm nature from her mother. Gloria, at fifty-one, was a strong, yet slimly built woman with a strength and determination characteristic of so many women in the Philippines. She had been a widow for the past six years, after her husband died in a fishing accident, yet she had insisted on staying in Cebu, even though Dolores and Floriza had wanted her to move to Marbel to be closer to them. All four of Gloria's daughters had a happy but strongly religious upbringing, where discipline had always played an important role within the family.

Gloria had intended to stay at Floriza's house, which had more space than at Dolores', for at least two weeks, as she rarely travelled the long way from her home in the southern region of the Philippines. Although Gloria and Dolores had always kept in touch by letter, they had much to talk about. Both knew it would be a few years before they were able to see each other again and made the most of this time together.

The older children amused themselves, playing party games, yet remained close by, allowing Dolores to keep a watchful eye on them all. Meanwhile, Lisa slept soundly through the noisy celebrations, occasionally accompanied by the usual crowing of cockerels, which went on well into the night.

Chapter Three

BY THE AGE of three, Lisa's true beauty was even more apparent. Her thick, black, silky hair was now shoulder length, framing her beautiful, delicate face, and her smile was guaranteed to melt the hardest of hearts. Not really a shy girl, she always seemed to have something to say for herself.

Lisa was very attached to her mother, following her everywhere, much to the annoyance of her elder siblings. In truth, all the children loved Lisa, yet petty jealousies were forming even at this early stage, their impression being that Lisa managed to get more attention from their parents than the rest of them.

Breeza, who was nearly five, felt the jealousy most and on many occasions showed open hostility towards her younger sister. She was careful not to let her parents or older siblings see her punishing the three-year-old. She would pinch Lisa's arms or legs until tears started to flow and would then deny any responsibility when questioned by her suspicious parents.

One day, as Breeza pinched Lisa's legs, their mother entered the room, heard Lisa's squeal of pain and saw what her older daughter had done. Breeza laughed at her younger sister's anguish, unaware that her mother was right behind her. Dolores bent down and pinched Breeza's leg, making the young girl howl in pain.

"Just how do you like it, Breeza? I knew you were telling lies when you denied hurting Lisa! Now I've caught you in the act. No more! Do you hear me? No more!"

Tears running down her flushed face, Breeza replied, "Yes. I'm sorry, Nanay! I won't do it again!" before running swiftly out of the room.

Around this time, Pedro had four pigs, earning a living from buying them cheap as piglets, and after fattening them, he would sell them at a good profit. He also had, in the past, a few goats, but had never made much money from them so had sold them without buying any replacements. The pigs were in a fenced-off area behind the house, their smell a constant reminder of their proximity. One morning, Pedro was outside the house, calling for Dolores to join him urgently.

Hearing the anxiety in his voice, she ran out. "What's wrong, Pedro?"

"Look!" He pointed at the pig pen.

At first, Dolores was uncertain about her husband's request, but when she looked into the pen, she gasped. "Where are the other two pigs?"

"I wish I knew. There were four pigs last night. Someone has taken them out of the pen while we were asleep!"

"But who would do such an awful thing?" Dolores was as stunned as her husband.

"It's obvious. The pigs were almost fully grown and ready for selling, so some thief must have decided it was the right time to steal my best pigs! Whoever did this left the two smaller pigs that are not yet ready for the market!"

"Oh, no!" Dolores cried in dismay, already calculating in her mind the sacrifices they would have to make. This theft would have a significant effect on the family expenses.

At that moment, Lisa ran out of the house, following her mother. She stared at the two remaining pigs. "Where are the other, fatter pigs, Tatay?"

"A bad man has taken them away while we were sleeping, Lisa. A very bad man! Now I will have to buy two more piglets to fatten. We must all keep watch to stop any more pigs being stolen."

This was Lisa's first lesson in the basic dishonesty of man, perhaps even neighbours, and would certainly not be the last.

Chapter Four

THE UNIQUE BOND between Lisa and her grandfather remained with her for all of her life. Allan visited whenever he could, and as Lisa grew older, her favourite treat was to visit him at his mango plantation. Shortly after her fifth birthday, she visited Allan, and it was to be a very special occasion. For the first time she would be allowed to stay overnight at her grandfather's house.

When Allan called to collect Lisa, she ran excitedly towards him. Typical of her Christian upbringing and a mark of respect for her elders, Lisa took her grandfather's right hand and touched it to her forehead, eliciting from him a fond smile. "Lolo! I'm ready. Shall we go now?"

The old man laughed. "Soon, Lisa, soon. Give me chance to say hello to the rest of your family. It wouldn't be very nice if we left without greeting them, would it?"

Dolores came out of the house and gave Allan a welcoming hug. He always insisted on greeting all of the children and brought each one a small present. Allan was very much aware that he paid far more attention to Lisa than any of her brothers or sisters. There was some rivalry between them, but Allan's gifts of colouring books and crayons helped to placate them.

Dolores looked down at Lisa. The little girl waited with an obvious sense of great importance and urgency, clutching a bag containing a few of her possessions and a change of clothing. Dolores bent down and kissed her daughter.

"Now, Lisa, be a good girl for Lolo, won't you?"

"Oh, yes, Nanay. I promise to be very good. Lolo will send me back if I don't behave."

"Please take good care of her, Tatay."

Allan embraced his daughter-in-law warmly. "Don't worry, Dolly. I shall take the greatest of care with my youngest grandchild."

"And don't be too soft with her. You always spoil the child." She smiled and gave him a wink as she continued, "Make her work hard, won't you?"

Smiling, he said, "Oh, yes. She'll be kept very busy while she's staying with me. Right, little one, let's be going. Do you want me to carry you on my shoulders?"

Boldly, Lisa replied, "No, thank you, Lolo. I am five now and can walk many miles without needing to be carried. Bye-bye, Nanay."

She skipped and danced along as they began their journey. Dolores watched and gave an occasional wave as her daughter gradually disappeared through the trees and into the distance.

***

Allan's plantation was about three miles away, and he was not surprised when Lisa's initial burst of energy petered out and her feet fell heavier. It was hot, even though there were still three hours before the midday sun.

Lisa kept going as long as she could but eventually had to admit defeat. "Do you think I could ride on your shoulders now, Lolo?"

He smiled at her admission. "Of course, Lisa. You've already walked about two miles, which is a long way for such a little girl."

He bent down, placed his hands under her arms and lifted her high. She giggled happily as he tickled her. Lisa liked to ride on his shoulders, as she could see more from such a height.

After a short distance, Allan felt her playing with his hair. "What are you doing, child?"

"It's all right, Lolo. I'm just trying to cover your bald patch with the little hair you have left." She giggled again, knowing that her grandfather did not like to be reminded that he was losing his hair.

Allan laughed at her innocent reply. "Lolo is growing old, Lisa. That's why my hair is getting so thin. A few more years and it will all have gone."

Allan was forced to stop several times during their journey to let his many friends and relatives see Lisa. They all remarked on what a beautiful girl she was. The smooth curves of her soft cheeks, her large, innocent eyes and her long, silky, black hair were so perfect that she almost seemed unreal, like a perfectly sculpted statue.

At last, they reached Allan's house. It was a large timber building with several rooms and had the luxury of electricity. In comparison to Lisa's ramshackle hut, it was an extremely comfortable home. Once inside, they had a cool, refreshing drink of mango juice. Lisa was longing for him to show her around the large plantation. The heavy, sweet smell of mangoes ripening on the trees was enough to make Lisa's mouth water, eager to devour the delicious fruit.

Allan had three workers helping him. The two women, Melissa and Ivy, were high in the trees picking fruit, while Ricky moved heavy cartons of mangoes, preparing them for later collection by market traders.

Lisa wanted to climb the ladders to pick fruit like the others yet knew she would not be allowed, as it would be far too dangerous. Instead, the women showed her how to inspect the fruit for quality and ripeness then wrap each mango in paper to protect the skin and finish the ripening process.

It was almost midday, and the sun's fierce rays could turn a Filipino's usually pale skin black. Aware of this danger, everyone on the plantation kept in the shade of the trees or the house whenever they could.

Allan had a maid, Marlyn, who cleaned the house and prepared all the meals. Now thirty years old, she had worked for Allan since the age of sixteen. When the smell of freshly boiled rice wafted through the window openings, Lisa began to feel quite hungry. Although she was slim and petite, she had a very healthy appetite and always looked forward to meals. Today, the exertion of her long walk and running through the trees had made her hungrier still.

When Marlyn called that lunch was ready, Lisa ran to the house, keen to satisfy her appetite. The table was on a small terrace at the side of the house. It was a cool, sheltered area covered by the roof and open at the sides to allow the flow of the gentle breeze.

Everybody took their place at the table, and after Allan had said a short grace, they all ate heartily.

Lisa enjoyed the small pieces of fried pork with boiled rice and a glass of cool fruit juice. It was especially enjoyable for her, as she felt she was being treated as a grown-up, eating with everyone else. Best of all, she did not have to compete for attention with her older brothers and sisters. She chatted happily with everyone and made them laugh with her innocent, naive responses to their questions. A transistor radio played music quietly in the background; nobody paid much attention to it.

"What shall we do this afternoon, Lolo?" Lisa, her stomach now full, was excited to continue with her day.

"First of all, we shall have a short rest. It's too hot to go far just now, but later, we shall sell some fruit to the traders, and then we'll visit a friend of mine who has a pineapple plantation."

Although the heat, humidity and her exertions had made her quite tired, Lisa had difficulty sleeping, as they wrapped themselves in blankets on the floor. Allan, who did not have such problems, was almost asleep when Lisa asked yet another question.

"Lolo, how far away is the pineapple plantation?"

"Not very far. Just about ten minutes' walk."

"Why don't you grow pineapples as well as mangoes?"

"Because I don't have enough money to own enough land to grow both fruits. And mango is definitely my favourite fruit."

"Yes, it is mine too."

Allan's eyes closed again, yet the inquisitive child still continued.

"Do you have a friend with a papaya plantation?"

"Yes, I do, but that is a bit too far for us to walk today. So many questions, child. Why don't you try and get to sleep?"

"Sorry, Lolo. I'm trying."

Allan smiled as he lay waiting for the next question. It did not take very long.

"Lolo, do you have many friends?"

His eyes closing, he sleepily replied, "I seem to have."

"More than a hundred?" she persisted.

"I do know many people, but it is sometimes difficult to know if a person is really a genuine friend or not." This answer seemed to give Lisa something to think about, giving Allan a chance to fall into a light sleep.

They rested for about an hour, Lisa eventually falling asleep for long enough to regain her usual energy. It was time for the traders to start calling. Ricky had stacked many cartons of mangoes, ready for display. Lisa watched with fascination and curiosity as the buyers started arriving. Her grandfather had a reputation for quality and fairness, which always ensured steady business. There was never much bargaining, as the traders knew if they did not buy the fruit, others would still pay his prices. Allan had plenty of fruit juice for refreshment, which made the traders feel welcome and trusting. An occasional inspection of the mangoes was sufficient to satisfy the traders, and soon all the cartons had been sold.

When everyone had gone, Allan and Lisa counted their takings. It was more money than the little girl had ever seen before, and she carefully piled all the notes of the same denomination into neat bundles. "What do you do with all your money, Lolo?"

He laughed. "Don't think all that money is for me. It helps to pay the wages for Ricky, Melissa, Ivy and Marlyn. Then I have to buy food and clothes. And pay taxes to the government. It does not leave much when all the bills have been paid."

Lisa looked quite downcast and disappointed by this answer. The reality of finance had spoiled her simple, idealistic impressions. Seeing this, Allan added, "Don't worry, Lisa. I have everything I need. And I manage to save some to last, if times should become difficult. The most important thing you must remember is that money can't buy you happiness. It just helps to make life a little bit more comfortable."

He gathered all the notes together, leaving just two ten-peso notes on the table.

Spotting these, Lisa said, "You've missed some, Lolo."

"Have I?" He pretended he could not see the two notes. "I don't think so."

"There, Lolo, there!" The little girl pointed at the money, not understanding her grandfather's ploy.

Again, he pretended not to see them.

"No, there's definitely no more of *my* money on the table. If there is any there, it must have come out of your pocket. So you had better put it away before it gets lost."

Lisa's face lit up as she finally understood the game he had been playing. She picked up the two notes, folded them neatly and tucked them into the pocket of her dress.

"Oh, thank you, Lolo. You are really so nice and very kind." Allan chuckled as she gave him a hug and a kiss.

"Right, now, little one, come on. Let's go and see my friend, Francisco."

The two set out on the walk to the neighbouring pineapple plantation, Allan carrying a bag of mangoes. It only took them around ten minutes for the walk, and as they arrived, Francisco, a short, well-built man about the same age as Allan, greeted them with a cheery wave.

He had been harvesting pineapples yet hurried across the huge plantation to where Allan and Lisa were standing. He took hold of Allan's hand and shook it vigorously as though they had not seen each other for many years.

"So this is the granddaughter you have been telling me all about. Now, let me see—it's Lisa, isn't it?"

She nodded. Her soft, tiny hand seemed to disappear within the big, calloused hand of Francisco as he welcomed her. Although she had never met him before, she took an instant liking to him. He did seem to be a very jovial, friendly character. It gave her a shock when she noticed that the little finger on Francisco's left hand was missing.

Brazenly, she asked, "What happened to your finger, Francisco?"

The two men laughed at her question.

"I was cutting some old branches off trees on the plantation. My hands are so old and gnarled that I mistook it for part of the branch. The machete cut clean through finger and branch alike."

The little girl stared incredulously at the mutilated hand. "Really?" The smile on Francisco's face made her wonder if he was joking.

"It is true, Lisa," her grandfather confirmed. "Francisco is a man who has many accidents. Almost every week, something else happens, but he just smiles and carries on with his life." Allan handed the bag of mangoes to his friend. "Here's something to keep you refreshed, Francisco."

"Thank you so much, Allan. Let's sit on the veranda and eat a little pineapple, shall we?" As they walked to the house, two teenage girls, busy cutting pineapples from the low-lying plants, waved and smiled at Lisa. She returned their smile and gave a little wave. The atmosphere seemed so pleasant and friendly that Lisa felt comfortable and very happy.

Once they were seated in the shade, Francisco went inside the house, soon to return with a large plate piled with slices of pineapple. Lisa ate the beautiful, sweet fruit. It was impossible to stop the abundant juice from dripping, but Lisa was careful not to spoil her bright-orange dress. The three chatted for a while. Francisco told Lisa a few stories of some of the many accidents he had suffered. On more than one occasion, he had fallen off a ladder while carrying out maintenance on his house. Lisa laughed when he told of a time, many years earlier, when he had been working on a different plantation and was knocked almost unconscious when a large coconut fell straight out of a tree, hitting him squarely on the head.

The time passed quickly, and before long the sky began to darken as dusk approached.

"Come on, Lisa. It's time for us to return home. Thank you, Francisco. We've enjoyed our little visit, haven't we, Lisa?"

Lisa gave a beautiful, heart-warming smile. "Oh, yes. I like you, Francisco. You are so funny.

The honesty and innocence of the little girl's remark made the two men laugh again. "If I can bring a smile to your face, then I am happy. You are very welcome to come again, Lisa. Any time you wish."

Francisco had a bag of pineapples ready for them as they prepared to leave. Little of significance happened from day to day, so people in the neighbourhood knew of Lisa's visit and almost everyone was pleased to see the little girl. In a land where most families were large, the Filipinos loved young children.

Yet there were two individuals who were not as pleased as the rest. Alberto and Dominic, two workers recently sacked by Allan, lurked in the undergrowth by the path. Their watchful gaze followed the happy youngster skipping and dancing around her grandfather as the pair made their way slowly along the dusty track.

"Not yet, Alberto. We must wait until the time is right."

Allan and Lisa arrived back home to be greeted by the delicious smell of cooking. Marlyn had been preparing a dinner of chicken and rice. The chicken portions were covered in flour and fried in oil, making the skin crisp and tasty. This was a favourite of Lisa's, and she hungrily devoured everything except the main bones. She chewed the smaller bones in the wings and breast along with the meat, leaving very little on her plate. All Allan's helpers lived at his house since they were unmarried and would have had to travel too far each day to their family homes.

With six people eating and talking happily, the atmosphere was quite festive, and everyone was determined that Lisa's visit should be an event to remember. But sadly, it would not be remembered for the happy meal times.

After supper, Allan, his workers and special guest talked together for a while. Ricky played his guitar and sang ballads. Everything seemed perfect to Lisa. With a satisfied stomach,

Ricky's gentle serenade, the bright full moon lighting the darkened room, Lisa's eyes were feeling quite heavy, yet still she chatted and asked many more probing questions.

As she was lying down to sleep, Lisa plucked up the courage to ask, "Lolo, why haven't you got a wife?"

"I have, dear." Allan had been expecting this question from his inquisitive granddaughter at some stage.

"Where is she?" Lisa asked with great curiosity.

"In heaven, with God. And one day, I shall be joining her again."

"Do you miss her?"

"Yes, of course. Every day that passes, I think of her. Your grandmother was a truly wonderful woman who meant everything to me."

"What was she like? Was she very beautiful?"

"Oh, yes, so very beautiful." Lisa did not see the tears in Allan's eyes as he talked of his long-dead wife, though his voice was a little shaky as he continued. "She had such beauty...and eyes with a sparkle that seemed to come directly from heaven. I have never seen such eyes until..." A lump came to his throat, and he found himself unable to continue.

"Until what, Lolo?" The moonlight shone on his face. Large tears glistened as they ran slowly down his cheeks. "Why are you crying, Lolo?"

"I'm all right, child. Just the night air making my eyes water." He stood up and went into another room. Lisa lay awake, wondering what Allan was doing and why he was crying. After a few minutes, he returned, carrying an old photograph. "This is a picture of Monalisa, your grandmother."

Curious, Lisa sat up and, taking hold of the photograph, held it to catch the full light. It was now obvious why Allan favoured Lisa above all her sisters and brothers. The woman in the picture looked to be in her early twenties, and even allowing for the difference in age, she and Lisa were identical. The shape of her cheekbones, lips, chin and her forehead were the same as Lisa's, but most significant of all, so were her eyes. That same sparkle Allan had described made Lisa's beauty complete. Now the child understood everything, yet she said nothing as she put her arms around Allan. No words could fully express her true feelings.

They held this embrace for what seemed like an eternity. The sadness of the moment caused Lisa's eyes to fill with tears too. For a child so young, she understood that the old man was desperately missing his beautiful wife. "Why did Lola have to die?"

Allan had been dreading this question yet had known it would come. "I'm sorry, Lisa, I can't say. But when you are older, I will tell you the full story. Now come on, you must try and get some sleep."

Obediently, she lay down and tried to sleep, yet it was so difficult. She had so many questions to ask of her grandfather but knew she must wait. Wait for how long? Why was she not old enough now? The mystery surrounding her grandmother's death puzzled and intrigued her, and she longed for the day when the full story could be told. The face in the photograph would always be etched in her mind, a constant reminder of the looks she had inherited from her beautiful grandmother, who had died so young.

Chapter Five

LISA AWOKE EARLY the next morning to the sound of heavy tropical rain falling noisily on the timber roofs. As long as she was dry, she loved to see the rain and watched, spellbound, through the window. The nearby trees did not provide any shelter on the ground. Water streamed off the broad leaves, forming wide puddles on the rich soil. She marvelled at how this water would, in turn, help to make the trees grow stronger and the sweet mangoes bigger.

Lisa was thrilled by the beautiful synergy of life on earth. *God is so clever*, she thought. *More water makes more fruit to feed all the hungry people.*

By the time they had eaten breakfast, the rain had stopped and bright sunlight was already starting to dry the sodden land.

"Where are we going, this morning, Lolo?"

"I think we shall walk along the banks of the stream that runs past the plantations. It's a pleasant walk and should take most of the morning. We'll be leaving shortly."

Allan went outside to talk to Ricky, who was already hard at work, sawing some fallen branches into smaller, usable lengths of timber. The two men discussed the work of the day for a few minutes before Allan was ready to leave.

"Okay, Lisa. Let's get started."

Allan was carrying a walking stick. He did not lean heavily on it, only using it occasionally, helping him to walk safely over uneven ground. Lisa happily strolled along, chatting to Allan. As always, she had a hundred questions for him and a thousand observations to make. She had not forgotten the mystery of her

27

grandmother from the night before, but she knew it was pointless to mention it. Today she saw Allan in a different light. She had always liked and respected him, but now there was an even closer bond. He had brushed off the signs of sadness, evident the night before, and his handsome, weathered features showed how happy he was to be close to nature on a bright, new day.

They walked upstream, accompanied by the sounds of the gently flowing water as it tumbled over larger stones protruding through the surface. The river was shallow and about fifteen feet wide, but occasionally, it was much deeper. The path along the bank was quite stony and uneven and in places disappeared completely. From time to time, they had to cross the stream to the other side where the path was a little easier to navigate.

The bridges were quite makeshift, often simply a tree trunk resting on both banks. For his age, Allan was remarkably adept at keeping his footing on the slippery timbers. Lisa had a good sense of balance, almost dancing as she crossed over the swirling water flowing fast beneath her feet.

"Are we going to walk to where the water starts, Lolo?"

He laughed. "No, Lisa. That is much too far for us to walk. It starts about fifteen miles from here, high in the mountains. I'm hoping that we can walk as far as the falls. That is definitely a sight worth seeing and, with luck, should not take more than an hour."

"Can we go there one day, Lolo? I've never seen the start of a stream or river. I don't know what it looks like."

"In truth, there is not a lot to see. Just a hole in the ground where the water bubbles out from some deep caves. Sometimes the water just trickles out of a crack in a rock. It's only when you get further downstream that you see a lot more water, as many tiny streams merge into one. By the time it reaches the sea, that slow-running stream can become a huge, fast-flowing, dangerous river."

Listening closely to her grandfather, Lisa realised that there were many things she knew very little about. In her five years, this brief holiday with Allan was the furthest she had travelled. "Have you been all over the world, Lolo?"

"Good heavens!" he chuckled. "No, I've never been out of the Philippines. And I have only been to a small fraction of the seven thousand islands in our country."

Lisa's eyes widened at what Allan was telling her. "But the Philippines is the whole world, isn't it?"

Allan's face creased into a wide smile. "You have quite a lot to learn yet, Lisa. Our country is only a very small part. Have you never seen a map of the world?"

The child, becoming more aware of her ignorance, shook her head. At home, talk was only of minor domestic matters. She found it hard to imagine that, beyond the sea, there were other countries and many more people.

"When we get back home, I'll show you my atlas. That's a book full of maps showing all the countries of the world. Would you like that?"

Lisa, keen to extend her knowledge, answered, "Oh, yes, please, Lolo. I would love to learn more about the world."

After walking a short way, Allan paused to look at the path in front of them. "The ground is becoming very difficult to walk on around here. I think we'll go back to that last bridge and cross to the other bank. It looks a bit easier on the other side."

As they turned around, out of the corner of his eye, Allan saw something move. Just for a brief instant, he thought he had seen someone in the distance. It was there and then it disappeared. Perhaps it was just his imagination. He said nothing about it and continued towards the bridge. This was wider and sturdier than most of the others spanning the water, allowing them to walk side by side. Farmers probably used this bridge to take their cattle to graze further away as local areas of grass became scarcer.

Once they were across the water, they continued their journey upstream. They made better progress on this side, with the ground more even and level for walking. After another twenty minutes, they rounded a bend, and there before them was the waterfall. It was the most spectacular, wondrous sight Lisa had ever seen.

"Oh, Lolo, it's so beautiful." She stood motionless, examining every minute detail. From a height of at least thirty-five feet, water cascaded over and down glistening black rock. The sound of the gushing water was almost musical as it snaked its way through the craggy rock surfaces, eventually dropping vertically into a pool at the base of the fall.

Allan smiled. "It looks even better than I remember it. The rainfall this morning must have added to the water flow." Both Lisa and her grandfather made the sign of the cross, sensing something almost spiritual in what nature had provided in front of their own eyes.

"Look—there are some steps to climb. We'll just go to the top and then down again. This is as far as we must go."

With the roughly cut, deep, uneven steps, Lisa's short legs made the ascent difficult, yet she was determined to do it without any assistance or complaint. Once they were at the top, they looked downstream into the distance.

"Lolo, I can see for miles!" The new experience made the little girl almost burst with sheer happiness. Shielding her eyes from the bright sunlight, Lisa gazed, spellbound, into the distance. After a few minutes, the two came down, picking their way towards the lower level.

"Lisa, follow me, but be very careful."

She wondered where he was taking her as they stepped onto large, rough boulders at the base of the fall.

"Keep your back to the rock face, hold my hand and step sideways, just like me." Allan noticed a sudden look of anxiety appear on her face. "Don't worry, Lisa. You'll be quite safe. Just watch where I put my feet and follow me."

They inched their way along the narrow ledge, closer and closer to the water thundering noisily past. Lisa felt she was only seconds away from certain death by drowning in the deep, swirling pool below and prayed for God's assistance.

"Lolo, I'm frightened!" She began to cry, wishing that she was safely back on the riverbank.

"Just a few more steps now, and we'll be there." Allan held her hand firmly and hoped her courage would last for just a few more seconds. His son and daughter-in-law would be horrified if they thought he was putting Lisa's life in danger, but he believed the experience was worth the risk. To his relief, the rock face began to curve inwards, away from the torrents of rushing water. A few more steps and they were able to walk safely into the cave, its entrance shielded by a watery curtain.

"Where are we, Lolo?" Lisa's eyes were wide in amazement as she looked around the space where they were now standing. The cavern was about eight feet high, seven feet wide and perhaps twenty or thirty feet deep. The surface of the rock glistened with countless water droplets as the walls close to the entrance were constantly covered with spray from the waterfall, encouraging the growth of a light, green moss over the rocky surface. Strong sunlight filtered through the water screen, creating patterns of all the colours of the rainbow dancing and shimmering in the cool air of this magical place.

Allan was delighted to see the wonderment in his granddaughter's eyes. "I haven't been here for over forty years.

31

It was purely by chance when, as a small boy, I discovered this cave. I played and hid here many times. My best friend Michael and I kept this place very secret."

"But who made it?" Lisa asked, innocently. It was clear she had never seen anything like it before.

"God did. That's what makes it so special. The water has been flowing here for millions of years, and in that time, it has carved this hole in the rock. All this just from the constant wearing effect of water." He wandered around, looking closely over the rock surface. "Yes! Here it is! Come and have a look."

"What have you found, Lolo?" She advanced as Allan pointed to one part of the wall surface.

"Look! This is where we carved our names."

She peered more closely. It was faint, yet Lisa could just make out sufficient letters to know that it said 'Allan Tiguelo'.

Allan brushed the surface, trying to remove some of the mossy growth, which had partly obscured the writing. Nearby, there was another name.

"Michael Sanzhes. "Was that … ?"

"My best friend? Yes. We always played together. Poor Michael is dead, now. Died over ten years ago." The old man stood silently, deep in thought. The experiences of his childhood came flooding back as he remembered his school friend.

An idea sprang to his mind. "I'll tell you what we'll do. If we can find a sharp stone, we'll put your name here as well."

The idea of having her name immortalised in this way appealed to the little girl. Eagerly, the two scrabbled about, looking for a suitable writing tool, until Lisa found a small piece of flint towards the back of the cave in an area where Allan had difficulty bending because the roof of the cave was quite low. It was then that she noticed a flat, metal plate covered the very

32

back of this space. Gingerly, she knocked on the plate, producing a deep, hollow sound.

"What are you doing, Lisa?"

"It's very odd. There's something metal right at the back of the cave. Why would it be there, Lolo?"

Allan bent down, trying to see what she had found, but the darkness and his height made it difficult. "Never mind, Lisa, it must have been there for a very long time. Now, let me see the flint you found."

Excitedly, she asked, "Will this do, Lolo?"

Allan closely inspected the flint. "Yes. Good girl. That's perfect. Would you like me to write your name, Lisa?"

"I think that I would like to try and do it myself, please."

"Okay, be very careful not to cut your hands. It's a very sharp piece of stone."

She soon realised it was not as easy as she had expected, and only a very faint impression of 'Lisa Tiguelo' appeared under her grandfather's name.

Seeing her disappointment, Allan said, "It's okay. I'll make it a bit easier to see for you."

Taking hold of the flint, he gouged deeper into the rock surface, carefully following the finely engraved outline made by his granddaughter. After a few minutes, the name was even more distinct than Allan's.

"Michael Sanzhes, Allan Tiguelo, Lisa Tiguelo," Lisa read aloud as she inspected their work. "Thank you so much, Lolo. That's great."

"You are now a member of the secret Hall of Mary. That's what we called it—after the Virgin Mary. It is such a spiritual place, so full of many happy memories. Now, I think we had better be going."

Lisa looked a little disappointed at the suggestion of leaving. "I really like it here, Lolo. Can we come here again, please?"

The old man smiled at her enthusiasm. "Yes, of course. Next time you stay with me. Don't forget to watch your step as we leave the cave. Just follow me."

They squeezed against the face of the rock as they inched their way back towards the riverbank. Lisa was not as frightened as she had been earlier when they had first entered the cave. Now she knew what to expect, it was a great deal easier, and they soon reached the safety of the bank, their clothes soaked from the spray of the water.

Allan had enjoyed reliving his childhood experience, yet the effort had tired him.

"We shall rest here a little while."

He had hidden his walking stick and small canvas bag behind some rocks before their expedition into the Hall of Mary. Now he retrieved them and opened the bag. Inside, he had some fresh mango and pineapple. Once they had found a shaded place to sit, he handed Lisa some sticky rice and pieces of fruit.

"I think we'll stay here a little longer, Lisa, and rest for a few minutes before starting our journey home. Be careful not to go too near the water's edge."

The exercise and the heat from the tropical sun had made Allan tired, and within a few minutes, his heavy eyes had closed.

Excited at the new experiences of this beautiful, sunny day, Lisa had no similar plans to sleep. She wanted to see as much as possible during her stay with Allan and played happily while keeping close to her grandfather.

Chapter Six

LISA WAS FASCINATED by fish and knew there must be many in the river. She found that by lying on the riverbank with her face looking downwards into the water, she could see the bright, silvery bodies of hundreds of small fish as they searched for food in the shallows close to the bank. Absorbed in this aquatic examination, Lisa did not notice a figure slowly approaching.

When two strong hands took firm hold of her waist, she knew straight away that it was not her grandfather and screamed, using the full strength of her infant lungs. She continued screaming as the hands lifted her from the ground. Using her arms and legs, she struggled violently, kicking in all directions, but could not match the strength of her abductor.

The sound of her cries woke Allan with a start. Jumping to his feet, he saw Alberto and Dominic by the riverbank. Alberto was carrying the fiercely struggling Lisa.

Picking up his stick, Allan ran towards them. "Leave that child alone!" he yelled, but taking no notice of him, they ran with Lisa, who was still screaming loudly.

Allan was fit for his age, and spurred on by the desperate situation, he caught up with them. He hit Alberto hard on the head with his walking stick. The shock was sufficient to make him lose his grip, allowing the frightened girl to fall to the ground.

"Run, Lisa! Run!" Allan shouted.

Jumping to her feet, Lisa wasted no time, heading upstream, sprinting towards the falls. Feeling slightly dazed by the blow on his head, Alberto, somehow, managed to follow.

35

Meanwhile, Dominic turned on Allan and tried to overpower him. The two men were of similar strength and struggled together. Allan tried to use his stick, but his assailant was too close.

By chance, two workmen emerged from the heavy wooded area and ran to assist Allan, quickly overpowering the attacker and holding him close to the ground as the man cried out in pain.

Meanwhile, Lisa had reached the falls and jumped onto the rough, rocky ledge leading to the Hall of Mary, her fear of falling into the water replaced by the desperation of her situation. She moved faster than even she had thought possible, side-stepping towards the falls. In an instant, she had disappeared behind the watery curtain, yet Alberto was still in hot pursuit.

Lacking Lisa's agility, he had to take his steps more carefully. He edged closer and closer towards Lisa, whose frightened face peered through the misty curtain of water. Alberto was within three feet of the cave entrance and, seeing how close he was to his quarry, turned sideways to make the last few steps. This was his biggest error. His foot slipped on the wet surface, and he reached out wildly for some support, his arms flailing, but could find nothing to hold on to. He let out an anguished wail as he fell heavily into the deep, swirling pool, his head disappearing under the surface.

Allan and his two helpers had seen how the small child had cleverly outwitted her attacker and laughed as they watched the figure struggling in the water. One of the workmen ran towards the pool and dived gracefully into the river. He was a strong swimmer and soon reached the struggling Alberto. Taking firm hold of the now-defeated attacker, he swam towards the riverbank. He climbed out, dragging Alberto behind him and continued this undignified treatment until they had reached Allan and Dominic.

Lisa, meanwhile, seeing that she was now safe, quickly returned to the riverbank and rushed back to her grandfather. She threw her arms around Allan, thankful to be reunited with him.

"Thank God you're safe, Lisa." He picked up the child and held her close. "I would never have forgiven myself, if anything had happened to you." Turning to the two brave helpers, he said, "I can't thank you enough for what you have done. Without your help, these criminals could have murdered my granddaughter."

"It's okay. When we heard the girl screaming, we knew someone had to help. We were working on the plantation, over there." He pointed towards the trees. It was a blessing that, even in such a remote area, there had been someone nearby and able to help.

"What are your names?" Allan asked.

"I'm John. And this is James." John gestured to the man who had dived into the dangerous waters to rescue Alberto. Both were broad-shouldered, strong men in their mid-twenties.

"Perhaps I should have left this miserable scum to drown." James used his foot to turn the still gasping man who lay before them on the ground. Alberto had swallowed a great deal of water.

"Who are these guys, anyway?" John asked. He was still holding Dominic, making certain that escape was impossible.

To Lisa's surprise, Allan said, "They are brothers. Alberto and Dominic. They worked for me a few years ago, until I fired them. They were fruit pickers on my plantation and decided to sell my mangoes privately, pocketing the takings for themselves. I never thought I would see them again."

"So, they are thieves as well as child abductors! I think they deserve to be hanged for what they have done."

Helpless against their stronger captors, Alberto's and Dominic's faces showed real terror.

"We...we wouldn't have harmed the child. We only wanted to hold her for ransom until the old man paid up."

Dominic's pleading did nothing to soften the minds of John and James.

"And you think that is good reason to spare your lives?" John's contempt for the two opportunists was evident. "I still think they should be hanged." He began to drag the now wailing Dominic towards the trees. James picked up Alberto as though he were a limp rag doll and followed John. He soon found a rope, ready to carry out the gruesome execution.

Allan, still holding Lisa in his arms, watched as his former employees pleaded for their lives. The ropes were prepared. Everything was ready.

"That's enough, now, John, James," Allan said firmly. "No matter what they've done, I don't want them to be hanged." With his strong Catholic upbringing, he could not condone such severe punishment for his ex-employees and knew the anticipated executions were enough to frighten the two men. "I do not want to see them, ever again."

John and James stopped, respecting Allan's clemency.

With sudden inspiration, James said, "I know what we'll do. We can still make good use of these ropes." He whispered a few words to John, whose face broke into a broad smile at the suggestion. James took charge of both criminals, while his partner disappeared into the dense growth. A few minutes later, he returned, dragging behind him a broad wooden palette. Together, they placed the two helpless men face-up on the palette and used the rope to fasten them to the timbers. Once they were secured, John and James lifted the palette shoulder high and walked towards the river.

Lisa's young eyes were wide with anticipation as she watched this strange exercise. "What's going to happen to those bad men, Lolo?"

Allan laughed as he realised their intentions. "I think those two criminals are just about to be launched."

Sure enough, the makeshift raft was heaved into the fast-flowing water and submerged enough for its unwilling passengers to disappear below the surface. They strained their necks to keep their heads up as the raft was caught by the current and began to turn and twist its course along the river. Soon, it was out of sight, around the bend of the river, but the shouts from the helpless men could still be heard for several minutes.

Lisa joined in the laughter with her grandfather and their two newfound friends.

"I hope you don't see those guys ever again, er…" John realised that he still did not know the names of the people he had helped to save.

Allan placed Lisa on the ground and offered his hand in friendship. "I'm Allan Tiguelo. And this…" With obvious pride, he put his hand on the little girl's shoulder. "This is my granddaughter, Lisa."

"I'm so pleased we were able to help, Allan." John shook his hand firmly and bent down to the shy, smiling Lisa. "And such a good-looking granddaughter, too." Her tiny hand disappeared inside John's massive paw. She could tell from his face and voice that he was a good man.

"Thank you for helping us," she said politely. She had a burning question on her mind yet was not certain if she should ask it. Overcoming her reticence, she asked, "John, would you really have hanged those criminals?"

"Hell, no!" He laughed. "The trick is, with men like those two, you really have to convince them that you mean to do it.

Sometimes fear of what might happen is the best punishment of all."

Adding his contribution to the conversation, James said, "And it worked, too. We really scared the shit out of them. Oops, sorry, Lisa. Please excuse my language."

She giggled shyly at the indiscreet expression. Somehow, use of this normally banned word did not sound so vulgar in this context.

"Whenever the two of you have time," Allan said, "you are welcome to visit me on my mango plantation. It's about four miles downstream. Just mention my name to anyone in the area and they'll point you in the right direction. Now, we had better be getting home, Lisa."

"Thanks. We'd like to visit you." John smiled broadly. "Take care on your journey home."

Lisa waved to the two workmen as she and her grandfather began their homeward journey. "I liked John and James, Lolo. Did you?"

"Yes, I did. They are good men. These days, you can never be sure just who to trust, but they were okay."

"What about the two criminals on the raft? What will happen to them?"

"By rights, they should be carried down the river, all the way to the sea. But I have no doubt that someone will see them and rescue them."

"Are they very bad men?" Lisa, at the age of five, had never previously seen the darker side of man. Now, she had firsthand experience.

"When they worked for me, I trusted them. I paid them well and always looked after them. They used to laugh and joke with everyone, but their greed got the better of them. You see, Lisa, even at my age, I'm still learning."

"What do you mean, Lolo?" She was puzzled by his admission.

"Well, somehow, you have to know the difference between a genuine smile and a false one. It's not easy, and even I was fooled. You must always be careful whom you trust and look deeper into them, way beyond their smile."

Lisa understood now just what he had meant. The lessons of this eventful day would serve her well in the future. During the walk home, she did not say very much but thought about the two men who had come to their rescue and what Allan had told her about understanding the true character of a person.

Chapter Seven

MARLYN WAS RELIEVED and pleased to see Allan and Lisa on their return. She had felt that something must have gone wrong, as her employer was normally well-organised and very punctual. The helpers had already eaten and all were curious about the cause of the delay.

Too hungry to wait, Allan and Lisa told their story as they ate, having already agreed not to mention the Hall of Mary. This place had been a secret during Allan's childhood, and both decided it should stay that way. When they reached the part where the two men had been launched into the river by their newfound friends, everybody laughed, but they were also shocked. Melissa recalled hearing some shouts from the river, probably as the raft was floating past. The two ex-workers were well-known in the area. Allan would make certain everyone knew what had happened in case Alberto and Dominic ever decided to return to seek revenge. From that day on, they would be treated as lepers.

When they had finished their meal, Allan said, "We had better get you home to Nanay and Tatay now, Lisa. I promised to have you back before sundown."

It was pointless to argue, Lisa knew. She had really enjoyed staying with her grandfather, partly because with him, she was treated as a grown-up, while at home she was still the baby of the family.

With a pleading look in her eyes, she asked, "Lolo. Can I have a look at the maps of the world before I go home, please? You did say that we would look at them."

42

Allan checked the time. "Perhaps, just for a few minutes. It's after four now, so we shall have to leave soon." He found it very difficult to resist the charms of the little girl. He went into another room and soon returned with a large, thick book. Clearing a space on the table, he placed the atlas where Lisa could see it clearly.

, "This book is the biggest I have ever seen!" Lisa's said, her wide eyes scanning the brightly coloured pages as Allan opened the atlas. "I think it is even bigger than the Holy Bible at church."

Allan smiled at this unusual comparison. "It has to be big, so that all the countries of the world can be seen. The world is a big place, you know. Bigger than you can ever imagine. For today, we shall just look at the pages showing all the countries together." He found the part where the world was condensed into two pages. "Now, where the map is coloured blue, that is the sea and all the land is yellow."

Fascinated, Lisa stared at all the strange shapes and sizes of the many different land masses. "But how can that be? There is so much blue."

"Yes, that is true. Two-thirds of the world is covered by sea. Now, can you guess just where the Philippines are?"

She closely scoured the different countries, looking for her homeland. Although she could read a little, the words she could see meant nothing to her infant mind. She felt certain that it must be one of the larger areas of yellow and, after a few moments thought, pointed to one that had an interesting shape. "I think this is where we live."

Allan smiled at his granddaughter's choice. "No, child. That is the United States of America. The Philippines is a much smaller country."

When he pointed to the insignificant dots representing the Philippines, Lisa, in amazement, said, "But it's so very tiny, Lolo."

"Yes, it is small compared to the rest. The world is a very big place, and I feel certain that one day, you will visit many countries, far further than I have ever been able to travel."

"Are there people just like us in all the other countries?"

Allan was enjoying this teaching exercise, especially as Lisa showed so much enthusiasm and curiosity, her small brain ever ready to absorb new facts. "There are people in all countries, who are almost like us, but they have different-coloured skins and looks. They even talk in different languages." He could almost see her imagination as she pictured people of different colours.

"You mean like Tagalog?" Even at five years old, she already understood the concept of different languages. With over a hundred languages in the Philippines, it was essential to have a common tongue. Tagalog was the most common language used to communicate with people from other islands within the Philippines, while a native dialect was kept for everyday use.

"That is the idea, but other languages sound very different from Tagalog. It is thought that thousands of years ago, people came from other countries to live in the Philippines, and we are all related to those people.

"But where did they come from, Lolo?"

He pointed to the countries as he mentioned their names. "It is said that people originated in Africa millions of years ago. From there, they spread to India, China, Malaysia and possibly even Australia. In more recent times, many people from Spain have settled here. Our country is named after King Philip of Spain, and most people's names, including ours, are Spanish." Carefully watching the time, Allan said, "I think that will have to be all for today. Next time you come here, we shall look at the atlas again.

Lisa was disappointed but knew that she would soon have to leave. Allan, taking great care of his precious book, returned it to the other room before gathering Lisa's few possessions.

Marlyn and all the helpers gave Lisa a farewell hug and kiss, urging her to come again. She felt sad at leaving and waved vigorously at everybody as she began her journey home. It was, by now, late afternoon and soon the sun would be setting. The effects of the heat, combined with missing her afternoon sleep, had sapped Lisa's energy. She tried to keep up with Allan, but before they were halfway home, he noticed she was going to need some help. "Would you like me to carry you, Lisa?"

"It's all right, Lolo. I think I can manage." She was trying to be grown up, but Allan knew that before very long, she would accept his offer. A few minutes later, she said, shyly, "I think I would like to be carried now, please, Lolo. My legs feel so heavy and tired."

He admired her strong determination, but Lisa's eyes were heavy and the croakiness of her voice indicated the extent of her fatigue.

"That's okay, Lisa. You tried your best. Come here." He lifted her off the ground, and with Lisa's arms around his neck, they continued their journey. "My, you are getting to be a heavy girl." Within a few minutes, she was asleep in his arms. The twilight emphasised her angelic features. Allan could not help but marvel at how closely she reminded him of Monalisa, his long-dead wife.

Although he was a fit man, his exhaustion was quite apparent as he arrived at Lisa's house. Dolores carefully took the still-sleeping child from him and laid her on her blankets.

"You look as though you should be asleep yourself," she remarked to her father-in-law. "You're welcome to stay here overnight if you want."

"Thanks, Dolly, but I'll just have a rest and then I must be off home. We have had quite an exciting day."

"Well, if you won't stay, you must have a drink and something to eat. What's been happening?"

As Allan recounted the day's events over a welcome meal, Lisa awoke and, with slightly renewed energy, added her enthusiastic comments to the tale.

"I think those two bad men will be swept out to sea by now, Nanay. They could be hundreds of miles away, never to return to the Philippines. Perhaps they will float all the way to America."

They all laughed, although Dolores was concerned when she realised how close her daughter had come to facing real danger. Still, she could not blame Allan. "I think those men would soon have returned you, when they got tired of your endless chatter."

Ignoring her mother's comment, Lisa said, "I feel very hungry, Nanay."

"I'm not surprised, after what's been happening to you, today."

Standing, Allan said, "Well, it's about time I went home. Thank you for a lovely meal, Dolly." As he was ready to leave, he turned to her. "I'm sorry about what happened to Lisa today, Dolly. I hope it won't stop her from being allowed to stay with me again?" There was sadness in his question, at the thought of no future visits.

"Don't worry." Dolores gave Allan an affectionate hug. "You're not to blame for what happened, and Lisa is quite safe, so don't worry. Of course she can stay with you, whenever you want."

The old man smiled at his daughter-in-law. "Thanks so much, Dolly. It means a lot to me, and I do enjoy her company."

Lisa gave him a farewell hug and kiss. "Thank you, Lolo. I've really enjoyed myself."

It was quite dark as Allan began the trek back to his plantation.

***

46

After all the excitement, Lisa slept very soundly that night. For days after, she recounted her adventures to anybody who would listen, yet she never once mentioned the Hall of Mary. That was to remain a secret just between her and her grandfather. The little girl looked forward to the time when she could return to see him again.

Her older brothers and sisters, especially Breeza, were beginning to resent her special relationship with their grandfather, a resentment which would, in time, result in many conflicts.

Chapter Eight

LISA PROBABLY DID have more attention than any of her sisters or brothers before her, but it was not until she was about six years old that her rebellious nature became more apparent. When she was not with her grandfather, Lisa always tried to be near her mother, even though this was not always wanted or convenient.

Often, Dolores had to buy provisions from the market, which was too distant to walk. She always travelled by tricycle taxi, and her shopping expedition would have been hampered by having a small child in tow. However much Lisa pleaded, Dolores remained adamant. "No, Lisa, you have to stay at home with your sisters and brothers. I'll soon be back."

Lisa clung to her mother's dress, tears running down her face. "Nanay, please take me with you. I don't want to stay at home."

Dolores knew how to make her daughter release her grip. She bent down and pinched the flesh on the inside of Lisa's thighs. The little girl let out a howl of pain and ran away to escape her mother's strong hands. Sobbing, she ran into the bushes and hid behind a coconut tree, watching her mother prepare for her shopping expedition. It was not long before the motor tricycle appeared in the clearing near their house. Lisa watched as her mother took her seat and talked to the driver, presumably giving him directions for her journey.

The vehicle started moving, and Lisa stepped out from her hiding place and ran down the road in pursuit; with her strong legs, she soon caught up with it. As she drew level with the tricycle, she grabbed hold of the handrail and heaved herself up onto the rear-facing seat attached to the back of the tricycle body.

It was quite a hot day for such exertions, and breathing heavily, she sat back in the seat, happy now that she was going to market with her mother. Although she could not see the child, Dolores had realised that Lisa was sitting at the back of the tricycle but decided against sending her home. She had noticed the impact as Lisa had landed on the vehicle and smiled to herself at the boldness of the six-year-old. *That child has far more spirit than all my other children put together.*

When they reached the market, Lisa jumped down from her seat and ran around to help her mother, saying, with a mischievous smile, "Can I help to carry some of your bags, Nanay?"

"Now that you're here, yes, you certainly can help. And just look at your dress! You'll make me feel so ashamed, walking with you, wearing that dirty dress." Dolores brushed the dust off her daughter's dress, then tugged at the hem in a vain attempt to smarten her appearance. This was only a mild scolding, and Lisa was relieved that her mother was showing no real anger at her misbehaviour. She would be quite happy just helping to carry some of the smaller items. She loved to see how her mother selected fish, fruit and vegetables.

There were many whole fish, laid out before them, all of which looked appetising to the young girl, so it came as a surprise when her mother turned her back on the stall to find another.

"Why did you not buy any fish from there, Nanay? Are they too expensive?"

Dolores smiled at her daughter's questions. Lisa was a bright child and keen to learn. "They were cheap enough, but they weren't fresh. You can tell if a fish is fresh by looking at its eyes."

Lisa had great admiration for her mother's knowledge and wanted to know more. "How, Nanay?"

"The eyes should be bright if the fish is freshly caught. If they look red, then I will not buy them. You must also look at the skin. If a fish is fresh, the skin is still shiny, so you have to look at both skin and eyes to be certain that it's worth buying."

When they found another fish stall, Lisa carefully inspected the fish laid out before them. She bent her head, peering intensely into the eyes of the dead fish. "I think this fish is fresh, Nanay." The child's clear voice could be heard by several shoppers and traders alike.

"Yes, Lisa. A little quieter, next time, please."

Her mother did buy some from this trader, who smiled at the newfound expert. From there, they visited the fruit and vegetable stalls. Lisa was equally fascinated by what made a good bargain and discovered that a mango's skin was smooth when it was fresh. Since Allan always kept them supplied with mangos, they would not need to purchase this fruit, yet it was a useful lesson to learn. Any signs of roughness indicated that it had been off the tree too long. A pineapple with a light-yellow skin and strong leaves would be fresh, while older ones had a deeper yellow skin and softer leaves. Vegetables such as eggplant, beans, alogbate and malunggay similarly could be assessed for quality by looking at their skin texture and leaves.

By the time Dolores had made all her purchases, they had several bags full of rice, fish, meat, fruit and vegetables. True to her word, Lisa offered to carry some of the shopping. Picking some of the lighter bags, Dolores handed them to her daughter, making sure she didn't overload her.

Lisa made no complaint and slowly walked behind her mother, her arms straining with the weight of their purchases. She breathed a sigh of relief when, at last, they were able to bundle all the shopping into the tricycle taxi. Her legs aching from the effort, Lisa sat next to her mother and, within seconds, was fast asleep from her exertions.

When they arrived home, Lisa awoke from her slumbers and noticed a familiar figure near their open front door. Allan had called with a bag of mangoes from his plantation. On seeing him, Lisa jumped out of the taxi, ran up to Allan and threw her arms around his neck. "Lolo! I've been helping Nanay with her shopping at the market."

The old man put his arms around her and lifted her off the ground. She gave him an affectionate kiss. "I hope you have been a good girl for Nanay, Lisa."

"Oh, yes. I know how to choose the best fish. Nanay showed me. And fruit. And vegetables too."

He smiled at the child's endless enthusiasm. "That's good. You must always listen to your Nanay. She's a very clever lady. Now, perhaps you had better check these mangoes I've brought."

He placed her on the ground and offered her the bag of mangoes. With great concentration and deliberation, she looked at each one, turning it over and over again. Proudly, she proclaimed, "They are all fresh, Lolo."

Both he and Dolores laughed. "They should be. I picked them myself only this morning. Now, how about tasting one?"

Dolores took a mango and sliced it into many thin pieces, handing some to each member of the family. The juicy, soft, creamy, orange-coloured flesh melted in the mouth and was a favourite fruit of many Filipino families. Lisa, in particular, loved the flavour of the fruit more than any other.

After this unauthorised shopping expedition, Dolores realised it was better to let Lisa accompany her at other times. At least that way, she could keep a watchful eye on the rebellious youngster. In fact, Lisa learned very quickly and was a great help in selecting the most suitable purchases. On many occasions when the trader was imploring them to buy his products, the little girl would say, quite boldly and in a clear voice, "No, it's not fresh enough for us, thank you." She received many an angry stare from traders desperate for their business, yet she would always remain adamant.

Lisa was as beautiful as people had predicted she would be on seeing her as a baby. She had a classical Filipino facial profile with high cheekbones, large eyes that held a mysterious depth and blackness, contrasting with smooth, golden skin and snow-white, perfectly set teeth. Her smile was positively enchanting, making it very difficult to be angry with her. Her heavy, wavy hair hung down to her shoulder blades and, with just a little grooming, framed her face so perfectly that her beauty was beyond question.

She was also a very strong-willed child, possibly as a result of being slightly built. In effect, her determination was compensation for her lack of stature. Lisa's mother spent many hours brushing and combing her long tresses, but this had to be preceded by careful head inspection.

While Lisa was at play, many insects sought refuge in her thick hair, and every afternoon, Dolores would carefully search through it, looking for kuto, kuyamad or lusa—tiny flea-like insects. When found, they would be crushed between fingernails and ejected from their nesting place. Lisa did not mind this ritual, as it was comforting, almost hypnotic, leaving her with a strange feeling of tranquillity, after which she would usually fall asleep.

Chapter Nine

THERE WAS QUITE a bit of jealousy shown by Lisa's sisters, particularly from Breeza, who was eighteen months older. Arguments constantly broke out between the two girls, usually over something trivial or insignificant. If there was any lapse in supervision of the two, they would often start fighting, with much scratching and hair pulling, but however fiercely Lisa fought, it was her bigger and elder sister who would win the fights. If caught, both of them would suffer the wrath of their parents, and punishment could be very severe.

On one occasion, their father caught Lisa as she was running from Breeza's attention. Pedro lifted the girl off the ground, her legs still pedalling in the air, while Breeza, who had seen what had happened to her sister, attempted to escape. He called her back, and obediently she followed as he carried the struggling Lisa out to the back of the house. Putting her down, he ordered, "Don't either of you dare move from there. I don't want to hear a sound from you girls!"

Pedro took two machetes and sharpened them on a large stone he used for all their knives. The little girls watching on in horror, not knowing what to expect from their angry father.

Was he going to kill both of them and cut their bodies into little pieces? Surely, he would not end his daughters' lives so brutally.

"Why are you two so much trouble? I think it is better that you fight it out until we never have any problems ever again."

The gleaming metal blades sent a shiver of terror through the two children. Fear rooted them to the spot as tears ran down their young faces. Pedro calmly offered each girl a machete. Breeza held her hands firmly by her sides and shook her head, too frightened to speak, and refused to even take hold of the handle.

The spirited Lisa, however, took firm hold of the lethal weapon and looked down at it. In her little hand lay the means to swiftly end her sister's life. With wide eyes, she looked at the trembling Breeza and then at her seemingly unconcerned father. Yet another look at Breeza. Was the six-year-old capable of hacking her elder sister to death? The air was electric as the thoughts in the little girl's mind assessed this dangerous situation. Everything was silent, no birdsong. Not even the usually noisy cockerels could be heard.

Time seemed to stand unnervingly still for this macabre spectacle until, at last, Lisa gave an anguished scream of frustration. Breeza felt sure that she was about to die a horrible death and made the sign of the cross, audibly praying to God for his help.

It was all too much for Lisa. Still holding the machete, she ran away from the house, still screaming and with tears streaming down her young face. She ran to her aunt's, where she hammered on the front door. When Floriza came and saw Lisa, who by now was wailing loudly, she ushered her indoors. The first priority was to take the dangerous machete out of her hand before any harm could be done.

Through her sobbing, Lisa explained to her aunt what had happened. Floriza was aware of all the fighting between the two sisters and showed little surprise. She was concerned, though, that her brother-in-law could have allowed such a potentially dangerous situation to arise.

It was nearly six in the evening, and she agreed that Lisa could stay with her until the following morning. The child needed a lot of consoling and clung to her aunt all through the night. It was a long time before Lisa fell into a troubled sleep. Floriza had a strong affection for her niece and did her best to calm the frightened child. The ever-patient Alfredo kept quiet and let his wife take care of the situation.

Sheepishly, the repentant girl returned home the next morning and carefully placed the machete back into her father's care. Nothing was said about the incidents of the previous day. Breeza was very aware of how close to death she had been and, understandably, avoided going anywhere near to her strong-minded sister or a machete. For a while, hostilities between the two girls were reduced to mere angry words and cold, penetrating stares.

However, it did not take long for this to return to full-scale hostilities, evident by their faces being covered in many scratches and scars, and Pedro decided that severe punishment was necessary yet again. The sound of Lisa and Breeza shouting at each other could be ignored no longer.

As Pedro came out of the house, the two girls were fighting like cats, scratching, kicking and pulling hair. They saw their father approaching and tried to run away, but it was too late. He grabbed one in each hand and roughly dragged them along to the back of the house.

Releasing his hold, Pedro, in a voice which commanded attention, said, "You two little monsters have gone too far this time. I thought you would've learned your lesson by now, but apparently not. Well, I've had enough of both of you."

With memories of the machete incident still fresh in their minds, the girls felt convinced that they were about to die.

"Don't you dare move, either of you."

Not knowing what to expect, the two girls watched, horrified, as Pedro took hold of two large, empty rice sacks. He placed one on the ground and pulled back the neck of the sack. "You!" He pointed to Breeza. "Get in here!" Reluctantly, she stepped forward and stood within the opened sack. Pedro took hold of the top of the sack and lifted it, until Breeza had disappeared completely from view.

Taking some strong cord, he tied the neck tightly. Placing the other sack ready for Lisa, he pointed to her. "Now, you."

Lisa's whole body was trembling, yet she made no movement towards the open sack. Pedro grabbed hold of Lisa so hard she screamed. Ignoring her protestations and cries for mercy, he lifted her and placed the wriggling bundle inside the second sack.

It amazed Pedro that his six-year-old daughter had so much more spirit and strength than her elder sister. It was completely exhausting to keep her under control, as she continued to wriggle and squirm within his grasp.

"Tatay, don't. Please don't. Not in the sack, Tatay!"

Her pleas were ignored. Quickly, Pedro pulled the sack up over her head and tied it firmly.

Inside her sack, Lisa, who was afraid of confined spaces, prayed for her very life. She feared that her father would take them to the pond and throw them in, where they would be left to drown. Problem solved! Fortunately, this dark vision was only the creation of Lisa's vivid imagination.

His two youngest daughters now secured in their prisons, Pedro took them to a mansanitas tree at the side of the house. He lifted one sack high off the ground and secured it with the strong cord to a sturdy branch. Similarly, he suspended the other bag on another branch of the same tree. Feeling quite breathless from his exertions, Pedro calmly walked back towards his house, oblivious to the anxious cries of his two youngest daughters.

The two terrified girls were left there overnight. Lisa's muffled cries could be heard coming from her hanging prison as she found it impossible to sleep. The confines of the sack made her breathing very laboured, and in the heat she sweated profusely. Both girls were aware that, during the night, bats, large insects and, most frightening of all, large snakes would be active in the branches of the trees. If a huge, constricting snake were to discover the hanging cocoons, that would be the end of their short lives.

When morning came, Pedro unfastened the sacks from the tree and released the girls. They blinked as the strong sunlight hurt their eyes. They smelled of urine, were filthy, and where the tears had run down their faces, streaks of pale skin showed through the grime.

"Now, listen carefully, you two. Both of you are going to promise not to fight ever again. Right?"

The girls nodded obediently.

"A nod isn't enough!" Pedro shouted at them. "Stay there!" He disappeared into the house and soon returned with a Bible, handing it first to Breeza. "Breeza, do you promise to God not to fight your sister ever again?"

"Yes, Tatay. I promise."

Taking the Bible from her, he passed it to Lisa and glowered angrily at her.

In a very subdued voice, she said, "I promise not to fight Breeza." Both girls looked exhausted.

Dolores had been watching this spectacle, careful not to interfere with the punishment her husband had administered to their children. She took the still-sobbing girls indoors, made them strip off and gave them a thorough bathing. She was not particularly gentle with them, making it more like an extension of the punishment rather than a welcome-home gesture.

Although Pedro and Dolores would have been surprised if either of their daughters ever changed their natures, they hoped that the experience would subdue them for a while.

All the children were expected to help with the farming and housework, but Pedro decided that it may reduce the chances for further hostilities if he placed more responsibility on Lisa. He made it clear to her that every day, before she was allowed to play, it was her responsibility to feed and clean up after the pigs. Unfazed by this, she took her role very seriously and carried out her chores without complaint.

Even after she had removed the foul-smelling manure to the compost, she would stay with the pigs for hours. If her brothers or sisters crept quietly near to the sty, they would giggle on hearing Lisa holding lengthy conversations with the pigs. She certainly had an affinity with animals and enjoyed their company more so than humans.

One day, as her sisters were watching from behind some trees, they were amazed to see Lisa sitting proudly astride one of the pigs, riding it as though it were a horse. The pig was, seemingly, unconcerned, and Lisa appeared to be quite happy. The story soon spread around the whole community, and she was teased by everyone.

On Saturdays, Lisa and Breeza were despatched into the fields to cut tangkong leaves, used as feed for the pigs, but it proved to be too much of a temptation for the small children. In the field where the leaves could be found, there was also a shallow pond. The two girls, still fully dressed, would wade into the water and enjoy themselves. Their laughter could be heard for quite a distance as the two splashed each other. They would also swim in this natural waterhole, their original mission pushed to the backs of their minds. Slurry from caribou, grazing nearby, ran into the pond, ensuring that when the girls emerged, their dresses and bodies would be absolutely filthy. The hot sun would soon dry their clothes but would do nothing to improve their appearance or smell.

Dolores would be furious with them on their return, not only because of their dirty appearance but also because their sack would only contain a small amount of tangkong leaves. Clothes were a precious commodity, and new dresses could only be purchased when a pig was sold. A four-month-old pig could realise three to four hundred pesos, enough for food and clothing for a little while. It was a very unreliable form of income, and if they had no animals to sell, there would be no money for anything. There were no further thefts of the pigs, thanks to improved security.

The financial situation in the country was becoming ever more desperate, especially since President Marcos had introduced martial law after the attempted assassination of Defence Minister Juan Ponce Enrile.

Lisa's aunt Floriza, always ready to comment on the corrupt dictator, felt certain that the assassination attempt was staged, purely to prolong Marcos's presidency.

Chapter Ten

WHEN LISA WAS nearly seven, in late 1972, there was a great deal of unrest in the Philippines as Muslim groups, and others opposed to the Marcos regime started using military force to make their voices heard. After this, Marcos declared a state of emergency and put the whole country under martial law. So began his reign of terror as a dictator.

Many lives were lost, but Marcos showed little concern, as his forces had brutally crushed any opposition. He plundered the government vaults and, it was rumoured, had vast wealth, stolen from the very people he was meant to serve. The lifestyle of Marcos and his wife Imelda was becoming more extreme and extravagant as he used his fortune to do absolutely anything he desired.

To the six-year-old Lisa, all this meant nothing, yet most adults were aware that, in time, everybody in the country would suffer as a result of Marcos's power and greed. Although everyone had to be careful what they said, there was a great deal of discussion amongst families, all of whom were fearful for their future.

During her many visits to her grandfather's house, Lisa heard talk about the many and varied excesses of their brutal dictator. Even for her tender age, Lisa understood far more than the adults realised, and she hoped that when she was grown up, she could do something useful to bring back hope and peace into the lives of ordinary people.

Although Lisa loved animals, she also had a morbid curiosity about them. Chicken formed a very important part of the

Filipino diet, but someone had the awful task of killing the poor birds. As Lisa approached her seventh birthday, she decided that she wanted to copy her parents and kill a chicken. The thought of tasty chunks of chicken meat and soups made her mouth water and inspired her decision. With her father's assistance, they selected a suitable bird.

Pedro grabbed hold of the chicken and carried the struggling creature into the tiny kitchen area. A sharp knife was placed ready for the kill, but first, Lisa had to take hold of the bird. She crouched while her father handed the chicken to her. Her thighs trapped the wings while her feet were standing on those of the unfortunate bird.

Although it was trapped, the bird still struggled violently, but Lisa was determined in her efforts at execution. Under her father's instruction, she pulled some feathers out from the scrawny neck. When the skin was exposed, she took hold of the knife and drew it quickly across the neck.

"Is that okay, Tatay?" The little girl was excited.

As blood trickled from the wound, Pedro said, "No, Lisa. You need to cut the neck right in the middle. It will take too long for the bird to bleed to death. Try another cut."

With great determination, she picked the centre line more precisely and swiftly drew the blade across the neck. This time, there was a spurt of blood, indicating that she had been successful. Lisa grinned, "I've done it now, haven't I, Tatay?"

He smiled at his daughter's enthusiasm. "Yes, that's much better." He caught the blood in a small container. "Now, Lisa, put the chicken straight into the water. Quickly in, then out again." There was a large pan in which water had been gently boiling. Taking care that she was not scalded, Lisa dipped the bird into the pan and, on Pedro's instruction, removed it after a few seconds. This immersion made the process of removing the feathers much easier.

The little girl showed great concentration as she plucked the chicken bare. Dolores, keen to impart her culinary knowledge to the youngster, gave Lisa instruction on how to clean and dissect the chicken. Soon, the smell of cooking filled the air as the bird was boiled.

During this time, Pedro took the container of blood, dipped his finger in and painted a cross on Lisa's forehead. As it was her seventh birthday, this was meant to bring her luck, a custom derived from Philippine culture long before the Spanish, with their Catholic doctrines, had set foot in their country.

Lisa felt very proud of her efforts, and her parents praised her newfound skill as they hungrily devoured the meat. There were set rules on how the chicken should be shared. Again, according to Philippine custom and traditions, eating the kidney helped to ensure a man's potency, while the wife would eat meat from the rump to maintain her fertility. The youngest child, in this case, Lisa, would have the liver and feet. Nothing was wasted, and many of the bones would be used to make tasty soups.

Lisa was a quick learner and enjoyed helping her parents, both with killing and cooking chickens from that day on. This domestication of Lisa Tiguelo gave her an absorbing interest, yet it did not make any difference to her rebellious nature.

Chapter Eleven

IN HER EIGHTH year, there would be many other distractions, as she was now the age to start her primary education. Although the family was still poor, they managed to scrape enough money together to cover the fees. There was no free education in the Philippines, which meant that families with little or no income could not afford a formal education for their children.

When it came to the first day, Lisa and her mother walked the mile-and-a-half journey to the nearest school. Lisa, not quite knowing what to expect, was unusually quiet and very nervous, fearful of the unknown stresses of having to conform to a formal school education.

Her full lips began to tremble as the time came for separation. Clinging to her mother's dress, she cried, "Please let me come back home with you, Nanay. I don't want to go to school."

Dolores tried to comfort the sobbing girl. "Don't worry. You will be all right, Lisa. It's the first day for all the other children as well. Just wait and see. I'm certain that you will make new friends here and begin to enjoy school."

Lisa was not convinced but reluctantly had to leave her mother and join the stream of tiny, unhappy children. The school was a single-storey, metal-clad building with a separate room for each grade. As a grade-one pupil, Lisa was in a class of around sixty children, all of similar age to herself.

In this school, there was a uniform, which for the girls was a white blouse with a blue skirt and straps. At eight o'clock, the class started with the teacher, a strict-looking woman who seemed to be even older than Nanay, welcoming the children.

63

Lisa did not think much of school and would much sooner have been at home with her family or, even better, with her beloved grandfather. Lessons finished at eleven but commenced again at one o'clock, lasting until four.

It did not take long for the mischievous child to realise that avoiding class was much more fun than sitting obediently and being taught things she really did not want to know. Not surprisingly, she much preferred to learn from her grandfather rather than in the formal setting of a schoolroom.

Each day, Lisa would leave her mother at the entrance to the school, but instead of passing through, she would slip quietly into the wooded area surrounding the school. There, she would climb a tree and, sitting high in the branches, would watch her mother disappear into the distance.

Sometimes, with the few cents given by her mother, Lisa would wander to the nearby market to buy a mango, then return to the trees to devour her purchase. She became fascinated by spiders and spent many hours watching them closely. It seemed like magic to her when the insect started to spin a new web. The intricate, organised pattern of fine thread would take shape before her infant eyes, her body frozen to avoid frightening the spider. She continued watching as more small insects became entangled in the sticky web. The frantic struggles of the trapped insect to free itself were always fruitless, and then, most excitingly of all, the helpless victim was eaten by the hungry spider. Lisa's keen eyes did not miss a detail as she watched this macabre spectacle.

In her mind, she could hear all the insects.

"Come on and taste my delicious silk threads," the spider would say in a deep, sinister voice.

Many tiny voices would say, *"Come on, everyone! Who is going to be the first to reach the web?"* Panic would then strike the tiny insects as they became stuck, trapped in the web, followed by the sound of them crying for help to escape their prison. Lisa really did enjoy adding the various voices to all the creatures, but she also realised that if this departure was done every day, her truancy would soon be discovered and she would be in big trouble.

On the days she did attend classes, she would frequently anger her mother by taking a long time to return home, when school finished at four o'clock. Trees and water seemed to attract the child's attention, neither of which was conducive to cleanliness. As punishment, Dolores would pinch the flesh on Lisa's thighs, which was guaranteed to make her cry. It did not, however, stop her from doing the same again a few days later.

On one occasion, when Lisa did not arrive home until nearly six o'clock, she was both surprised and puzzled when her mother greeted her with a cheerful, broad smile. The reason soon became apparent. Instead of being offered food and drink, she was taken by Dolores to a corner of the room. Liberal amounts of salt were sprinkled into a small area of the floor and Lisa was forced to kneel, the coarse salt biting into her bare skin. She had to face the wall and hold both arms outstretched. On the upturned palm of each hand, a heavy book was placed.

"Now, young lady. You will stay in that position until I say you can move. And keep those arms straight! If you drop either of the books, the time will start over again." Every time the girl's arms began to droop, Dolores would say, in a firm, uncompromising voice, "Get those arms back up, girl."

Lisa had to stay in this uncomfortable position for at least thirty minutes, her knees becoming excruciatingly sore from the salt, but it had the desired effect of making her hurry home from school the next day. Alas, as with all punishments, the impact diminished with the passing of time. The punishment would then have to be repeated. As for her school lessons, Lisa had the ability to learn quickly yet had little interest in broadening her education.

In her ninth year, Lisa showed quite a talent for business. She had ready access to fresh fruit from plantations owned by relatives, particularly mangoes from her grandfather. She would take some bananas, boil them at home and then sell the fruit to her classmates. She would charge just a few cents, and this would be used to buy either writing paper or bread. This entrepreneurial talent also extended to other fruits and rice, and while it did not earn her a fortune, it gave her a good grounding in business economics.

Lisa was still able to visit her grandfather every so often and looked forward to these special times. Allan and Lisa spent many happy hours together going for walks or just talking, allowing Lisa to learn from her grandfather's vast wealth of experience. True to his word, he showed the knowledge-thirsty youngster his atlas of the world, teaching her about different countries. Allan was well-read and told Lisa about the inhabitants of countries such as America, Africa, India and Australia.

"Why are there so many people in India but not in Australia? They are both much bigger than the Philippines."

"That's a very good question, Lisa." Allan scratched his forehead, trying to think of a satisfactory answer. "You are right, they are both very big. I think, perhaps, that Australia is so far from other countries that it was much more difficult to travel there by sea."

This satisfied Lisa's curiosity for a moment, but it was not long before she had thought of another equally difficult question. "Which country did Adam and Eve live in, Lolo?"

Allan never ceased to be amazed at the variety of questions she asked. "Now, that is a very difficult one to answer. The Bible, sometimes, is a bit general in its stories. Even the people who wrote the Bible could not have known how life began and just made a convenient story to illustrate how life could have started."

Surprised, she asked, "You mean that it's not really true?"

"I don't know. I still believe that life is God-given, but the scientists say life began in Africa millions of years ago and that we all developed from apes."

Lisa giggled at this idea yet was disappointed that a part of the Bible may be false. Still, she accepted that it was such a long time ago, it would have been very difficult to verify all the facts.

As she was looking at all the different countries, Lisa spotted one area on the atlas which she had not previously noticed and spelt out the name, "J-A-P-A-N. Which country is that, Lolo? I don't remember you telling me about that country."

Allan's mood and attitude changed instantly. "That's Japan." The name was said so dismissively that it took Lisa quite by surprise. "I think that is enough for today. We'll put the atlas away now."

Lisa noticed this sudden change in her grandfather and it puzzled the innocent child. "What is wrong, Lolo? We were having such a good time, weren't we?"

"Yes, but Lolo is tired, Lisa. Come on, let me take the atlas away now."

She knew it was pointless to argue and obediently helped him to tidy the table. Something about Japan had touched a raw nerve, and even at nine years old, Lisa was wise enough not to ask about that country ever again.

Chapter Twelve

THE BIGGEST SHOCK of Lisa's life came from Mother Nature and made her realise that the punishments meted out by her parents were mild by comparison. She was at school, when, without warning, the ground, the building, everything began to shake violently. All the children were terrified and started to scream. Their teacher, having had past experience of earthquakes, quickly assessed the situation and said in a loud voice, "Quickly, children. Leave everything in here and walk, as quickly as you can, out of the building and into the playground."

Obediently, the children, ushered by their teacher, filed out of their room, along the corridor and out into the open air. They did not dare stop to see what was happening to their school behind them. The tremendous, terrifying forces beneath their feet were shaking the whole building and ground. The sound of smashing glass, ripping metal and frightened screams filled the air. Violent movements beneath them made it difficult to stand or walk as the youngsters struggled to escape. For Lisa, as with many of the younger children, this was her first experience of earthquakes and was made even worse by not having their parents close at hand. When the frightened group reached the centre of the playing field, well away from both buildings and trees, they were told to sit on the ground and wait there until it was safe to move.

As the shocks came to a stop, hundreds of frightened children and anxious teachers huddled together, hopefully in a safe area. After a few more minutes, the only sound that could be heard was that of a few crying children. Most of them were too afraid even to cry. Lisa looked back at the buildings. As she did so, the ground began to shake again, and Lisa watched in horror as the roof of her classroom collapsed in a tangled mess. The whole building heaved up and down as if shaken by some huge, extraterrestrial force.

Convinced that the end of the world was coming, Lisa held her hands together and prayed. She knew how much trouble she had caused her parents over the years and felt that the time had now come for divine retribution.

"Heavenly father, please have mercy upon me. I don't want to die. Please tell me what I must do to seek your forgiveness."

It had been only that same morning when, before leaving for school, she had taken some coins, which her father had kept on a high shelf. She hadn't taken all of them; that would have been far too obvious. Just the odd coin or two, she thought, would never be missed, but as her mother and the Catholic Church kept impressing upon her, God saw absolutely everything. To her youthful mind, this could be the only explanation. In her prayers, she confessed and repeatedly asked God for his forgiveness.

The tremors stopped once more. Everybody waited, anxiously, in silence, wondering if the earthquake was going to start again.

Thirty minutes passed without any further movement. At this point, the teachers decided it was safe to move from the playground. It was two-thirty, and as the school buildings were in a dangerous condition, it was decided that the children should be sent home to their parents. It was a great relief to the whole family when everyone arrived home safely and that the Nipa hut was still in one piece and habitable.

This new, unpleasant experience had a profound effect on Lisa, who was convinced she had brought it on by stealing money from her parents, and this was God's punishment for her actions. She showed more respect for them after that day and decided that she would never again take any money without their permission.

Lisa would experience many other earthquakes over the years, but one never became used to them. Each had its own characteristics and degree of devastation, and this first terrifying experience of earthquakes would remain with her for the rest of her life.

It was within that same year that nature played its destructive hand yet again. This time, Lisa and all her family were asleep in their house when disaster struck. She awoke abruptly as the tremors began. The whole family knew what they had to do. Nothing should be taken with them, as they were to leave the house to find a safer area. Human life was far more important than any possessions, or, at least, that was what Lisa had understood. This was to be a night when she would learn something new.

The floors, walls, everything was shaking as they struggled, with great difficulty, to their feet. Dolores reached the door first but found the straining timbers had jammed it firmly shut. She tugged with great determination on the handle yet knew it to be a hopeless task. Her children were behind her, trying to help their mother.

Frantically, she screamed, "Pedro, where are you? Help us all to get this door open!" Pedro had disappeared into the other room and returned clutching a struggling cockerel under one arm.

His wife repeated her frantic pleas. "For God's sake, Pedro. Help us, please help us!"

Realising there was no way he could keep hold of the cockerel while forcing the door, he turned to Breeza, who was closest to him, and thrust the frightened, squawking bird into her hands, saying, "Don't let go of it!"

It took all of Pedro's strength to force the timber door open, but after what seemed like an eternity, the door fell inwards, its hinges torn off their mountings. In their frantic dash to escape, several of the children fell upon the still-heaving ground. Breeza, struggling once more to her feet, was unable to keep a tight hold of the bird.

Confused, it flew around and disappeared back into the room from which Pedro had just rescued it. With frightened cries, the children ran, terrified, away from the house, along with Dolores and Pedro. Neighbours were similarly trying to reach safer ground, leaving their homes to be tossed around like tiny boxes in the palm of some giant's hand.

On seeing his precious bird return to its home, Pedro ran back towards the house. Dolores screamed at him, "Pedro! For heaven's sake, leave the bloody bird where it is!"

Ignoring his wife's pleas, he reached the doorway, but before he had chance to enter, there was a tremendous crash and his family home was demolished in front of his eyes. A tall tree, its roots weakened by the tremors, had fallen, crashing heavily through the roof.

Unaware of the danger he was facing, Pedro climbed over the now-flattened walls, searching through the wreckage. He tore at the timbers with his bare hands, frantically looking for the prized fighting bird. With the house now destroyed, the tremors stopped as abruptly as they had started. The only sounds were those of crying, frightened people. Amazingly, he found the cockerel, but it had fought its last fight. The lifeless body hung limp as he picked it up. Clutching it to his chest, he let out an anguished wail of desperation.

Pedro, tears streaming down his face and still carrying the bird's corpse, walked slowly towards his family. It was the first time Lisa had seen her father cry, yet she was unable to understand why any tears should be spent over a dead cockerel.

As he reached the now-silent family, he walked straight up to Breeza and slapped his hand so hard against her cheek that she was physically lifted off the ground. She fell awkwardly, in obvious pain. Screaming with rage at the fallen child, he shouted, "I told you to hold on to the damn bird! Why the hell didn't you do as I told you?"

In that instant, Lisa lost all respect that she had ever had for her father. Nothing could justify such cruel treatment.

"Leave my sister alone, you pig!" she screamed angrily, all thoughts of previous conflicts with her sister now forgotten as she bravely defended the older girl. Breeza was crying loudly and holding her leg, injured in the fall. Everyone felt the same distaste at what had happened, but it was Dolores who took the action.

Pedro was about to hit Lisa for supporting Breeza when his normally subservient wife marched up to him and slapped her hand squarely on Pedro's cheek. "Don't you ever dare hit my children again or we are finished! Do you hear? Finished!"

Pedro, realising that he had made a serious mistake of judgement, stepped back in a shame-faced, sullen manner. Dolores held great control over her voice, emphasising every syllable, making certain that Pedro understood her determination. The firmness of her manner demanded such authority that it could not be ignored.

Dolores' use of the word 'my' instead of 'our' when referring to the children had not been missed by any of the onlookers. Close neighbours who had fled their homes when the earthquake struck had also witnessed this deeply embarrassing spectacle.

In probably what had taken less than a minute, Lisa now felt a far greater closeness to Breeza than ever, her admiration for

Dolores had strengthened immeasurably, and Pedro, the man who had fathered her, had now been justifiably disgraced. She thought back to the times she had feared her father. One stern word from him had been enough to make her lips tremble and her legs turn to jelly. The memory of being left hanging in the sack from the tree branch after Lisa and Breeza had been fighting had caused her to experience nightmares for years. Now, strangely, she felt no fear, only contempt for a man who put the life of a fighting cockerel above the safety of his family.

Pedro, smarting from his wife's blow, held a hand to his cheek. "But my cockerel is dead. And it is her fault!" He pointed to poor Breeza, who was still wailing. This was not the act of a brave man but a desperate last excuse for his selfish actions. There would be men pleased with the news of the cockerel's death—men who had lost a great deal of money and their own fighting cockerels after they had been pitted against Pedro's champion rooster. For over twelve months, it had fought many battles, beating all of the opposition. Pedro had pampered the creature, giving it a special diet, and to avoid danger from jealous rivals, he kept it in a storeroom inside the cramped house. The family had not been happy with this privileged treatment, not least because of the smell from the bird's droppings.

"Are you really so stupid, man? It's nobody's fault that the bird died, and it can be replaced. You should be thankful to God that all of your family are alive and safe! If you have any sense of responsibility left, you had better find somewhere for us all to stay, now that our home is gone."

Humiliated, he slunk away to find out if other relatives' houses had survived the tremors.

Dolores carefully inspected Breeza's leg. Although the young girl found it extremely painful to stand, her mother was satisfied and relieved that there was no fracture. It had been badly sprained in the fall and would cause her some discomfort for several days until it had healed. There was also some bruising and one eye was blackened from the force of her father's blow. None of the family would ever forget or forgive what he had done that dreadful night.

Pedro returned, after a few minutes, to declare, in a sullen, bad-tempered voice, that the house of Floriza, Dolores' sister, was safe enough for them all to stay there. Wearily, they set off, in procession, towards Floriza's. Breeza's elder brothers were unusually supportive to the twelve-year-old. Two of them offered to carry her between them, to prevent any unnecessary weight being placed on her sprained, swollen joints. Lisa did not mind the attention Breeza was receiving as the injured girl held on tightly to her brothers for the short trek.

Floriza's house had not escaped completely from the earthquake, but the damage was quite minor since it was of stronger construction than their Nipa hut. The bright moonlight shone through the roof where, in places, the timbers had been ripped off by the twisting forces as the house shook. All the family was made welcome, and Dolores' sister managed to find sufficient blankets for everyone. Everyone, that is, except for Pedro. He did not stay with them, preferring instead to remain at the ruins of his own home. There would always be some individuals who would try to turn natural disasters to their own advantage. Pedro and his family did not have many possessions, but he intended to make certain that what they did have would not be taken by ruthless looters.

Floriza was shocked when she learned how Breeza had sustained her injuries and showed great sympathy towards the young girl. She bathed Breeza's face and ankles with a cocktail of herbs and potions, saying, "I'm sorry, Breeza, but this will sting a little while I'm bathing your face, but it will help the flesh to recover more quickly." Floriza was a great believer in the healing properties of herbs, her medicines proving very popular with all the villagers. She seemed to have something for every ailment from relieving girls' period pains to arthritis for the elderly.

With no medical qualification to her name, the local doctor saw her as unwanted competition, yet nobody could deny the efficacy of her treatments.

Next day, when the full damage could be assessed, every able-bodied person helped to clear the wreckage and begin the task of rebuilding their homes. Some government help may have been available, but the villagers knew this could be a very slow process, preferring instead to do the work themselves. Many of the timbers could be reused, but in Pedro's case, the roof and some of the other timbers had splintered into smaller pieces, making them only suitable for firewood.

Reconstruction of their house, by Pedro and the older boys, took only a few days, during which time Dolores and the rest of the family stayed at Floriza's house. There were insufficient funds to purchase new timbers, making it necessary for Pedro to scrounge materials from wherever he could. The rebuilt house was quite a patchwork, yet it was sufficient to serve them as a home once again.

Breeza's leg recovered from her injuries, thanks to her aunt's herbal remedies, but she walked with a noticeable limp for quite a while, a useful reminder, if one was needed, of her father's cruelty. He never apologised to any of the family for his selfish actions and remarkably, under the circumstances, found enough money to buy a new cockerel. It would be a long time before any of the family discovered that he had sold some of the girls' clothes to raise the money. He spent many hours training his new bird and sharpening its claws, getting it ready for its first fight. Pedro spent little time with his family, knowing he no longer commanded their respect, and if the truth were known, he did not really care.

It must have been a morbid curiosity which drew Lisa to the first cock fight of Pedro's new, potential champion. A licence for the fight should have been issued by the police, but Pedro and his opponent chose not to use the formal legal procedures. Instead, a clandestine meeting was arranged on the outskirts of the village. It was due to start thirty minutes before dusk, hopefully a time when officials had decided they had done enough for that day.

A group of about ten men, all hoping to win money on their chosen combatant, were talking excitedly as the two birds were readied for the fight. Pedro's new bird had a red plumage, while the opposition was all white. The colour was used as a distinguishing feature for the placing of bets. Seven placed money on the red bird, knowing that, even for its first fight, Pedro's reputation as a ruthless trainer was definitely worth a gamble.

Lisa watched, spellbound, as the two birds were simultaneously released. A flurrying of feathers, accompanied by a loud squawking, filled the air while the onlookers shouted encouragement to the two fighters. Pedro praised his bird as it dug its sharp talons into the opponent's flesh. The white bird retaliated with a sharp peck of its beak. Feathers were lost as the audience kept a tight ring to enclose the fighters. Lisa found herself shouting support for her father's rooster, as the atmosphere of the combat excited her. The birds were fairly well matched at this stage, but the fight had to continue until one of the birds was mortally wounded. It was impossible to know how long this would take, but everyone was prepared to stay until the death. Again, the red bird's talons caught in the firm flesh of the opponent, drawing a little blood, yet there was still plenty of fight left in it.

The warning, shouted by an observer, was only just audible above the noise of the fight and spectators, but it was enough to cause a quick reaction. "Look out! The police are coming!"

Pedro grabbed his bird, held it in his arms and ran, while the other was withdrawn by its owner. There was a general panic as everyone ran in different directions. Lisa had been warned that this could happen and did not waste any time asking questions. She ran into the jungle, trying to keep her father in sight as he headed, indirectly, for home.

By the time the policeman arrived, the only signs of the fight ever having taken place were a few scattered feathers, some splashes of blood and disturbed soil.

The policeman was quite used to this situation. Officially, he had to pursue anyone holding an unauthorised cock fight, but he ignored them most of the time, even though he was aware they were taking place. It was more a case of having something in the records to show that he was doing his job. Wearily, the hapless policeman returned to his office to record notes of the incident before finishing for the evening. He omitted to mention that his brother had been one of the onlookers at the fight. In fact, he was more than an onlooker. The police officer's brother was the owner of the white bird. Fearful of losing his rooster, he had asked his brother to intervene so that the fight could be stopped after only a few minutes. In this way, he could assess the fighting qualities of Pedro's new champion without the fight ever needing to reach its deadly conclusion. Cock fighting was a very serious business in the Philippines and a sport which, not surprisingly, caused many an upset to marital life.

Although Lisa had enjoyed what she had seen of the spectacle, she did not bother going to any further fights. In a way, she was relieved that she had been spared from seeing the agonising death of the losing cockerel.

Over the coming years, Pedro had some success with his new bird, and the Tiguelo family often feasted on the remains of cockerels torn to death by Pedro's champion. Traditionally, the owner of the losing bird would hand over the corpse of his fighter to his lucky opponent, to be consumed by the family.

Pedro never sought any forgiveness from his wife and children for the assault on Breeza, knowing that it would never be granted. He became a remote figure who spent little time at home, preferring to be with his men friends, gambling, smoking and drinking. Sometimes their discussions would be political, complaining about the corruptness of the Marcos dictatorship. One of the biggest disappointments of recent times was when the leader of the Democratic opposition, Benigno Aquino, was arrested and charged by a military court with subversion.

The majority of the people in the country had been hopeful that Aquino would topple Marcos, but with the threat of a death sentence, any effective opposition against Marcos was impossible. Instead, inflation rose further, increasing poverty for most while the privileged few improved their wealth by plundering the natural resources of the country. For those with a lot of time and little to do, such as Pedro, all they were capable of was discussing the impossible situation.

Lisa and Breeza were now changed sisters, having only the occasional minor tiff, the ruthless antagonism of their earlier years completely forgotten. Dolores was the undisputed head of the family, making decisions for all of them, many of which, in earlier years, she would have left to her husband. It saddened Dolores to know that the man she had loved and married had become a stranger within their family and was not to be trusted ever again.

Chapter Thirteen

LISA'S SCHOOLING WAS progressing well, her quick mind soaking up the wealth of information presented to her by, mostly, quite strict teachers. Her main fascination was with geography, a subject inspired by her grandfather. When he had shown her, at the age of five, an atlas of the world, she had realised how insignificantly small her village was, not just to the Philippines but also in comparison to the rest of the world and even beyond that. When she learned of the many other planets in the solar system, the magnitude of God's creation had truly astounded her.

In her twelfth year, Lisa had managed to make a good, close friend at school with whom she shared a similar background and many common interests. Jessica, a girl about seven months older than she, had two brothers and no sisters and needed someone close at this difficult stage of her life; Lisa was the one with whom she found true friendship and a close affinity. The two girls, on occasions, would visit Allan's plantation and spent many happy times together, becoming almost inseparable.

Dolores would smile to herself as she listened to the girls happily singing songs as they walked home from school together. She was pleased Lisa had found a good friend to associate with during her formative years.

Around this time, Lisa became aware of another girl who always seemed to follow her. Lea, a thin-looking, untidy ten-year-old, for some unknown reason seemed to be fascinated by Lisa. Wherever she went, the younger girl would always be there. Once she knew that she had been seen, Lea would smile. It was

79

a knowing, rather unnerving smile, and at first, Lisa tried to ignore her, thinking that, in time, she would tire of this stupid, pointless game.

The persistence of the younger girl proved Lisa wrong, as Lea's presence was not only near school but also around the neighbourhood, in church, at the shops—in fact, everywhere Lisa went. Although Jessica told her to ignore the girl, it was beyond a joke and she knew she was going to have to do something about it.

One day, as she was walking home from school on her own since Jessica was ill, Lisa, feeling the presence of her quarry, suddenly stopped and turned around.

"Why are you following me?" she demanded so that Lea would understand how angry this fruitless pursuit had made her. Yet the girl did not seem afraid or surprised.

"Don't you know, Lisa?" she asked with a cheeky smile.

"Haven't you anything better to do with your time than follow me everywhere?"

"Not really. I want to be with you. I like you."

A sick feeling filled Lisa's stomach. She was aware that some girls had strong feelings for others of the same sex, yet Lisa had never expected to be the object of such a strange, unwanted desire. "Just leave me alone, please?" Lisa turned, resuming her homeward journey.

"Don't you want to know why I like you?" Lea persisted, but Lisa ignored her, continuing to walk onwards and trying desperately to think of a way to stop this unwanted pursuit. She had no interest in close relationships with other boys or girls, but she knew that she was incapable of loving another girl.

"Shouldn't sisters love each other?"

At this unexpected question, Lisa stopped dead in her tracks. Turning slowly to face the girl, who was obviously enjoying this

80

game, with a sinking feeling in her heart, Lisa asked, "Sisters? What are you talking about, you stupid girl?"

"Don't call me stupid! It's true! You're my sister. Well, half-sister, anyway!"

Stunned by this declaration, Lisa stared at the young girl in disbelief. It was the first time she had looked properly into her face and, sure enough, Lea did bear some family resemblance. "But how can ... ?" She could not bring herself to ask the obvious question, but the younger girl was not as reserved as Lisa.

"Now who's being stupid? Your father, Pedro Tiguelo, had an affair with my mother, and I'm the result. Is that clear enough for you?"

Tears welled up in Lisa's eyes at this unexpected revelation. She stammered, "But ... but he couldn't have!"

"Of course he could. And it wasn't just once. My mother has been your father's mistress for much longer than twelve years."

That had been the last thing Lisa expected or wanted to be told. With tears running down her cheeks, she asked, "Why are you telling me this now?"

"Because, dear sister, our father has not given us any money for over six months. My mother cries herself to sleep every night, not knowing how we're going to survive. You don't know what it's like to have no money at all!" Lea was becoming quite emotional as she told of their poverty and her mother's anxiety over their lack of financial security and support.

Lisa could not help feeling sorry for her newfound half-sister but knew there was nothing she could do. "I ... I'm sorry. I don't know how my family can help. We have very little money ourselves. Tatay gambles and drinks all of our money, so we're also struggling to survive."

Although not completely surprised by this, Lea had been hoping for better news and promptly burst into tears. On that dusty road, on a hot, summer afternoon, the two girls held each other close in an effort to provide some common comfort.

Wiping her eyes, Lisa said, "Listen, I will speak to my mother and see if there is any way we can help. But I can't make any promises. Do you understand?" The younger girl nodded her head. "Now, you must go home and give us time to see if and how we can help, okay?"

Lea nodded once more. The brash youngster, who only minutes earlier had been taunting Lisa, had now turned into a very sad, tearful little girl. Quietly, she turned away, slowly heading in the direction of her home. Lisa watched as her newly revealed half-sister disappeared from view and felt a great sadness overcome her, mixed with intense anger towards her feckless father.

As soon as she arrived home, Lisa approached her mother, telling her of the bizarre meeting with Lea. It came as a surprise when Dolores said, "I've known about Tatay's other woman for many years. And of her daughter."

"You knew?" Lisa found it hard to believe how calmly her mother was treating the situation. "But why didn't you stop him? Why didn't you do something to end his affair?"

"What could I do? Tatay is a typical man, never satisfied with what he has here. As I grew older, he wanted someone younger and better looking. If I made a lot of fuss about it, he would probably have left us for her. And then our situation would have been even worse. Do you understand what I'm saying?" Her mother held Lisa close, annoyed that she had discovered her half-sister in such a way.

The logic of the explanation was very clear to Lisa and difficult to argue against. She now realised how, for many years, her mother had endured this painful situation for the sake of keeping the family together. "How can we help?"

Her anger rising, Dolores said, in a firm, uncompromising voice, "We can't. It is difficult enough looking after ourselves without having even more mouths to feed. Besides, it's Tatay's problem. Nothing at all to do with us."

Although Lisa loved her mother dearly, she was ashamed of Dolores' indifference. The revelations of that afternoon had made her feel some responsibility towards her half-sister, but there was nothing more to be said, so she quietly left, and her mother, busy preparing a meal, failed to notice.

Lisa had to get away. Somewhere, anywhere. She needed to think. The sky was darkening from the approaching dusk, yet she still walked on, oblivious to her surroundings. Without realising, she had walked in the direction of her grandfather's plantation and remembered nothing of the journey as she arrived at Allan's house.

Her grandfather was sitting quietly on his veranda, reading a book, and did not notice his granddaughter approaching.

"Lolo!" Lisa's voice trembled with emotion as she spoke.

He dropped his book in surprise. "Lisa! What are you doing here?"

"I...I had to talk to someone. I couldn't think where else to go. Please help me, Lolo. Please help me!" The tears ran freely down her face as she threw her arms around the old man.

"Whatever has happened to you, child?" Many worried thoughts raced through his mind as he realised the depth of her depression. Had she been raped? Had one of the family been killed?

She sat on his knees, burying her head in his chest, desperate for comfort.

"Tell me what has happened, Lisa. Take your time. Don't worry, everything is going to be all right."

Slowly and painfully, she recounted the story of her meeting with Lea, her half-sister. Allan waited patiently until she had finished before saying anything. It did not surprise him to learn of his son's infidelity, yet he felt a deep, unrelenting anger at the way Lisa had learned the sordid truth. Puberty was not the best time to learn of such indiscretions.

"You must try not to let it upset you so much, Lisa. These things do happen."

"How could Tatay love someone else when he was married to Nanay? How could he?"

"That's a difficult one to answer." Allan paused for thought. "Perhaps he did not really love this other woman."

"What do you mean?"

"Well..." He had to choose his words very carefully in this difficult situation. "In our culture, there are many pressures on a man to live up to an image. To have another woman as well as a wife is a symbol of man's potency. He is considered to be macho if a husband takes a mistress, especially if it results in another family."

Lisa stared at her grandfather in amazement. She understood what he was saying yet found it difficult to accept.

"Some men even have more than one mistress, which could mean several families all related to each other through their father."

"But how could Nanay just accept that Tatay has another family? Why didn't she stop him?"

"What could she do to stop him? As long as your father continues to support all of you, it is better to accept and ignore the situation."

"How would she have found out?"

Allan considered how to answer without being crude. "It is not difficult for a wife to know when her husband is having an affair. His attitude changes, he even smells different and makes many excuses for long absences. The guilt of what he is doing may even improve the marriage, by showing more care and attention to his wife."

It was obvious from Lisa's expression that there was still another question burning in her mind, yet she was uncertain about asking it. Seeing this, Allan said, "It's okay, Lisa. You know you can ask me any question you want and I will always give you an honest answer."

She took a deep breath. "Lolo, did you have a mistress when you were married to Lola?"

Allan smiled. It had taken a great deal of courage to ask such a bold question of him, a fact which earned her his admiration. Firmly, he said, "No, Lisa. I never could cheat on your grandmother. There was only one woman in my life, and that was my wife."

"But if you have managed for all these years without somebody else, then why couldn't Tatay?"

It was such a logical question, yet one without an obvious answer. "I wish I could tell you, but I do not know. It could be that your father was trying to be like his friends, not wanting to appear a lesser man in their eyes. Such pressures never bothered me. I was also committed to God's scripture, which clearly shows adultery to be a sin against God. I could never have treated your grandmother in such a way, even after her death."

Lisa knew then that her father was a much weaker man than Allan and despised him more than ever. What her grandfather had told her made great sense, although it did not lessen Pedro's crime nor her own hurt feelings. Her thoughts returned to that of her half-sister and the desperation Lisa had seen in her eyes.

"What about Lea? What can I tell her?"

He countered by asking, "What would you like to tell her?"

A look of deep concern crossed her young features. "I don't know. I just feel that something should be done to help her. After all, she is my half-sister and it's not her fault."

"Yes, but you must understand how Nanay feels. To you, Lea is related by blood. To Nanay, she is nothing. Just the result of her husband's adulterous affair. She hardly wants to be reminded of that, does she?"

Lisa began to understand how her mother must be feeling, yet she still had a sense of responsibility to her newfound relative. "Perhaps I can help her a little. If I take some food to school with me, I could give it to her there."

Allan was very proud that, at only twelve years of age, Lisa was prepared to make sacrifices in this way for her half-sister. "That's okay if you want to do that, but you must be careful not to upset or anger Nanay. You already know how she is feeling."

"I do love Nanay, but I wish she would understand how I feel. I can't just forget all about Lea."

"Listen, Lisa. You tell Lea that she and her mother must come here to see me. I will do what I can to help them. After all, Lea is still my granddaughter and nothing will change that."

On hearing this, Lisa brightened up. She gave Allan a kiss. "Thank you so much, Lolo. You're an angel."

He laughed. "Oh, I'm certainly no angel, Lisa. I just feel the same sense of responsibility as you." Allan was ashamed of his son, who had, over many years, caused him numerous disappointments, but now that the heavy burden had been taken off her shoulders, Lisa felt much happier and relieved.

"Now, young lady, I expect you didn't tell Nanay that you were coming here, did you?"

Lisa lowered her eyes and shook her head, knowing what Allan was going to say.

"Do you not realise how concerned Nanay must be feeling? You must never go anywhere without telling her first. She will be worried sick."

Tears again began to flow. "Please don't send me home, Lolo. Can't I stay here tonight?"

Allan took a handkerchief out of his pocket and wiped Lisa's eyes. "Of course you can, but we still have to let Nanay know where you are. I'll ask Ricky to walk over and put your mother's mind at ease."

***

When Dolores had become aware of Lisa's disappearance, she asked the other children if they had seen their sister. None of them had even noticed but could see the worried expression on their mother's face.

"Why would she run away?" Breeza asked.

"I…I don't know," Dolores lied. She knew exactly why her daughter had walked out and felt some responsibility and shame for not showing enough understanding for her daughter's feelings after discovering her half-sister's existence. Knowing how close Lisa was to her grandfather, Dolores hoped that her daughter had gone to him, but she still wanted to be certain of Lisa's safety. When Pedro came in, she spoke to him quietly so they would not be overheard by their other children.

"Pedro, Lisa has found out about her half-sister."

He looked alarmed. "How? Did you tell her?"

She retorted, angrily, "No, of course not! Perhaps I should have told her before she found out in this way, but that's not the point. She's disappeared. I think she must have gone to your father's. You had better go and find her. I can't rest until I know where she is."

87

Chapter Fourteen

WITH SOME RELUCTANCE, Pedro agreed to look for Lisa. He was in a foul mood for most of the time, and this was now made worse by the need to locate his missing daughter. He was a lazy man by nature, sparing little effort for anyone or anything except his precious fighting cockerel.

Dolores could see this and reminded him, "Pedro, when you find Lisa, treat her very gently. Don't you dare think of hitting the child like you did with Breeza. After all, if you'd kept your otin in your pants, this would never have happened."

This painful reminder of his infidelity ringing in his ears, Pedro slunk away, muttering curses under his breath. He did not really hurry along the track, preferring instead to think of the relationship he had with Lea's mother over a period of many years. There had been numerous occasions where he had slipped away from home to see his lover and enjoyed the illicit love-making. His mistress, Annalita, without the burden of many children, was exciting and much more passionate than Dolores had ever been. Annalita was also far more sexually exciting, teaching him many more positions to achieve maximum sexual satisfaction. He felt no guilt whatsoever and had, in fact, grown tired of both his family and his mistress. Pedro's love life was now non-existent, as he found much more enjoyment from training his fighting cockerels.

He reached Allan's house just as Ricky was about to leave and cursed himself that he had made the journey instead of the younger man. There were no smiles from either his father or his daughter to greet him on his arrival.

As soon as Lisa saw her enraged father and his undisguised hatred directed towards her, fear engulfed her, and she quickly disappeared inside the house.

"Please don't let him take me home, Lolo! He'll beat me, like he did to Breeza."

"Don't worry, Lisa. He's not going to touch you. I'll speak to him."

Pedro saw his daughter disappear into the house and shouted, without making any effort to disguise his anger. "Come here, girl! Have you any idea what trouble you've caused?"

Allan stood directly in Pedro's path. "She's not going anywhere tonight. The girl is upset after discovering her half-sister."

"What about her mother? Lisa should never have run off without saying where she was going!"

"I know. She was wrong to do that. But now you can tell Dolly she's perfectly safe and with me."

"Don't interfere, Tatay. She had better come home with me. Now!" Pedro tried to pass his father to enter the house. "Come on, Lisa! We're going home!"

The old man was not going to give in so easily and stuck out his leg. His reactions slowed by the constant abuse of alcohol, Pedro fell over the protruding limb, crashing heavily to the floor.

"I told you, Pedro. She is not going anywhere today! Now go home and calm yourself down!"

When Pedro managed to get back onto his feet again, there was pure hatred in his eyes. Smarting from this humiliation, he glowered at his father and raised his fist.

For a moment, it looked as if Allan was going to receive a hefty blow from his own son, but then a voice, clear and authoritative, rang out. "Don't you dare touch him or you're a dead man."

It was Ricky. Allan's faithful assistant had heard all the shouting and was ready to defend his employer if the need arose.

A gleaming machete was held in a threatening gesture, leaving Pedro in absolutely no doubt about his intentions.

Lisa watched from a window and gave a happy shout of relief at Ricky's timely intervention. She did wonder if Ricky would actually have killed her father. In her mind, he would have deserved it, and she certainly would not have missed him.

Pedro knew he was powerless against the stronger, fitter man. In an instant, Ricky could have leapt upon him, using the sharp, steel blade to swiftly end his life. He stood motionless, as Allan took control of the situation.

"Now, listen to me, Pedro. You go home and tell Dolly that Lisa is safe and staying here with me. I will bring her home tomorrow morning. But if you harm the girl in any way, I'll kill you myself, and that is a promise! This whole problem is because of you and your other family. If you had any decency, this would never have happened. I never want to see you at my house again. Dolly and all of the children are welcome at any time, but from this moment, you are no longer my son. Do you understand?"

The burning menace in Pedro's eyes remained. He hated his father for humiliating him, yet knew he had no choice but to leave. He turned, angrily spat on the ground and, without another word, slowly walked away.

"Thanks, Ricky."

The young man smiled. "It's okay. He needed to be taught a lesson."

Lisa ran out of the house and threw her arms around Allan. "Oh, Lolo, Tatay frightens me. Please, don't let him kill me!"

"Don't worry, Lisa. He's a coward. I really meant what I said, and he knows it. If he does anything to you, he will pay for it with his own life. Now, come on, dry those eyes, little one. Then we'll see what Marlyn can cook for us." He put a comforting arm around her shoulder as they walked into the house.

Lisa made the most of that evening, feeling very safe in her grandfather's care. Marlyn prepared a splendid meal of rice, chicken livers and vegetables, all made hot and spicy by the addition of chilli peppers. She made certain that the little girl had plenty to eat, piling her plate high. With cool, fresh fruit juice to refresh her, Lisa felt very full, satisfied and comfortable after such a fantastic meal. Allan knew she would soon fall asleep, the traumatic events of the day being temporarily forgotten.

Her eyes were very heavy as she gave Allan a goodnight hug and kiss. "I love you, Lolo. I wish Tatay was more like you."

Her affectionate statement brought tears to his eyes. She was so precious to him, he would gladly give his own life to protect her. As expected, Lisa soon fell into a deep sleep, lasting until six-thirty the next morning.

After a light breakfast and a quick wash, Allan walked her home. To the little girl's relief, Pedro was nowhere to be seen on their return. It was Dolores who welcomed them, happy to see her daughter return home safely.

Lisa put her arms around her mother. "I'm sorry I ran away, Nanay. Lolo has been looking after me. He even stopped Tatay from hitting me."

Dolores' eyebrows rose on hearing this. That would explain the foul mood Pedro was in the previous evening. Not surprisingly, he had said nothing about the incident on his return, simply telling her where her daughter was and that she would return home the following morning. Dolores had had an uneasy feeling that Pedro was not telling her everything but hadn't pressed for further details.

She felt such anger toward the man she had once loved and married. He had changed so much over the years. Where there had once been honour and tenderness in his character, there was now cowardice and so much bitterness, she was afraid that, one day, his hot temper would result in someone's serious injury or even death.

"It's okay. I should have listened more when you told me how you had discovered your half-sister. It hurts me to be reminded of your father's adultery."

"Lolo is going to help Lea," Lisa said excitedly, and Allan visibly winced, belatedly realising he should have stressed to the innocent twelve-year-old to keep the assistance a secret from her mother, expecting some possible hostility.

"Why?" Dolores looked with sharp, angry eyes directly at Allan. "It's Pedro's problem, not yours."

Patiently, Allan replied, "We all know Pedro is not capable of looking after her, and I could not see her starve, could I?"

"You're a good man, Tatay, but too soft. You don't know where this help might end. For all we know, there could be a trail of other illegitimate children all coming to your door for help."

"Don't worry, Dolly. I'll make certain they don't abuse my generosity. They shall help on the plantation and earn their support. I could do with some extra help at the moment."

Dolores was not convinced he needed any more help and was certain he had said it to placate her. She felt slightly easier, but warned, "Just be careful, please, Tatay. I don't want to see you hurt." Turning to Lisa, Dolores said firmly, "Now, young lady. We'd better get you ready for school. You've already missed some lessons."

"Oh, Nanay! Do I have to go to school? Can't I stay off, just for today?"

Dolores stood her ground. "Certainly not! Get your books together and I'll walk to school with you." Aware of the temptation in her daughter's mind to try to avoid school, Dolores was determined to ensure Lisa's attendance. "Thanks for looking after Lisa, Tatay. She is very lucky to have such a good grandfather."

"Oh, that's okay. She can come anytime, as long as she gets your permission first. Anyway, I won't be here forever, so she might as well make the most of it while I'm still alive."

This last statement by her grandfather worried the young girl. The thought of Allan dying had never crossed Lisa's mind before and the possibility absolutely horrified her. Without him, who could she turn to for genuine paternal love and moral support?

"Oh, Lolo, I want you to stay alive forever."

Allan laughed. "I'm not certain that's a good idea. I'm getting old, and just as night follows day, death will come to everyone when their time is up. Now, come on, Lisa. You had better go to school."

Allan walked for part of the way with his granddaughter and daughter-in-law. He gave Lisa a parting hug, saying, "You be a good girl for Nanay and do what she tells you. Promise?"

"I promise, Lolo."

Turning to Dolores, he said quietly, "Let me know if you have any trouble at all with Pedro. He's a man of many different moods, and I don't want anything to happen to any of you because of his temper."

Dolores appreciated his concern and gave Allan a parting hug before continuing towards school.

***

Later that day, when Lisa saw Lea, she told her of how her grandfather was prepared to help a little and how she could find him. Lea seemed genuinely thankful and very different from the bitter little girl who had stalked Lisa so ruthlessly.

Lisa's friend Jessica listened, spellbound, as the story of the previous day was recounted in great detail. During their walk home from school, the two girls discussed the problem of having an uncaring, sometimes violent father such as Pedro. Fortunately for Jessica, her father did not have the same characteristics as Pedro and appeared to be a genuine family man.

Pedro did not pose much of a threat to any of the family after that day. Instead, he became even more insular and remote, spending most of the time with his male friends and concentrating his efforts towards gambling on cock-fighting. Dolores was not only the head of the household but now also had to earn a living to feed and clothe her children. She took in sewing work, cleaned other people's houses, looked after children—in fact turned her hand to practically anything that would earn her a few pesos. In addition, she was helped by her sons and daughters. Antonio and Enrico, now in their twenties, could not find any work, even though Antonio was married and had a small daughter of his own. Around this time, there were several outbreaks of dengue fever, usually caused by being bitten by infected mosquitos. Antonio had been bitten and had been quite sick but thankfully managed to recover from the illness.

Lisa's aunt Lucia, at the age of forty-five, was not so fortunate. After several weeks of sickness and swollen stomach, she died in terrible pain. Lisa wept at her loss and hoped that nobody else would catch dengue fever.

It was a difficult time, during the late 1970s, for the fast-expanding population of the Philippines, with poverty spreading at an alarming rate. To add to the country's problems, there was a great deal of political unrest, with Ferdinand Marcos's popularity at an all-time low. In the area where the Tiguelo family lived, there were many activists willing to take arms against government forces. In an attempt to crush any opposition, Marcos ordered the military to send heavy armour into the region.

Lisa and her family were disturbed one night by the sound of tanks moving slowly through the area. When they realised that some houses were literally being crushed, they fled without gathering any of their possessions and ran into the jungle in a desperate effort to remain alive. For several difficult days, they survived within the densely wooded confines of the jungle, temporarily safe from the troops and existing on what little food could be found in the undergrowth, using Dolores' skills to know what was safe to eat. They even resorted to eating grubs hidden behind the crumbling bark of rotting trees. Although this was preferable to starving, Lisa and her sisters could not bring themselves to eat some of these unsavoury sources of nutrition.

It was a miserable time, trying to avoid dangerous reptiles and the military alike. Lisa, in common with many others, lost weight through this enforced rationing and appreciated the help and comfort given by her best friend, Jessica, whose family was also trying to survive by living in the jungle. Two of Lisa's brothers would, on occasion, creep back towards their home in an attempt to determine when it would be safe to return.

At last, the troops and their heavy armour seemed to have moved on to different areas, allowing the Tiguelos and many other families back into their homes. A great deal of looting and damage had been caused by the oppressive action, and it took considerable time for the people to recover.

Chapter Fifteen

1981 WAS A very significant year in Lisa's life. She was now fifteen, a happy, carefree girl, who was physically maturing yet retained the natural innocence of a child. She was well-liked by everyone and still held a special relationship with her mother and grandfather. In common with many others in the Philippines, money was in very short supply, yet somehow, they managed.

Whenever she could, Lisa and her friend Jessica would stay with her grandfather on his plantation. He was a man of such knowledge and experience that their times together were an education in themselves.

The fourteenth day of May 1981 proved to be a significant day for many. It came as a tremendous shock when they listened to the radio that morning. The newsreader, speaking in sombre tones, reported that an assassination attempt had been made on Pope John Paul at five nineteen the previous evening, leaving the revered head of the Catholic Church critically ill in hospital.

Although he had been pope for just two and a half years, everyone in the Philippines held the Polish pontiff in such high esteem that this attack was taken personally by everybody. The family sat in stunned silence as they listened intently to the tiny, crackling radio. Dolores and her children all made the sign of the cross and prayed that the Holy Father would survive his injuries. Apparently, a twenty-three-year-old Turkish terrorist had fired several shots at the sixty-year-old pope while he was surrounded by thousands of followers and worshippers in St. Peter's Square in Rome. Some of the bullets had penetrated his abdomen, which made the chances of recovery much more difficult. It was with a very heavy heart that Lisa started her daily chores, and worse was yet to come.

That afternoon, Lisa was busy helping her mother with washing. She was outside, squeezing the water out of the heavy clothes before hanging them to dry, when she heard her name being called. Dropping the clothes with a loud splash back into the rinsing water, she rushed to the front of the house to see what was happening.

It was Ricky. The man was breathless, obviously having run the three miles from Allan's plantation.

"What's wrong, Ricky? What's happened?" She felt terribly afraid of the answer.

"It's your grandfather," he gasped. "He's not been well for a few days, but last night, he became far worse. He wants to see you as soon as possible."

Lisa's stomach turned. She knew that at sixty-seven, Allan was lucky to still be alive, since many in this poor country commonly died in their forties or fifties. Although she knew it to be impossible, she wanted him to live forever.

Having heard Ricky, and knowing how close her daughter was to Allan, Dolores said, "Go quickly, Lisa. I'll come as soon as I can, but my legs are not as young and as quick as yours."

Lisa had never made the journey as fast as she did that day. The lush vegetation of the jungle and the numerous, fruity aromas went unnoticed as she raced along the dusty track, accompanied by Ricky. Usually, she would linger on such a journey, soaking in the delights of this beautiful tropical setting, but now, only one thought occupied her mind. She prayed out loud that the one man she loved and admired would be saved. The sweat poured down her body from her exertions, soaking her pale-blue shirt. It was fortunate that she was wearing jeans, as a skirt would have hindered her progress. Ricky ran beside her, saying little.

They were both exhausted when, at last, they reached the plantation. With great urgency, Lisa rushed straight into her grandfather's room, desperately hoping he could be saved.

Allan lay quietly on his bed as Lisa approached. His eyes were closed but flickered open as she put her arms him, and a smile appeared as he recognised his granddaughter.

"Lolo, it's Lisa. How are you feeling?"

"Not good, Lisa, not good." His voice was weak and his ashen appearance was enough to leave Lisa in no doubt about his condition.

Allan had always been slim, but now, what little flesh he had in the past was gone, leaving him gaunt and skeletal. Huge tears welled in Lisa's eyes. "What is making you ill, Lolo? Has the doctor been to see you?"

"Yes, he's been. There's nothing he can do. He tells me that it's cancer in my bowel, but it is too late for any treatment. I'm dying, Lisa."

"Don't say that, Lolo. You can't die. I don't want you to die!"

He held her close as she sobbed uncontrollably. "You must never be afraid of death, Lisa. I heard the news about our Holy Father, but I feel certain that he will recover. It is God's will that I should leave this earth. I'm ready to join my Monalisa."

The fifteen-year-old was surprised by her grandfather's calmness and buried her head in his chest as she sobbed gently. She could not find the words to express her feelings.

Allan patted her reassuringly on her back. Noticing Ricky, he said, "Thanks for bringing Lisa. You're a good man. The plantation is yours now. You are like the son I wished I had. Please, take good care of it."

The young man, normally so brave, quiet and impassive, looked as though he was ready to burst into tears. Since the age of fifteen, he had worked for Allan and had great respect for his employer. Allan's kindness and honesty were qualities that would be difficult to equal.

Before Ricky had chance to speak, Allan said, "It's okay, you don't need to say anything. I know that if Pedro were to get his hands on this plantation, it would be bankrupt and ruined in less than six months. All I ask is that you retain and take care of Marlyn, Floriza and May. Also, I want you to pay a ground rent of eight hundred pesos a month to Dolores. That will give her a little income and still leave plenty for you."

Ricky knew this was a very fair offer, as he could earn at least fifty thousand pesos a year with a reasonable harvest.

"Now, Ricky, will you leave me to talk to my granddaughter, please? Don't let anyone else come in until I am ready."

Obediently, Ricky left the room, closing the door behind him.

"Little one, I have much to tell you, while I still am able. I promised, many years ago, to tell you about your grandmother and how she died. I still don't know if you're ready to hear it, but it seems I have no choice. There is little time left."

***

When Dolores arrived, Ricky politely explained that Allan had not wanted to be disturbed. Patiently, she waited, curious to know what was being said. She strained her ears to try and catch a few words, but Allan was talking too quietly for her to pick anything up.

After about twenty minutes, Lisa appeared, tears still flowing from her blood-red eyes as she stood sobbing in the doorway. Seeing Dolores, Lisa walked slowly towards her, seeking the comfort only a mother could give. "Lolo's dying, Nanay. I don't want him to die."

Dolores put a comforting arm around Lisa's shoulders. "God will take care of him, Lisa. Don't worry, he will be in good hands."

99

Together, they walked back into the bedroom. When Dolores saw how grey her father-in-law looked, she wondered if he was already dead.

The old man's eyes flickered open. "Dolly." His voice was barely audible, but a smile crossed his features as he recognised his visitor.

"It's okay, Tatay. You don't have to talk. I'm just happy to see you." She bent over and gave him a kiss on his cheek. His skin was cold and clammy to her moist lips.

"You have been good to me, Dolly. I shall miss you."

There was no doubt in anybody's mind that life in Allan's frail body was ebbing away fast. "I shall miss you too, Tatay. You have no idea how much I will miss you." Tears were now freely flowing down her cheeks as the emotion-charged setting absorbed her feelings of love. In the thirty-one years she had known her father-in-law, she had never seen him angry or ill-tempered. His manners were always impeccable, and she found it quite remarkable that he was the father of Pedro, as their characters were so fundamentally different and opposite. Pedro had been loving and good to her all those years ago when they had first met, but with the passage of time, greed, laziness and selfishness had overtaken her husband's character.

Allan's breathing was quite laboured as he said, "Take good care of all the family, Dolly. Especially Lisa. You will be very proud of her one day."

Dolores was puzzled by this statement, unsure what he could mean. She had always been baffled by this strange bond between Lisa and Allan but had never questioned it.

Pain crossed his face. "God have mercy on me!" With this last utterance, the life left his body, and silence replaced the irregular gasping breaths, yet both Dolores and Lisa were happy to see the smile return to his ashen face. That would be how they must

100

remember him. The man with the dignified smile who was known to many people for his generosity and kindness.

Dolores, quickly followed by Lisa, made the sign of the cross and bent their heads in silent prayer. Lisa felt the loss, not only of a grandfather but also of her very best friend. Their special relationship meant so much to her and she would never forget him or what he had told her, in confidence. Lisa took a last look at Allan and gasped in amazement.

Dolores looked with curiosity at her daughter and saw nothing out of the ordinary, realising that whatever Lisa had seen must have been for her eyes only.

Lisa blinked, yet the figure was still there. Standing behind her grandfather's head was a shimmering, golden angel. The beautifully serene face was unmistakable. It was the face of Monalisa, her grandmother. Her smile gave Lisa a feeling of calmness, comfort and reassurance that everything would be all right.

As she walked out of the room, Lisa thought of what her grandfather had told her in his last dying moments. His secrets would be safe with her, and when the time was ready, she would do her best to fulfil his final requests.

**

Dolores took full charge of the funeral preparations, willingly assisted by Lisa, who was determined to show a fitting tribute to the man she had idolised for so many years. The young girl had suddenly, with Allan's death, matured into a responsible young adult.

Pedro, on the other hand, had showed no grief at the loss of his father, even expressing bitterness at being denied his inheritance. "Why the hell should Ricky have the plantation? He's just an employee, not a blood relative."

"He may only have been an employee," Dolores countered, "but he has done far more for your father than you ever did. He has been a good, hard-working man and close friend of Allan's and deserves his reward. If you had any sense, you would have learned a few lessons from him."

Pedro, once the respected head of the family, now had to endure the cutting remarks made by his recently emboldened wife, who now always seemed to have the last word.

Although Pedro was Allan's only child, the elderly man came from a large family, with many sisters, brothers, nephews and nieces. Many of them did not live locally but would, no doubt, wish to be present at Allan's funeral.

Dolores, accompanied by Lisa, travelled to each relative, informing them of Allan's death and inviting them to the funeral. Francisco, a close friend for many years, was noticeably shaken at the news of Allan's death and offered to help in any way he could. It would take ten days before the ceremony could be held, allowing time for everybody to make their arrangements.

Allan's sisters, particularly the younger ones, were shocked and saddened by the news, causing many tears to be shed. He was well-loved by all his relatives, and without exception, every person informed of the tragic death had wished to attend the funeral. The words of affection spoken about him were genuine and not the sycophantic platitudes often heard on such occasions when greed motivates people to battle for their expected share of the inheritance.

Allan's body had been suitably prepared to withstand the fast-decaying effects of the tropical heat. His corpse remained at his house, on view in an ornate, polished casket for any of the grieving friends and relatives to show their last respects. A glass panel above the corpse provided some protection to assist in its preservation. The room was transformed into a miniature chapel, with ornate candle holders adding to the effect. The white curtains were replaced with rich, deep-purple material, and a large rug covered the floor around the casket.

Ricky was worried about the potential fire hazard and made many checks to ensure safety. Ancient myths combined with the dominant Catholic faith to create a strange set of rules and superstitions. The house and the people in it were supposed to remain dirty and unwashed for the whole nine days of the mourning period, yet Dolores and Lisa felt that this was a custom which could be ignored for the sake of hygiene and cleanliness. Every evening, the local church deacon would arrive at the house and say prayers for the deceased, followed by hymn singing, assisted by as many relatives who could fit into the room. On the seventh evening, this was extended to a full Mass by the arrival of the priest. Dolores, Lisa and her sisters took turns to keep a vigil for the body throughout the night, again following ancient customs that defied any sense of logic.

When the day of the funeral finally arrived, the population of this part of Cotabato was swollen by the many mourners to an extent it had never seen before. Those who had travelled any distance were given temporary shelter in the large grounds around the house. Marlyn had the task of providing food and refreshments for the many visitors, and on the actual day of the funeral, pigs were slaughtered to provide a feast for all the mourners.

Lisa felt unable to view the body of her grandfather, as she preferred to remember him as she had last seen him on the day he had died, feeling certain that what was now lying in state was just an empty shell of the man she so deeply loved. She felt extreme guilt as she asked over and over why God had spared Pope John Paul yet had failed to save the most important person in her life. It was a terrible, selfish thought, but she could not help herself.

If only God could have spared him for a few more years, they could have enjoyed so many more good times together. Could it be that God was so busy caring for John Paul that he overlooked the failing health of Allan Tiguelo? It was, undoubtedly, the most testing time for Lisa's beliefs. She felt let down and deserted by both the Catholic Church and God alike.

The coffin was placed in a hearse, which had been richly decorated with silks and flowers. As the sombre procession, headed by the hearse, passed through the village on its mile-long journey, many additional mourners joined those walking. By the time they reached the church, there were so many wishing to pay their last respects to 'the man with the dignified smile' that it proved impossible to accommodate them all within the ancient church. People were tightly squeezed into every single pew, while others were standing along the side and rear walls of the church. Those unable to fit inside had to be content to amass around the open doors, listening intently to the priest's words. It could well have been a recipe for trouble, with tempers flaring as people fought for a privileged viewpoint, but remarkably, everyone was on their best behaviour.

Lisa even spotted Lea, her half-sister, amongst the crowds of mourners. The girl had grown quite fond of the man who had been such a great help for her family.

A notable exception was Pedro, who still bore a grudge against his father, even in death. Many were surprised by his absence and asked Dolores if he was too ill to attend. It made the funeral even more upsetting for her, having to make excuses for her ill-mannered, thoughtless husband. He was probably hiding somewhere, drinking heavily. In truth, Dolores preferred him to be absent, as he would only have caused more trouble if he had been there.

104

The sadness of the occasion caused many to weep openly. Lisa's head was bowed, her shoulders gently shaking as she sobbed over the loss of the most important person in her life.

The priest spoke many kind words about the man whose generosity had touched so many lives in this part of the Philippines. All Allan's relatives and many of his friends were dressed in black as a mark of respect. Lisa and her sisters wore sombre black dresses and a small lace headpiece covering their hair, while Dolores' headpiece extended into a full shawl. Around her neck, Lisa wore a fine, gold chain, from which was suspended a locket. Inside the casing were two photographs: one of Allan, as a young man; the other of Monalisa, his long-dead wife. Allan had given the locket to Monalisa many years ago, shortly after their marriage, and then had presented it to Lisa, asking her to take great care of it. There was no doubt in his mind that she was the only one worthy of receiving such a personal keepsake. Lisa promised faithfully to treasure it, knowing how important it had been to her grandfather. She also had the world atlas to remind her of the many happy hours they had spent looking through its pages.

The priest's words drifted in and out of Lisa's mind as the memories of the times she had spent with her grandfather, flooded back. The many hours they had just talked of anything and everything, his books, full of history and geography which so fascinated her, their long walks along the river and, of course, the secret Hall of Mary, so cleverly concealed behind the waterfall. All of these were moments in her life, so full of happy memories.

When the ceremony was complete, the coffin was loaded back onto the hearse and the procession started once again, this time heading towards the cemetery. It was a beautifully hot, sunny day, their black clothing absorbing the sun's strong rays. There was no proper highway in this part of the hilly province, their route taking them along a rough, stony track. It almost seemed a shame to drive such a prestigious vehicle over uneven ground, but with some complaining from the engine and occasional crashing of gears, it managed to move slowly along the route to the cemetery. The procession of mourners did not find it an easy trek either, many of them, particularly the elderly, having to stop for the occasional rest. There was no hurry, and the burial did not commence until most had arrived. Four of Allan's brothers lifted the coffin from the hearse and carried it, shoulder-high, towards the open tomb. The casket was lifted into the tomb, after which the open end was sealed by a workman, using bricks and cement. An engraved marble headstone was finally placed in position, marking the end of the official burial.

It was no secret that Allan was closer to Lisa than anyone else, giving her the right to assume the role of chief mourner. Standing near the headstone, she held a single, red orchid, which she had picked that same morning. After saying a silent prayer, she placed the flower in a small container in front of the headstone. Tears streamed down her face as she said in a loud yet trembling voice, "I love you, Lolo! Dear God, please protect and take into your care, the soul of Allan Tiguelo."

This simple, symbolic gesture touched the hearts of all the mourners, and an eerie silence fell upon the large group.

The priest began, "Heavenly father..." but Lisa did not hear any of his words, her mind still reliving all the happy times she and her grandfather had spent together. What haunted her most, though, was what he had told her only minutes before the life had drained from his body. She did not know how she could carry out her grandfather's wishes and prayed for God's future guidance.

The mourners set off once again, but this time in a less-ordered procession. People chatted in small groups as they made their way back towards Allan's plantation. After the sadness of the formal occasion, it was custom to hold a fiesta, usually at the home of the deceased person. It took quite a while for everyone to reach the plantation, but as with many aspects of Filipino life, there was no need to rush. Marlyn, assisted by friends, had prepared a massive collection of foods to refresh the mourners after their long, tiring day. There were barbecued pigs, chickens, vegetables and, of course, masses of rice. Fresh mangoes, pineapples and papaya were all in abundance and a poignant reminder of the man who had devoted his life to growing such tropical fruits. True to his word, Francisco had not only supplied some of the food but had also asked his own helpers to assist with the preparations.

Like all such gatherings, after a while, the people separated. The men sat around in groups, drinking, smoking and laughing noisily, while the women and children kept themselves in a less self-indulgent assembly. Occasionally, a few women would start singing, soon joined by other women and girls. There were many songs reserved for funerals, and they would be repeated several times as the mourners sang deep into the night, even through to the following morning. Lisa felt there was something very special, almost haunting, about the sound of so many female voices singing unaccompanied. She had invited Jessica to the funeral and, together, they sang their songs along with the others.

When dawn finally broke, most were asleep and would stay that way for a great part of the day. Seven days later, prayers would again be said, usually followed by the men drinking and gambling. By this time, those mourners who had travelled any distance would have returned to their homes.

Chapter Sixteen

BY THE AGE of sixteen, Lisa's full beauty was apparent. It was a natural, uncultivated beauty that attracted many admiring and, not surprisingly, some jealous glances. Even with her good looks, she showed little interest in boys and in many ways enjoyed life as a bit of a tomboy. She had become very close to her mother and seemed content just to be with family and friends, especially Jessica. Life, however, could hardly be described as peaceful for any of the Tiguelo family.

There had been much unrest in the Philippines for several years as Ferdinand Marcos and his friends did their best to plunder the natural riches of the country. Many people were willing to challenge the corrupt government as they joined forces to create the New People's Army. The area in this southern part of Cotabato had become popular as a training ground and hiding place for the rebels, making it impossible for anyone living in the community to escape the troubles. The tension throughout the country had even been picked up by the children, and over the year since Allan's death, the time had passed without any happy events to break the tedium of poverty and shortages for Lisa and her family.

The Catholic Church, never afraid to speak out against the Government, had turned many of the usual religious sermons into political gatherings. In this way, they managed to get the message out to the masses, but careful not to overstep the mark, ministers had appealed for peaceful protest. There were members of the congregation who knew it would take more than peaceful protests to solve the country's many serious problems. Dolores and Pedro, along with most of the Church members, had decided to join the NPA, yet they had stopped short of actually taking to arms, preferring instead to help in any peaceful way possible.

Dolores, and even Pedro, had discussed their thoughts with the whole family before committing themselves to the NPA. They stressed that this was no ideological game and the possible consequences of membership could prove fatal. They all knew that government forces would not hesitate to kill anyone found to be a member of the NPA, which was a sobering thought.

All the family was unanimous in their decision and decided to risk the consequences. They would have to undergo an initiation ceremony where they would swear allegiance to the rebel forces. The air was tense in the tiny house of the local leader as the initiation ceremony progressed. It only needed a single person to inform the authorities of what was happening and they would all be ruthlessly killed.

It was late at night as the family gathered together in the Nipa hut. A dark, wet and windy night, the candles flickered angrily with every chilling draught, eerily lighting the faces of each person as their turn came to take part in the ceremony.

After Jessica, Lisa was the last and keenly stepped forward when Romeo, the leader motioned to her.

"Do you understand the rules and aims of the New People's Army?"

Lisa's innocent, young features appeared almost angel-like in the light of the flickering candles. It seemed incongruous that a beautiful sixteen-year-old should be enrolling into such a dangerous organisation. "Yes, I do."

"Do you promise to support the cause of the NPA to remove the present government? Do you accept the principle of equality for every individual in the Philippines?"

"I do."

"Do you promise not to reveal the identity of any member of the NPA? I would remind you that the penalty for revealing a member's identity is death."

This was a very chilling reminder of the seriousness of her promises, yet she did not hesitate.

"I do."

"Do you accept that, when you are working on missions for the NPA, you will be away from your family and, if instructed, will never return to them?"

This was one of the worst conditions of joining, and Lisa hoped that it would never actually come to this. "Yes, I do."

"Welcome to the New People's Army, sister Julie." Romeo took hold of Lisa's hand and shook it firmly. Every member of the group had been assigned a new name, which should, hopefully, help to avoid identification by the authorities.

When the ceremony was over, the newly elected members slipped quietly out into the dismal evening air. Careful to avoid suspicion, they separated, each making their own way home. There was much talk that night about their new roles and responsibilities, which they all took very seriously.

After that day, Lisa became much more suspicious of strangers, constantly aware that they may be undercover government supporters. She was keen to have some useful role and became secretary of the local NPA group. She kept the records of how much money had been raised and also put every effort into enlisting new members, assisted by Jessica. This meant that she had to document a great deal of information, which put her at considerable risk. The notebook in which she kept all the information had to be securely stored in a plastic bag and buried in the ground close to her house.

Lisa particularly enjoyed the rallies, where many supporters of the NPA would gather to hear what visiting officials had to say.

They would tell of the latest excesses and atrocities of the Marcos government. After a rousing speech enthusiastically applauded by the audience, everyone would sing the songs of the rebel cause. This would be accompanied by the crowd raising their left arms in a clenched fist, an influence from the Maoist Communist revolution in China.

With the ever-increasing poverty of the population, it was not difficult to recruit new members at these rallies. There was no doubt that Marcos was responsible for all the country's problems and would have been lynched, had he dared to attend any of these meetings. There was always a noticeable increase in anti-government slogans appearing on buildings after a rally.

On occasions, Lisa would be sent on missions for the NPA to places like Davao, a large city high in the mountain regions and quite a distance from her home. It would take about four hours to travel there by bus, a hot uncomfortable journey along rough, narrow, twisting roads rising into the mountains. She set off on her mission early in the morning, her fare being provided by the NPA.

Before starting, she had folded the message she was to carry into a tiny rectangular package, which she concealed inside her bra. She also had a small container of antibiotics, helpful when treating wounded rebels, but she had no option but to carry them inside her bag. To provide some refreshment, she had taken with her some fresh fruit and chewing gum.

Fully aware of the potential dangers of what she was doing, Lisa's adrenaline levels were high and her heart pounded as the bus progressed on its laborious route. It was a hot, dry day and the bus was quite busy as it started its journey. The long, single-decker was full of men and women of all ages as well as a few children. Within a couple of hours, many had left the bus, yet it was still about half full. Lisa looked at the remaining passengers and wondered if there could be any other NPA agents or, even more dangerous, government agents.

A middle-aged woman sat next to her, but to avoid difficult questions, Lisa decided not to make conversation. Two young men, who seemed to talk incessantly, were sitting in front of her, while a woman with a small child was behind her. The beauty of the NPA messenger system was that the most unlikely people could be used. Simple, ordinary people were willing to risk their lives to help the rebel cause and, hopefully, rid the country of Marcos and his ruthless followers.

The chewing gum did help to keep Lisa's mouth moist as the old bus, its engine straining to heave itself along the twisting incline, raised huge clouds of dust from the road. The windows were openings with canvas roller blinds for simple protection from the sun and did little to save the passengers from all the dust and strong-smelling engine fumes. The suspension was nearly as hard as the seating, resulting in a very uncomfortable ride, but the patient Filipinos were quite used to such discomforts. Lisa had a small bottle of water in her bag, yet this did not last long as the sweltering heat did its best to dehydrate her body.

After nearly three hours into her journey, the bus pulled into an area at the side of the road. While it was not quite what could be described as a bus station, it provided access to a small community with facilities where the passengers could stretch their legs and use the toilets. Lisa took advantage of this comfort stop, knowing that she still had a long wait before she reached her destination. When she took her seat again, many young children had surrounded the bus, each holding a tray filled with a myriad of candies, sweets and drinks high above their heads. Every child was doing its best to attract the attention of passengers, by calling out their sales patter and holding the trays close to the open window of likely looking customers. Lisa bought some more gum and fruit juice, picking carefully from the brightly coloured selection spread out on the tray.

A few new passengers boarded the bus at the station, and Lisa studied their faces closely. She had learned not to trust anyone, no matter how innocent-looking a person may be, but still found it fascinating to analyse features and facial expressions. A heavily built man in his forties, an elderly couple, a single woman in her twenties and three women in their late teens all piled into the bus for its onward journey.

The old vehicle, its engine still complaining noisily, pulled away from the station, leaving the juvenile salespeople behind in a choking cloud of exhaust fumes and dust. The few grimy buildings soon disappeared into the distance and the rich, lush vegetation of the jungle crowded along both sides of the highway as if trying to consume it. No longer was it a solid, concrete road. The dirt track had, in many places, deep troughs where spinning wheels had churned into the soft surface. As the road climbed the steep mountain slopes and sank into valleys, many hairpin bends provided breathtaking, even frightening views.

It was as the bus rounded one such bend that the brakes were slammed on hard and it screeched to a sudden halt. The shock threw most of the passengers forward in their seats, but thankfully, nobody was hurt. The driver pressed his horn loudly. A fallen tree blocked the road, but from its position, it was certainly no accident of nature. This supposition was confirmed as many rough-looking men materialised out of the jungle. These men all carried rifles, and they meant business. This was not a road block by government troops but a gang of several potentially dangerous, ruthless bandits.

Lisa had been told that there were occasional ambushes by groups of bandits in the mountain regions, yet this was to be her first experience. They usually wanted money and jewellery, and as she had nothing of any value, they should have little interest in her. Still, it did not reduce the dread of what might happen to her, and she found it impossible to stop her legs from shaking.

The bandits quickly boarded the bus, pointing their weapons at the driver and some of the passengers. The driver was instructed to stop the engine, and the ignition key was taken from the terrified man. One of the bandits, presumably the leader, calmly climbed the steps as though he was just another regular, fare-paying passenger. He was a broad-shouldered, muscular, tough-looking individual and was far more menacing because of his relaxed attitude. His jet-black hair was untidy and quite long, while a scar on his left cheek revealed a man who had probably been involved in many fights. He smiled a wide, chilling smile that appeared to be pure evil.

"I'm very sorry to interrupt your journey, ladies and gentlemen. We are going to have a little collection, and as good Catholics, I feel certain that you will give generously to a very worthy cause." He laughed at his own joke, yet nobody else shared his humour. He noticed that a woman, sitting near the front, had a half-eaten mango. Afraid to move, she obediently allowed him to take the fruit out of her statue-like hands. He took a huge bite of the soft fruit. As juice ran down his chin, he used the sleeve of his green shirt to soak up the drips. After greedily devouring most of the fruit, he casually tossed the remains out of the window. He took his time, knowing that nobody would dare to challenge his authority.

"We won't keep you very long. Your money and jewellery are all we want. And please, no stupid moves by anyone—if you all want to stay alive."

He motioned to two of his men, who obediently walked down the aisle, stopping at each passenger. Roughly, they grabbed rings, earrings, pendants and watches off the subdued victims, stuffing the valuables into a bag. Greedily, they emptied wallets of hard-earned pesos, some of the passengers in tears. Lisa was wearing no jewellery and had little money in her purse, much to the annoyance of the bandit. Many, though, did have valuables, which were plundered irrespective of any sentimental value. Children cried as their mothers held them close, and an elderly woman was praying loudly while frequently making the sign of the cross. It made no difference as the criminal roughly removed a wad of currency and an elegant, silver necklace from the sobbing woman.

When the bandits were satisfied with their haul, they jumped down onto the road. All, that is, except for their leader. A showman to the end, he said, "Thank you so much for your cooperation, ladies and gentlemen. Your generous donations are very much appreciated. My men will now remove the tree so that you can continue on your journey. I do hope you all have a good day!"

Once the criminal was safely on the road, he casually threw the key towards the driver, who caught it, feeling very relieved that he had survived this unexpected attack.

Sadly, this was the cue for mayhem to break out. The sound of machine guns angrily ripped through the air. Instinctively, all the passengers ducked down between the seats to avoid being hit. There was a confusing cacophony, with shouts and terrified screams adding to the sound of gunshots. No-one in the bus dared to move until the noise had ended.

Lisa was as frightened as anyone. Eventually, she plucked up courage and peered over the windowsill. The carnage which met her eyes sickened her. All the bandits were dead. Some were sprawled over the tree they had started to move, their bodies torn by the mass of bullets fired at them. One or two had tried to run but had been caught in the hail of missiles.

The leader, who only a few minutes earlier had calmly been talking to the passengers, was now lying in an undignified heap on the road. His green shirt showed little of its original colour, now stained a deep red, blood still pouring from his many wounds. His eyes were wide open, as was his mouth. A shout, frozen in time, had never managed to escape his lips. The top of his head was shattered, making the scene the most gruesome Lisa had ever witnessed and would, forever, be etched deep into her mind.

The victor in this massacre was a small detachment of government troops. They were unceremoniously dragging the bodies to the side of the road, where they were left in a tangled heap like discarded dolls when new had been bought to replace the old. Other troops were moving the tree off the highway. It came as a surprise when Lisa realised that the middle-aged man who had been sitting only a few seats away from her was now talking to the captain. He must have been a government agent. They appeared completely unconcerned about the carnage surrounding them. There was something about the situation which really unsettled Lisa. She felt that it must be more than just the military taking out an opportunistic bunch of bandits, and she was soon to be proved correct. Just where had these troops come from?

The captain, still deep in conversation, casually held a cigarette, occasionally taking a long, deep draught on the weed. He dropped the stub on the road, crushing it lazily with the toe of his boot. It looked as though he had come to a decision and wandered, purposely but still casually, towards the bus.

There was a heavy silence as the captain boarded the bus. Unlike the leader of the bandits, there was no trace of humour nor smile on his weathered face. Tight, thin lips hinted at the cruelty within the man, but it was his eyes that sent a chill through Lisa. Even for a Filipino, they were unusually large, black pools that seemed capable of looking straight into one's soul, stripping off with ease any possible deceptions.

He strode purposely down the passageway between the seats, looking with those frightening, cold, merciless eyes at every individual passenger. After the trauma of being robbed by bandits and the gruesome way they had been sorted, yet another menace hung over the passengers as the captain studied each frightened face.

What was he looking for? Lisa's heart pounded so hard, she felt certain he must be able to hear it. Was he looking at her longer than any other passenger? This sinister man could make the most innocent of people feel quite guilty. Had there been a leak of information about Lisa's involvement and her mission for the NPA?

After what seemed like an eternity, he returned to the front of the bus. "I believe there is an enemy agent amongst you. All of you will leave this bus now and line up for searching by my men. If anyone makes a false move, they will be shot. I do hope that I make myself very clear!"

Lisa's face flushed with fear. How could they have found out about her mission? With a sick feeling in her stomach, she felt resigned to the probability that her short life was soon to come to a sticky end. Obediently, she followed the other passengers out onto the dusty, blood-spattered road. One of the soldiers split the passengers into smaller groups of three or four, for searching by several soldiers at the same time. At the front of Lisa's group was a young woman with a boy, about four years of age.

The soldier, machine gun in hand, did not waste any time. He ordered, "Strip everything off. You first and then the boy."

There was no room for any modesty. All knew the penalty for refusal, which helped to avoid any argument. As the woman began to remove her clothes, the soldier closely inspected each garment for any concealed item. When he was satisfied that she was 'clean', he allowed her to dress again and told her to remove the boy's clothing. They were not taking any chances. Agents could be the most unlikely of people and, presumably, had in the past used children to conceal information, possibly even without their knowledge.

The frightened boy started to cry as he was undressed by his mother. She talked reassuringly to the infant in an attempt to calm him, yet he persistently screamed as he was stripped naked. Happily, nothing was found on the youngster and he was allowed to be dressed again, his mother consoling him all the time.

While the old man in front of Lisa was slowly going through the same humiliating process, she noticed an anxious-looking woman, probably in her mid-twenties, being searched by another soldier. She had removed her blouse and skirt but was reluctant to remove her underclothes. The soldier cursed, shouted angrily at her and roughly took hold of her, ripping her bra off. While he was checking the flimsy garment, the woman, foolishly, pulled away and started to run towards the shelter of the trees at the side of the road. This was a signal to the troops that she had something to hide, and without hesitation or warning, the soldier raised his gun and fired a volley of shots into the woman's back. She screamed an agonising cry and fell heavily to the ground, blood pouring freely from her many wounds.

Her killer walked casually over to her prone body and unceremoniously pulled the woman's pants down. A triumphant smile lit his face as he found the tiny, folded paper which had been secreted in the woman's underwear. Lisa recognised it as being similar to that which she herself was concealing, and the tragic death of the young woman emphasised the terrible danger which now faced Lisa. The NPA had shown its messengers how to fold a piece of paper in such a way that it occupied the minimum of space.

The children and several women were wailing loudly, and all but the very hardened individuals had tears in their eyes, shattered by this tragic incident. The soldiers, seemingly unconcerned by this horrific killing, continued the searching process. The fact that a young life had so swiftly been cut short did not bother them. No-one even took the trouble to move the woman's naked body. To the troops, it was a useful warning that full cooperation was expected. If any of the civilians had attempted to cover the body, they would be treated as sympathisers of her cause and would suffer the same, horrific punishment.

When it came to Lisa's turn, her heart was pounding so strong and fast, she felt certain that it would reveal her guilty secret. She tried to avoid looking into the soldier's eyes as she unfastened the buttons on her blouse. She handed it to him, unfastened the belt on her jeans, slid the zip fly down and tugged the tight-fitting pants off her shapely legs. Was this young soldier turned on by seeing her undress, or was it such a frequent exercise that it was just part of his job? She certainly did not feel attractive at having to undress openly and in public.

Lisa felt her face flush as she unhooked her bra, revealing her firm, small breasts. The final embarrassment came as she slid her pants down and stepped out of them. The soldier checked every item of clothing very thoroughly before handing them back to her. As quickly as possible, she dressed again, having satisfied the soldier that nothing was to be found. The remainder of the searches passed without incident, and eventually, they were all allowed to return to the bus. The shock of the occasion was plain on everyone's faces as they silently resumed their seats in the battered old vehicle.

Before they were allowed to leave, the commander of the troops again climbed on board and addressed the passengers.

"You will now be allowed to continue your journey, but let it serve as a warning just what will happen to traitors. The government forces will hunt down and kill without mercy anyone opposed to the rule of law." This cold warning was the last thing said by the commander. He stepped down onto the road and motioned to the driver to move off.

Obediently, he turned on the ignition. It took several attempts before the ancient engine coughed noisily back into life. The gears crashed fiercely as he released the clutch, causing the bus to lurch forward. He carefully manoeuvred around the soldiers and the corpses and quickly built up speed to escape the gruesome scene as quickly as possible.

There were now two passengers less than before this unforgettable incident. The middle-aged man, who must have been an agent with the military presumably on the lookout for possible rebels, and the young, attractive woman whose life had been extinguished so brutally, purely because she had been caught acting as a messenger.

Lisa waited until the bus was well away from the troops before she leaned down to retrieve her own message. She had used the chewing gum to attach the folded note to the underside of the seat in front of hers. If this simple precaution had not been taken, she could also have been lying dead on that dusty road, ready to be reduced to a mangle of bones by hungry, wild animals. She would have to be very careful if she was not to suffer the same fate.

Nobody felt like much conversation for the rest of the journey, and all passengers spent the remaining time either sleeping or looking out of the windows in absolute silence.

Chapter Seventeen

WHEN LISA EVENTUALLY reached her destination, she was physically and emotionally drained by the horrific events of the past few hours. The carnage she had witnessed would remain with her for the rest of her life. She actually felt sorry for the leader of the bandits. Like most people in this poverty-ridden land, he was just trying to earn a living, albeit unconventionally. Somehow, there had seemed some warmth of humanity in his soul, unlike that of the military leader, whose compassionless demeanour still sent a chill through Lisa. She had memorised the name and address of the person with whom she was to make contact but felt it prudent not to go directly to his place, in case she was still being watched. Instead, she went to her aunt's house. It had always proved helpful to have a relative living in the province in which the NPA wanted her to deliver messages in order to create a feeling of authenticity.

The strain must have been visible on the teenager's face as her aunt greeted her. "Whatever has happened to you, Lisa? Come on in and have a rest."

This served to release her emotions, and she collapsed, sobbing, into the arms of her welcoming aunt. Through her tears, she managed to relate the events of the past few hours to her aunt and uncle, who listened with a fearful sense of foreboding. Lisa was given food and drink, for which she was extremely grateful.

"Please do be careful, Lisa." Her aunt looked very concerned. "These are very dangerous times. Only this last week, four people were dragged from their homes in the middle of the night

121

and brutally executed by the military. This is not the place for a young girl like you."

"But I have to do what I can to help," Lisa replied earnestly. "The lives of many people depend on messages getting past the military and through to the NPA. I must go and take my message during the next two hours. It is expected of me."

The older woman admired the courage of her niece after such an ordeal. "All right, but come straight back here as soon as you have finished your mission."

Lisa promised that she would and slipped out quietly into the hot night air. She knew the village well and knew how to reach her destination without attracting any undue attention.

As she drew near to her contact's house, she heard raised voices, starkly penetrating the stillness of the night. Lisa froze as she recognised the voice of the military captain who had so ruthlessly invaded her life earlier that day. The training she had received from the NPA was now being put firmly to the test, as she needed to observe without being seen. She crept as close as she dared and soon realised what was happening. The captain and two of his men were outside the house where Lisa was supposed to have delivered the message. She could only assume that the message taken from the young woman they had killed had given sufficient information to the soldiers to identify the contact within the village.

The captain was ordering the occupant of the house to come out and surrender. When he refused to emerge, the captain decided on an alternative, more dangerous course of action.

He ordered his men to pour kerosene around the outside of the house. No further chances were to be offered. He set light to the volatile liquid, and within seconds, the small wooden house was engulfed in flames. Her NPA compatriot did not stand a chance. His screams pierced the night air, sending an incredible shiver of horror through Lisa's veins. In one short, eventful day, she had witnessed human brutality in its worst form with fellow countrymen being burned alive and shot to pieces by so-called representatives of the Government, which was, supposedly, there to represent the people of the Philippines.

"Oh, God! Why don't you stop this madness?" Her mind returned to the time when she was a small girl attending church. Nobody had prepared her for this totally brutal way of life. She had been told that God would protect the innocent, but where was he now, just when she needed him?

Her mission was now in vain, with nobody to receive her message. She knew of no other contact to whom she could hand the information. For all she knew, they could all have been murdered by this insane, evil military captain who walked away so calmly from the terrible carnage facing Lisa. This brute of a man acted as though he had just crushed a cockroach under the heel of his shoe, yet he was some woman's son, perhaps even a child's father. It all seemed so incongruous. Lisa remembered the coldness in his eyes when he had boarded her bus earlier this same day.

She was about to return to her aunt's when she noticed the captain lean his rifle against a tree and go in to the jungle, presumably to relieve himself. Could she avenge all these deaths?

Plucking up all her courage, Lisa took out a small, razor-sharp knife she kept for her own protection and ran silently into the thickly wooded area where she knew the soldier would be. He owl-like eyes penetrated the darkness, as she looked for the man for whom she felt so much bitterness and hatred. She was in luck. He was crouching, his trousers around his ankles while defecating. Lisa's emotions were mixed as she struggled with her conscience. Her Catholic upbringing could not appease her anger at the brutality of this man. If she was able to stop him coldly murdering any other innocent people, then it had to be her duty.

Lisa approached him from behind and, with a swiftness that even surprised herself, drew the knife sharply across his throat while holding her left hand pressed tightly over his mouth to prevent his cries being heard. The years of practice in killing chickens under the expert guidance of her father had, at last, paid off. Sadly, this was the only benefit she had experienced from her father's instructions. She had been absolutely accurate in her knife cut, demonstrated by the spurt of blood that escaped from the open wound as a low croak left his mouth. She pushed his slumped body forward, feeling certain that he could never survive such an injury and ran, swiftly and silently, back towards her aunt's house.

It was not until she was safely inside the tiny Nipa hut that the full impact of what she had done hit her, and she burst into tears as she clung tightly to her surprised aunt.

"What's wrong, my dear?" There was great concern in her aunt's voice. "What's happened?"

"I...I have just killed the military captain. He burnt my contact alive, trapped in his house. I had to do something." Her body shook as the shock of her experience made its impact felt.

Her aunt was surprised at the bravery of her sixteen-year-old niece. "In that case, you are now in extreme danger, Lisa. You must go back home as soon as possible."

Lisa knew that by her action, she had also put her aunt and uncle in great danger. "I can get the bus back in the morning."

"No. The military will be stopping everything after such an incident." Lisa's aunt looked thoughtful. "The only safe way out of here is on foot. If you leave about three in the morning and use the side tracks, you could reach Marbel before dusk. At least it is downward all the way."

"But what about you and uncle? This place is not safe for anyone now."

"Don't worry about us, Lisa." She smiled at the girl who had grown into a young woman so quickly. "We are too old to leave our village. We will stay here, no matter what happens." Lisa clung to her aunt, fearing the worst. "You must try to get a little sleep. I will have some food and drink ready for you and will wake you up when it's time for you to leave."

Lisa put her head down on the soft blanket and closed her eyes but found great difficulty in falling asleep. The vision of her compatriot losing his life in such horrific circumstances constantly pervaded her mind. Somehow, she managed a little sleep, yet it seemed like only minutes before she was being shaken awake by her aunt.

"Come on, Lisa. It's time for you to be going home now."

The teenager wiped the sleep from her eyes and pulled herself up.

"There's some food and drink in this bag. I'll also give you fifty pesos just in case you need it." Her aunt pushed the notes into Lisa's hand. "Do you know which way to get back along the tracks?"

"I think so. It's quite a while since I tried it, but I can remember using the tracks before the main road was built."

"Good. I think it's time for you to get started. There's been much activity in the village overnight. The soldiers are probably not very well organised if they have lost their captain, but it's only a matter of time before they search all the houses."

Lisa gave both her aunt and uncle a big hug, knowing this might be the last time she would see them alive. "I'm so sorry, Aunt. I should have thought it through before killing that captain."

"You mustn't blame yourself, Lisa. What you did was so brave, and we are both very proud of you. The man really deserved to die. Now, come on, off you go. Send my love to your mother."

"I will. Thanks for all your help. Please take care." Lisa stepped out into the cool morning air. She would have to use all her skills of observation if she was to escape from this hostile area. Skirting the village, keeping in the thickly wooded parts, she hoped to avoid contact with anyone. In such a tense situation, nobody could be trusted, even if they were not wearing a military uniform.

Slowly, she worked her way downwards. In places, the track was steep and slippery, but the sure-footed teenager had no difficulty in keeping on her feet. She was more concerned, however, about the possibility of coming across the many snakes living in the jungle. There were both poisonous and constricting species, but they were only dangerous to humans if they felt threatened. To avoid this, she constantly scanned the path in front of her and overhanging branches, looking for the long, slithering creatures. She remembered the time her father had left her suspended in a rice sack from the branch of a tree overnight as punishment for fighting with her sister. As a result, she had suffered many nightmares from the age of six, in which snakes were attacking her as she hung helpless. Now she had a healthy respect for these magnificent creatures and would do her best to avoid coming close to them.

As she progressed on her arduous trek, she sometimes found the track disappeared as the road crossed the ancient route. When this happened, she would study the road carefully, looking for any signs of life, before running swiftly across the concrete highway. She was thankful that at this early hour, there was very little activity, and she pushed herself hard to make as much progress as she could before dawn. Lisa had no choice but to stop occasionally for a quick gulp of water, as her exertions made her very dehydrated.

Around five-thirty, the sky began to lighten, and the sun's rays tried vainly to penetrate the thick canopy of the jungle. At this time of the day, the temperature was quite comfortable, with a little breeze giving the air a slight chill. Lisa felt that this was the best time of the day, before the air became heavy under the hot tropical sun. The sound of cockerels making their piercing cries became more frequent as dawn broke.

Lisa noticed that for a part of her journey, there was a small stream running along the side of the path. Pausing for a few moments, she dipped her cupped hands into the sparkling, clear waters. It felt so refreshing to run the ice-cold water over her face and arms, removing some of the sweat and grime from her body.

She dipped her now-empty bottle into the cleaner, faster-moving water and filled it up, ready for the next part of her journey. Now that it was daytime and people were moving about, she would have to be even more careful. She must keep moving as fast as she could, without arousing any suspicion by looking as though she was escaping from the military. Most of the villagers in these areas were probably supporters of the NPA, yet many would betray her for a few pesos.

Experience had also taught her how to move in the correct direction by noting the angles of the shadows cast by the sun. Her life as a child had prepared her well for surviving alone in such difficult, possibly dangerous conditions. It still came as a relief when, around eleven o'clock, she reached a village which she knew to be only about twenty miles from home. Lisa was exhausted, having already walked about thirty miles since she had left her aunt's house at three o'clock that morning.

Feeling a little more secure now and quite tired, she decided to chance taking a tricycle taxi for the rest of her journey. It felt so good to sit down at last and let someone else do all the work. As she relaxed under the canopy to shield herself from the burning sun, she found it impossible to keep her eyes open.

Lisa awoke with a start as a gruff voice disturbed her slumbers. For a moment, she thought the military had caught her. It was a great relief to discover that it was just the taxi driver.

"This is Marbel centre. Where do you want to go?" He sounded quite impatient.

"Oh, this is fine, thanks." She thought it prudent not to have him take her straight to her house and would walk the last part of her journey. Sleepily, she pulled herself out of the seat and gave the driver his two-peso fare.

It felt so good to be back in her hometown, and she was eager to see her family again. After a quick drink from the bottle of water, she began the last part of her long, tiring trek. Twenty minutes later, the familiar and very welcome image of her family home appeared directly in front of her.

Lisa ran up to her mother, who was busy preparing a meal, and threw her arms around the woman she had missed so much over the last two days.

"Lisa! We did not expect you back so soon."

"Oh, Nanay! Everything has gone wrong."

Dolores put her knife down and rinsed her blood-stained hands in water. "What's wrong, child? Tell me everything." She listened intently as Lisa related her tragic story, her face showing great concern as the seriousness of the situation became fully apparent. "Oh, child! At least you are safe now. That is all that matters. May God protect us all!"

Surprisingly, her father was also home. When Pedro learned how Lisa had killed the captain, he showed great pride for his daughter's achievements. The fact that she was the first in the family to kill one of the enemy lifted Lisa's prestige in everybody's eyes, especially her father's. He found it particularly amusing that she had killed him while he had his trousers around his ankles. "You should have cut off his otin as a souvenir," he joked.

Dolores gave him a look of disgust, and Lisa, in her innocence, could not appreciate his crass humour either. The young girl was still in a state of shock. She ate well that night, though, and had no trouble sleeping. She would, however, relive the whole grizzly experience over and over again in her frequent nightmares.

Over the next few days, there was a noticeable change in the atmosphere throughout Cotabato. Many government troops poured into the area, heading towards Davao. Rumours abounded that the military were making a determined effort to find and disable NPA strongholds in the mountain regions. Apparently, one of the top military officers, Captain Antonio Rodriguez, had been attacked and brutally killed during a purge of NPA supporters. The whole Tiguelo family was elated to discover Lisa had killed such an important government figure, yet all realised the real dangers of boasting about the killing to anyone and kept this dangerous information to themselves.

Tensions were high in the city with the increasing presence of the military, and many people were afraid of possible violent reprisals. A great deal of pressure was being applied to the Catholic Church, and soldiers made their presence felt at most Masses to ensure that the sermons were devoted purely to religious matters and not criticism of the Marcos regime.

Many of the NPA supporters, particularly the Tiguelo family, were worried that some of those less enthusiastic than themselves may be persuaded to reveal their identities to the military, either through pressure or bribery. NPA political meetings had been abandoned, as the risks had become ever greater.

Lisa's friend Jessica, a determined anti-government rebel, visited the Tiguelo family on many occasions and always had some information about the current crisis. She knew of many people who had been arrested, and tales abounded of the tortures meted out to these unfortunate individuals.

It came as a terrible shock when Jessica was, herself, arrested. Her mother told Lisa how the military burst into their house one night and dragged Jessica away, screaming and shouting. Her mother sobbed as she related the story of Jessica's terrible demise. Lisa found it hard to believe that the girl she had known so well for over four years was now dead. Apparently, she had been raped by the military many times before being tortured and then shot dead.

To learn of such horrific punishment meted out to such a close friend was the final blow for Lisa and her family. They felt certain it was only a matter of time before they faced similar punishment and decided to get out while they still had a chance. Lisa's eldest brother and her sister, Diding, stayed in Marbel, much against their parents' wishes. They were both married with children and had their own small houses. Antonio promised to look after the family home and thought that he might even live there, as it was bigger than his own tiny Nipa hut.

Dolores could not hide the concern she felt about them staying in such a dangerous situation. She embraced Antonio, Diding and her grandchildren, fearing that she may never see any of them again. "May God protect you all," she said, tears filling her eyes as she bowed her head and made the sign of the cross.

Chapter Eighteen

THERE WERE MANY others in similar circumstances to the Tiguelo family, who felt it necessary to flee the turbulent areas surrounding the mountain region. Some chose to move only a short distance, intending to return when circumstances allowed, yet the Tiguelo family felt the need to travel further before a safe haven could be found. Government forces had been suspicious of the Tiguelo family, not just because of Lisa's own activities but also for her mother's deep involvement with the Catholic Church. Sadly, it was generally assumed that the Church and anyone closely connected with it had communistic tendencies. Nothing could be further from the truth with Dolores, yet her character was now tainted purely by association.

All the land and livestock, which had taken so many years to accumulate, had to be abandoned. They gathered what possessions they could carry in bags and slipped away from their village, heading down towards the sea.

With such difficult security problems, they could not even let friends know of their plans, and Lisa felt guilty for not telling her grandfather's faithful assistant Ricky what they were doing. She hoped that one day she would be able to return to the mango plantation where she had spent so much of her childhood. Lisa's aunt Floriza, a long-term critic of the Marcos regime, had already fled the region moving to a safer area near her husband's relatives.

There were many ferries moving goods and people between the numerous islands that formed the Philippines, the captains enjoying a good, steady income from all the frightened people.

Lisa noticed the look of hopelessness on the faces of the families who, like them, were forced to flee from the land where they had lived peacefully for many years. All were carrying heavy bags filled with pots, pans, dishes, clothes—anything that could be carried was carried.

One family was crying hysterically as they saw their precious possessions disappear into the murky dockside water when one of the bags burst open from the weight of its contents. The woman looked as though she was ready to jump in to retrieve what she could, but her husband, seeing what a hopeless task it would be, restrained her. It was common knowledge that many sharks swam close to the quayside almost in anticipation of and hunger for the unwary swimmer.

Eventually, the ferry, with probably twice as many passengers as the designed capacity, slowly moved away from the still-crowded jetty, leaving even more would-be migrants stranded. Many pitiful-looking groups huddled together with their meagre belongings on the quayside, waiting hopefully for the next available ferry. Lisa and her family thanked God that they had managed to get on board this well-used and over-crowded vessel. Privacy was not an available commodity on this perilous journey, and nobody cared as long as they had managed to escape their troubled homeland.

The whole family, together with another equally large family, somehow squeezed into a cabin normally meant for four people. Not a square inch of floor space was visible as bodies and belongings filled every possible space. Food was available but had to be rationed, as the ferry operators only had sufficient for the number of passengers it was designed to carry.

Progress was slow as the ancient vessel's engines strained to pull the hulk through the swelling sea. A strong wind made the journey an uncomfortable one, causing the ship to rise and fall with regular, stomach-churning movements.

Lisa was fine, the frail child having matured into a young woman who was strong both in body and mind. She attended to her mother, who was suffering intensely from motion sickness. Even Pedro, who was normally presented a strong, macho image looked very pale and said little. Lisa did not normally have much affection for her father, but on this rare occasion, she did her best to comfort him.

"Is there anything I can get for you Tatay?"

"No, no, don't worry about me. Just take care of Nanay. I'll be all right."

Lisa realised that much of his quietness was because he was leaving his homeland after so many years living in Cotabato. They were all refugees hoping for a more peaceful life and somewhere to earn a living without the fear of being murdered by either government or NPA forces.

The journey should have taken about twenty-four hours, arriving in Cebu at six in the morning. It came as quite a surprise, then, when at two in the morning the ship's engines came to a sudden stop.

Lisa and Breeza scrambled to their feet in eager anticipation. Her parents were sleeping. "Nanay, Tatay! We've arrived!"

Pedro drowsily opened his eyes and looked at his watch. "It can't be. There's at least another four hours' sailing yet. Let's have a look where we are." Since their cabin was deep in the bowels of the ship, there were no portholes to look through. "All of you, stay here. I'll go up on the deck to see what I can find out." Pedro squeezed his way through all the bodies covering the floor and managed to escape from the heavy, sweat-filled atmosphere.

The ship was still heaving from side to side as he walked carefully along the narrow passageway. It took what seemed like ages and many stairways for him to reach the open air. Everywhere he looked there were people, some sleeping, some eating and some talking. Surprisingly, there were few people interested in finding out what had happened. As he reached the side of the ship, there was sufficient light from the moon to show that they were surrounded only by dark, threatening, swelling seas.

At last, he found a member of the ship's crew. "Why are we stopped?" he asked, fearful of the reply.

"It's a fault in the engines. A fuel blockage, I think. Don't worry, sir. We're doing our best to repair the fault. I'm certain that we'll be on our way again very soon."

Pedro thanked the man and began to make his way back to the cabin where his family was anxiously waiting. He only hoped he could remember the difficult route through this rabbit-warren of a ship. He narrowly avoided being beaten up by a huge drunken Filipino looking for any excuse to start a fight. Pedro used his smaller frame to his advantage, slipping quickly away from the lumbering giant of a man. He breathed a sigh of relief when he eventually found his way back.

An air of despair quickly descended over the cabin as Pedro explained the situation to them. Over many years, there had been countless stories of overloaded, under-maintained ferries sinking with great losses of life for both passengers and crew.

Fearful of becoming yet another tragic statistic, Dolores suggested that they all should pray to God for his help in delivering them to their new home. They all knelt, making the sign of the cross, and bowed their heads in sombre reflection. Each had their own silent prayer, after which they all tried to get some sleep again.

It was another two and a half hours before the lumbering engines coughed into life once more. The family looked at each other, praying that this was not just a temporary reprieve. Even in the bowels of the ship, they sensed movement through the deep waters of the Pacific. Nobody wanted to tempt providence by appearing too optimistic, and all kept a hopeful silence.

It came as a great relief when, after another four hours, bells rang throughout the ship signifying their arrival in port. There was a frenzied scramble as passengers gathered their few possessions together and made their way towards the main deck. It was truly amazing to see just how many people had been crammed into the vessel. All passageways were packed tightly with families eager to start a new life in what should hopefully be a more peaceful part of the Philippines.

They had chosen this part of the country because Dolores' mother lived in Balamban, a tiny village on the outskirts of Cebu. It had been a few years since she had seen her mother, but Dolores had kept in touch with her through the occasional letter. From what she had heard, the areas surrounding Cebu were not as troubled as in southern Cotabato. It was over thirty years since Dolores had visited Cebu, but now they were hoping to start a new life there. To the Tiguelo family, it seemed as though they were travelling halfway around the world and not just a few hundred miles.

After more than twenty-four hours with only artificial light in their cabin, the bright morning sun hurt their eyes as they reached the main deck and joined the mass of people inching slowly towards the walkway, all eager to see this new land.

There were many impatient individuals calling for the slow procession to move faster, to no effect. The bottleneck was mainly at the head of the various walkways from the deck down to the quayside. Their movement had to be controlled by ship's officers to avoid overloading the walkways.

It took quite a while, but at last the Tiguelo family was standing on solid ground once again.

As the area was unfamiliar, they had to seek advice on how to find the bus station. Since it was not very far and they were all carrying heavy bags, they decided to use taxis. Even though it cost only a few pesos, they knew they would have to be very careful with what little money they had. The cost of the ferry had taken quite a big slice of their resources.

The taxi drivers were pleased with the increase in demand for their services and greedily accepted the few pesos from the many refugees. Once at the station, the family found that there was only one bus every two hours and they would have to wait until eleven o'clock in the hot dusty confines of the bus station. Little was said as they all waited patiently. There was a great sadness about the occasion, which affected the whole family.

They were all excited at the prospect of starting a new life, yet the sadness of having to leave Antonio, Diding, their grandchildren and the land they had known for so many years was overwhelming.

At last, the bus arrived at the terminal. As soon as it had emptied, they all piled in, eager to find seats where the whole family could sit close together. Lisa felt a chill of fear on boarding the bus, as it reminded her of her recent experience on her fateful day travelling to Davao when so many precious lives had been lost. The cold, emotionless eyes of Captain Rodriguez constantly haunted her. It seemed strange that the image of him striding down the bus looking into the souls of everyone was far stronger in her mind than when she had ended his miserable life by cutting his throat.

There seemed to be plenty of passengers wishing to travel to Balamban, yet the driver still waited well past the official leaving time to ensure maximum passenger capacity. The growing impatience of all those already on board eventually persuaded the driver into action, as he engaged the gears, released the brakes and manoeuvred the long bus out into the midday traffic.

All of the Tiguelo family was interested to see their new surroundings and, unlike most passengers peered through the window openings as the bus made its way out of the city. It did not take very long for the tall buildings of Cebu, the Philippines' second-largest city, to be replaced with grassland and wide-open areas. They all settled back in their seats once the scenery had become less interesting.

Lisa felt distinctly uncomfortable, as the memories of her previous bus journey kept flooding back into her mind. Every time the bus stopped, she trembled with fear, anticipating another military check on the passengers. Her mother sensed her anxiety and tried to distract the teenager by keeping her in conversation. After a while, the road cut a very long and straight path through the dense jungle. In places, there were pineapple and mango plantations, reminding Lisa of the times when as a young girl she had visited her grandfather. She missed the old man and remembered their many happy times together.

Lisa really wished she could return to those happy, carefree days before Marcos brought unrest and civil war to her country. If only her grandfather could still have been alive, she would feel much more secure. She was still not certain how she was going to fulfil his dying request yet had sufficient faith in God to know that he would guide and direct her to meet her obligations.

Chapter Nineteen

AFTER ABOUT TWO hours' travelling on the bus journey, Dolores began to look more closely at the buildings dotted along the side of the highway. Her mother lived on the outskirts of Balamban, and if they were to avoid a long walk, she must keep a watchful eye for the only landmark she could remember.

It was a big old house very close to the roadside. The fact that it was two storeys high had made it bigger and more noticeable than most. Of course, it could have been demolished, or there may now be many more houses of similar design, but to her relief, Dolores spotted it in time. She called sharply to the driver, who slammed on his brakes to stop where she had requested. The driver waited patiently as the family of eight with all their possessions climbed down the steep steps of the bus.

As soon as the last of the family was standing on the roadside, the driver pressed his foot hard on the accelerator, creating a huge cloud of dust, and the bus disappeared noisily into the distance.

Now the responsibility fell on Dolores to find the old family home. Everyone followed as she weaved her way through the maze of houses which ranged from the tiniest of timber shacks to large concrete residencies. Even after an absence of over thirty years, very little seemed to have changed.

After a few minutes' walking, they were confronted by a fairly insignificant single-storey timber house. "This is Nanay's. I do hope she's at home." The front door was closed, suggesting that there may be no-one inside. "Nanay!" called Dolores as she knocked loudly on the door. The whole family waited, anxiously listening for signs of life.

It took quite a while, but eventually, there was the sound of a bolt being drawn on the inside of the door. Gloria's tired face appeared as the door slowly opened. The old woman, now in her sixty-ninth year, stared in astonishment at the large Tiguelo family in front of her.

"Dolly? Is it really you or am I dreaming?"

Dolores stepped forward and gave her mother a warm embrace.

"I was just having a little sleep when I heard your voice. I felt certain that you were just in my dreams." The older woman gave an involuntary yawn and immediately apologised.

"No, Nanay. Except for Antonio and Diding, we are all here and are refugees from Cotabato. The military are making life unbearable for everybody back home. It would only have been a matter of time before they killed us. We have had to leave our house and land. We've little more than you see before you."

"Oh dear. I was afraid that might happen. There have been many stories of atrocities throughout the country. I'm so pleased that at least you are all safe. Come on in." She motioned to the large family to enter her tiny house. It was quite a squeeze, but somehow they all managed to find a little space on the floor for each of them to sit, the few seats she had being reserved for herself, Dolores and Pedro.

With an anxious tone in her voice, Gloria asked, "Why are Antonio and Diding not here with you? Are they all right?"

"Yes, they are fine. They wanted to stay there with their families," Dolores replied. The old woman breathed a noticeable sigh of relief.

Once again, Lisa found herself the centre of attention. "Lisa!" Gloria motioned to the teenager. "Come here, child. Let me have a good look at you."

Lisa stepped forward obediently.

"My, you are quite grown up now. You are a very good-looking woman." It had been six years since their last meeting, during which time she had grown much taller with an attractive figure that was both slim yet quite curvaceous. "I feel sure that you'll win the hearts of many young men."

Lisa blushed at this observation while her brother and sisters laughed at her. "I'm not particularly interested in men, Lola."

"You will be, my dear." The old woman laughed. Her wizened face cracked into a broad smile, showing a remarkably intact if somewhat yellowed set of teeth. "You must all be quite hungry. I think there is sufficient rice for us all to have a little."

Dolores moved into the small kitchen area with her mother, and the two of them started to prepare a meal of weak vegetable soup and rice for the whole family. There was just about enough to satisfy their immediate hunger, yet Dolores knew that she could not impose too much on her mother. "We shall buy some food from the market tomorrow, Nanay. Until we can find a place of our own, we will do what we can to help with the cost of everything."

"You really don't need to worry, Dolly. If you don't mind a bit of a squeeze, you're all very welcome to stay as long as you want." Gloria put a comforting arm around her daughter's shoulders. "Don't worry. You will have all you need, and I will do what I can."

"Thank you so much, Nanay. You don't know how much we all appreciate your help."

That evening, after a refreshing if somewhat meagre meal, there was a great deal of discussion as the family related what had been happening to them in Cotabato. When Dolores told Gloria of the way Lisa had killed Captain Rodriguez, her eyes widened in amazement. "I underestimated your talents, Lisa. That must have taken a great deal of courage. I understand now why you had to leave your home."

It seemed quite strange that night, as they all tried to sleep on the floor in their new cramped surroundings. In fact, most of the family had very little sleep.

Next morning, Gloria, Dolores and Lisa took a tricycle taxi for the four-mile journey to Balamban. Dolores noticed some changes and improvements in the shopping area since she had last been there. They wandered around both the open and covered markets looking for any possible bargains. She bought a big sack of rice and, after much searching and bargaining, some fish and cheap cuts of meat. There was so much she could have bought, but they had to be very aware of their limited resources. Sweet potatoes, basic vegetables and bananas completed their shopping. The bananas were under-ripe but would be cooked and served hot to provide a very simple, cheap yet nourishing and tasty meal.

Over the next few days, they began to feel incredibly homesick. Even with all the troubles in Cotabato, they all without exception wished that they could have returned but knew that to risk losing their lives would have been foolish and they had no option but to accept their current situation.

Pedro looked for a small plot of land nearby or preferably one with a house already on it but was very despondent when he realised that he could not even afford the smallest. Gloria was quite insistent that they could share her house. She owned enough land herself to allow her house to be extended to accommodate the larger family. This seemed to be an ideal solution to the problem. Pedro and his son Enrico began to purchase sufficient timber to enlarge both living and sleeping spaces, and after a few weeks of hard work, the bigger, more spacious house had been completed. It was very crude and simple, yet it meant that all nine of them could live and sleep without being too cramped and on top of each other.

Everyone except Gloria was also looking for employment of any kind. This proved to be even more difficult than they had anticipated. Jobs were very scarce at that time, yet they did manage to earn a few pesos by making food to sell to the children at the local school. It was not very satisfactory but somehow they made sufficient for the basic necessities.

Pedro was unable to continue his living as a farmer. Without money to buy land or livestock and no other skills but farming, Pedro had no choice. He became one of the countless unemployed in the Philippines, and with no social security benefits, the family was poverty-stricken.

Pedro was a changed man. The dominant, ruthless father and supportive husband had long ago turned into a weak shell of a man who showed very little interest in life. He could not afford to continue training cockerels for fighting, which had for some time been his only interest and passion. With the ready availability of tuba wine, Pedro frequently drowned his sorrows. The once-caring husband had long ago turned into a violent, angry man while drunk and a quiet morose person on the rare occasions when he was sober. He would sit for hours, never even bothering to utter a word but if irritated would fly into a violent rage. To add to the difficulties, the heavy consumption of alcohol had damaged his liver. With no money for medical treatment, he had no choice but to endure the pain.

Dolores had, for the past few years, been the undisputed leader of the family who made all the decisions and would try practically anything to earn a little money. Lisa helped her mother as much as she could, but the teenager's spirit seemed to have been broken by the boredom of every day being just the same. She longed to have something useful to occupy her time, yet there seemed to be no opportunities for employment.

It was nearly six months since they had moved into the area before a possible job was found. Gloria had heard of a family living a few miles away who had been looking for a housemaid. Lisa did not like the sound of the job, as it would mean living away from her own family, yet she knew that it was pointless to argue with her mother. She would be provided with living accommodation and food plus a monthly payment of one hundred pesos.

Lisa was very quiet as she and Dolores took the tricycle taxi for the fifteen-minute journey to her prospective employer. A quietly spoken, middle-aged woman came to the door of the large, imposing house and welcomed them inside. She was a friend of Gloria's and aware of the family's plight. Tina seemed quite pleasant and showed them around her house, explaining what Lisa's duties would be. Then it came to the most difficult part. Dolores was ready to leave Lisa in the care of her new employer.

Tears filled Lisa's eyes as she gave her mother a parting hug. "Oh, Nanay, I'm not certain about this. I really want to stay with you at Lola's."

"Don't worry, child. You will soon get used to it. I think you'll like working for Tina. She'll look after you."

Sensing the youngster's sadness, Tina put a comforting arm around her shoulder. "I realise how close you are to your mother, Lisa. You will still be able to see her every few weeks. Come on now. I would like you to make a start by dusting all the rooms."

Obediently, Lisa began her work, yet her heart was not in it. She did the task, thoroughly thanks to her upbringing, but there was a noticeable lack of enthusiasm. Tina understood her feelings and did not pressure the teenager, preferring instead to keep her busy with the household chores.

For Lisa, the nights were the worst times. As she lay wrapped in blankets on the living room floor trying to sleep, the tears would flow down her cheeks. If only she could be with her family, she would feel so much better.

This situation lasted for only seven days before Lisa felt that she could not stand it any longer. It was mid-afternoon and Lisa was on her own polishing the floor. She left everything as it was, walked out of the house and, with the few pesos she had, hired a tricycle taxi back to her grandmother's house. When she arrived, Dolores was outside washing some clothes.

She dropped the clothes back into the water with a loud splash as Lisa appeared in front of her. "What are you doing here, child?"

Lisa flung her arms around her mother and sobbed. "I can't stay there, Nanay. I want to be here with you."

"What did Tina say?"

Lisa hung her head. "She doesn't know yet. I ran away. I… I have left all my clothes at her house."

Lisa looked very sheepish as her mother scolded her. "Is this the way to treat her? She was good enough to give you a job, and you have let her and me down. Can this be the same woman who had such spirit in working for the NPA? Certainly not the one who had the guts to kill a military captain!"

Lisa could not argue against her mother's logic. Somehow, the excitement of working for the NPA had overridden all other fears and thoughts. "I'm sorry, Nanay. I didn't want to let you or Tina down, but please don't make me go back."

Dolores knew there was little point in forcing her daughter to do something against her will. "All right, but we must go there right now, and you will apologise to Tina."

Somewhat reluctantly, Lisa agreed, and after Dolores had finished all her washing, the two of them took a taxi back to Tina's.

The youngster's head was bowed in shame as she once again faced her employer. Surprisingly, Tina was very calm and understanding. After Lisa's mumbled apology, Tina said in a kindly voice, "I realised that your heart was never in the job, Lisa. I'm sorry to lose you, as I know that in principle, you are a good person. I do hope that you have more success in your future employment. Here, take this." She pushed a hundred-peso note into the teenager's hand.

Lisa felt that she could not accept the payment, but the kindly woman insisted. Lisa gathered her clothes and few possessions together and left with her mother.

When they had returned home, Dolores made it quite clear that she was still very angry with her daughter. She decided that if Lisa preferred to stay with her, then she would make her stay less welcoming. The family was still very short of money with only two having proper employment. Enrico did some building work but was also a tricycle taxi driver when he had enough money to hire a vehicle. Indai, one of Lisa's sisters, was a housemaid, and now Breeza would take over as housemaid at Tina's. Any earned income would be shared by the whole family to help reduce the burden of poverty.

Dolores' relationship with Lisa became very cool, and she constantly criticised and scolded the teenager. It was emotionally painful to treat her own daughter this way, yet it was a deliberate ploy to make Lisa feel more independent.

It took quite a while, but eventually the tactic proved successful when, several months later, Lisa announced that she wanted to go to Toledo where she understood there to be many more work possibilities than in Balamban. Everybody was surprised, but Dolores smiled to herself in satisfaction, seeing her daughter prepared at last to break her close, restraining ties with home. Pedro tried to talk Lisa out of the idea, as he feared for her safety, but Dolores persuaded him to let her go.

"Lisa has a spirit for adventure and unlike her sisters was not destined to stay with her family forever. This could turn her into a strong, determined woman," Dolores insisted. Between them, they managed to find one hundred and fifty pesos to provide food and shelter for a little while.

The air was very charged with emotion as they came to the time of Lisa's departure. Many tears were shed and a great deal of hugging took place.

Chapter Twenty

LISA LEFT HER home at eight o'clock in the morning of 7th January 1983, prepared for a long, tiring walk in preference to spending her money on a jeepney ride. She walked along the side of the hot, dusty road towards Toledo, wondering what fate lay in store for her. The prospects were not good for a seventeen-year-old whose meagre possessions did not even fill the small bag she carried. If only she could find a job that would pay enough to feed and house her and hopefully have some left over to send to her mother.

The road was already quite busy mainly with big, noisy, heavy trucks pouring filthy, choking exhaust fumes into the air. Even so, Lisa enjoyed walking along the side of the highway, as she was able to see everything around her better than if she had been travelling by jeepney, and at least she was not using her money on transport.

By late morning, her enthusiasm was flagging, as her legs began to feel much heavier, slowing her progress. She had some rice and water in her bag, which helped to provide a little refreshment, but these would be finished before very long.

It was while she was walking with heavy heart and legs that she first noticed the motorbike. The young man sitting astride the bike slowed down when he saw Lisa. Smiling to herself, she pretended not to see him. She held her head high and walked purposely onwards, a faster pace to her strides now, as though she were on some really important mission which could not possibly be interrupted.

"Can I offer you a lift?" he enquired.

147

"No, thanks," she answered with an indifferent air. At that moment, she would have been very relieved for some transport but was aware of the dangers of accepting a lift from a complete stranger.

To her surprise, he did not accelerate away but continued at walking pace alongside. At this speed, his bike was less stable, and with his eyes on Lisa, he failed to notice a deep pothole in the road surface. As the front wheel sank into the hollow, his bike tipped sideways, almost throwing him off. In an effort to prevent this, he opened the throttle sharply and accelerated out of the depression. Lisa noticed his frantic efforts to retain his 'cool' image and laughed openly.

He stopped his bike about twenty yards ahead and waited for her to catch up with him. As she reached him, she laughed and said, "Please don't have an accident because of me. You would do better to keep your eyes on the road."

"I know that to be very true. But it is difficult when a beautiful woman such as you is distracting me."

Lisa smiled shyly and blushed at this complement.

He held out his hand. "My name's Juan. What's yours?"

"Lisa." She ignored his outstretched hand. "Now will you please let me continue with my journey?"

He was not one to give up so easily. "It's a very hot part of the day to be walking. I would be very happy to give you a lift." Sensing her unease, he added, "And no strings attached. Where are you going?"

In a way, she admired his persistence. "Toledo."

"That is where I'm going too. Come on, Lisa. Let me be a Good Samaritan."

She laughed at his religious reference, yet there was something about him that attracted her. Perhaps it was the sparkle in his eyes or his smile that changed her mind.

"All right."

"Good. Have you ridden on a motorbike before?"

Lisa shook her head.

"It's quite easy. Come on, sit behind me. You will feel more secure if you squeeze the seat between your knees and hold on to me. When we're going around bends, lean over as I do." He secured her bag on to the back frame and sat astride his machine. "Come on, Lisa."

She felt shy and embarrassed as she lifted her leg to mount the bike.

"Are you comfortable?"

"Y…yes, I'm fine." Her mother would strongly disapprove of her accepting this lift from a stranger, but somehow, she felt quite safe in his presence. She did think that she could manage without holding on to Juan, but as the bike accelerated, Lisa found that it was necessary to put her arms around his waist to prevent her from being thrown off. The experience was exhilarating. The wind blew in her face, and the scenery flashed by her as they sped along the highway. Juan weaved his machine around some of the slower-moving vehicles, and within twenty minutes, they were entering the outskirts of Toledo. If she had continued to walk, it could have taken quite a few hours to complete her long journey.

Lisa thought that she liked the look of Toledo, as it was not as big and noisy as Cebu yet had far more activity than her local village of Balamban. The streets were bustling with many workers and midday shoppers as they pulled up in the centre of the town.

"Where do you want to go?" Juan asked.

"Oh, anywhere will do."

As though inspired with a sudden idea, Juan said, "Would you like to have some lunch?"

"Oh…I don't…" She felt it would be unwise to encourage this young man, yet she did feel quite hungry.

"Listen. I'm going to have some lunch myself in the little restaurant near the bus station. You're welcome to join me if you want. No obligation."

Lisa relented, feeling that it could do no harm to have some lunch with the man who had saved her from such a long walk. "Okay, I will eat with you."

Once again, he opened the throttle and drove along the streets of Toledo towards the bus station. As they pulled into the area near the restaurant, Juan parked his bike close to where they would be eating. From the greeting given by the restaurant owner, it was clear Juan was a regular customer.

"Who is your friend, Juan?" the man asked with a cheeky smile.

"This young lady is Lisa. And I want you to look after her with one of your very best meals."

The man offered Lisa a seat. "You know that everything here is very fresh and only top quality. That is why you keep coming back."

The restaurant owner—a rather rotund man in his fifties called Jose—handed Lisa a menu. This was the first time in her life that she had been in a restaurant, and her face coloured as she realised how expensive the meals were.

Juan, sensing her embarrassment, said, "Don't worry, Lisa. This meal is my treat to you."

"Oh, I couldn't—"

"Yes, you can," he interrupted. "I insist. What would you like—you can have anything from the menu."

Obediently, Lisa surveyed the choice of meat and fish dishes, eventually choosing fried fish, rice and a glass of mango juice.

"That's a good choice, Lisa. The fish here is superb. It's freshly caught, and Jose cooks it to absolute perfection."

Lisa looked at Juan, now facing her across the table. She thought that he was probably in his late twenties. He was quite attractive, fairly tall and strong-looking without being too muscular. His hair was short and black, and he had dark-brown, smouldering eyes and a smile that made her feel quite relaxed. She felt that he could be trusted and wondered why he had chosen her to befriend. "You are very kind to me, Juan."

"I could not let you walk all the way to Toledo. You really did look quite exhausted. Why have you come to Toledo?"

"I'm hoping to find some work here. There's nothing in the area where my family live."

"What sort of work? Secretarial?"

She blushed, laughing. "I wish I was that clever. No. I can only do cleaning or housemaid work."

"Really? I feel certain that you are capable of much greater things."

Lisa smiled shyly at this complement.

Jose brought several plates full of rice and fish, placing them on the table. "I hope that you will both enjoy your meal."

The platefuls of hot, savoury-smelling food reminded Lisa of the times she had spent with her grandfather when Marlyn would pile the plates high to satisfy her hunger. Meals at home were now more meagre and economic to be affordable within their limited resources.

"Help yourself, Lisa. Take as much as you want."

She did as Juan directed and ate the rice and fried snapper and mackerel as though she had not eaten for a week.

Juan laughed at the strength of her appetite. "You don't eat meals like this very often, do you?"

"No. My family has very little money. We eat just rice for most of the time."

"This is why you are looking for work, isn't it?"

She nodded her head in embarrassment.

151

"I might be able to help you. I run a small bar here in Toledo and could do with someone to keep the place clean. Would you be interested?"

"I...I don't know. You have been so kind to me already. Are you sure that you really need assistance?" Lisa still had to be very cautious and felt uncertain about this man whom she had known for just a few hours.

"Yes, I'm certain. Ask Jose if you don't believe me. He has known me for many years."

"It's all right, Juan. I believe you." She felt guilty at her obvious mistrust.

Understanding her embarrassment, Juan assured her, "You are right to be cautious. The job is there if you want it, but you don't have to make up your mind just now. If you decide to take it, you would earn three hundred and fifty pesos a month and have free accommodation. Anyway, take your time and think about it. Are you enjoying your meal?"

"Oh, yes, thanks. It's the best meal I've had for a long time."

Jose arrived at their table with more fruit juice and a fresh mango sliced into three pieces. By the time Lisa had finished, she was feeling very full. As well as the food, she had enjoyed the view since the little restaurant was very close to the harbour wall.

There was a pleasant, gentle breeze blowing from the sea, making the temperature quite comfortable. Lisa was fascinated by the scores of small fishing boats, moving slowly across the blue, tranquil waters of the Pacific Ocean. To her, there was something quite magical in such a vista. It was as though the scene was transformed into a slow-motion image, removing the need for any possible urgency in her life.

Noticing how she was transfixed by the scene, Juan asked, "Do you like the sea, Lisa?"

His question brought her suddenly back to reality. "I like to look at it, but I don't really know. I suppose it's because I grew up in the mountain region around Davao, and the sea is relatively new to me. It's hard to imagine that there are other countries somewhere out there far across the sea." Lisa remembered the ferry journey nearly twelve months earlier when she and her family had travelled to Cebu. The ferry seemed so big that she thought it would be a great experience to travel in a small boat to appreciate the sea properly.

Juan gave a little cough, which had the desired effect of bringing Lisa back to the present. She realised he had finished his meal and was ready to leave. "Oh, I'm so sorry. I was daydreaming."

He smiled at her obvious enjoyment of both meal and scenery. "I'm going to my bar now. You are welcome to come and look to see if you're interested in the job if you want."

Plucking up courage, she replied, "Yes, please, Juan. I would like to see it." They both thanked Jose for the fantastic meal and left the restaurant, walking back towards the motorbike.

Once again, Lisa held tightly on to Juan as he drove expertly through the busy streets of Toledo. He stopped outside a two-storey, white-painted concrete building displaying a large sign: 'Juan's Bar'. He asked Lisa to dismount from the bike and then pushed it along a narrow passage at the side of the bar and through a doorway, which opened onto a large, covered hallway. Lisa followed him into the building.

"I always keep my bike in here for security. It would be stolen within a few minutes if I left it outside in the street."

Lisa looked with interest at each room, following Juan as he proudly showed her around his place. "I won't take you in the bar itself, as it is open at the moment, but you can see it through this window. Don't worry, it's one-way, so nobody can see you."

153

Lisa found it fascinating that she could see into the bar without being seen by the customers. Men were sitting at tables, deep in conversation, most of them holding glasses of beer. Many were smoking, creating a heavy blue haze that made the scene almost unrealistic. Upstairs, there were three rooms where Juan lived: a spacious living room, tidy bedroom and a compact bathroom with toilet.

"What do you think of my place? Would you like the job?"

"I think so. Yes, please. When can I start?"

"Straight away if you like. I'm afraid that the place could really do with a good clean." Juan sounded almost apologetic.

Lisa had noticed from her brief inspection that there was a great deal of dust and grime around the place and assumed that it had not been cleaned for quite a while. "What happened to your last housemaid?"

"She was getting a bit elderly and the work was too tiring, so she decided to find something a little easier."

His reason sounded quite plausible. "What are my responsibilities?"

"To keep the rooms clean, cook most meals and wash clothing. Do you think you can manage it?"

"Oh, yes, I'm certain that I can." It would be hard work, but she was happy both for the challenge and the prospect of the money. "Where will I sleep?"

"In the same room as Rosa. She helps me in the bar serving drinks. You will meet her later. This is her room." He opened one of the doors, showing a small, quite basic room with no windows, illumination being only from a single electric light at ceiling level. There was a small table against one wall, two rough wooden chairs, a few shelves on another wall and a floor-level large sink in one corner. Lisa knew that this sink would serve many purposes. This would be where she would wash herself as well as washing clothing and bedding. It was certainly spartan, but it was better than in many Filipino homes, as it had solid walls and floors. Juan had already shown her the kitchen, which was a little better, as it also doubled up as a dining area.

"And the CR?"

Juan showed her the door to the toilet. This was close to the rear service entrance and backed onto the narrow passage separating this building from the next. In the Philippines, everybody referred to the toilet as the CR, copied from the abbreviation of the American 'comfort room'.

Lisa had noticed that the drainage channel was covered with concrete slabs unlike many buildings where one had to be careful, particularly at night, to avoid putting an unwary foot into an open sewage channel, something which would, at some time, happen to most people.

"Just one more point, Lisa. Please don't enter the bar area when it is open."

"That's okay, Juan." This suited Lisa fine, as she did not want to mix with rough, drunken men smelling of smoke and beer. "So is there just you and Rosa looking after the bar?"

"Yes, for most of the time, but my cousin also helps in the bar, usually when I have to go out to the bank or other places. He serves drinks and tries to stop any troublemakers before they can actually cause damage. But he doesn't live here. He has his own house a short distance away. Now, if you don't mind, I must go and see to my customers."

There were two doors separating the bar from the living area, which helped to keep the noise down to a reasonable level. Lisa heard coarse laughter from the drinkers as Juan opened the door leading into the bar. Background music could also be heard, presumably to create a welcoming atmosphere for the customers. Lisa could not understand why so many men spent such long hours drinking and smoking. To her mind, it was a complete waste of time and money.

At least she now had a job because of them and was grateful that she had been lucky enough to find work so quickly. Three hundred and fifty pesos each month was as much as she could expect for her age and experience, and even at this level, she should be able to send some money back to her mother to help with the family expenses. She was aware that her mother would probably not approve of her working in a bar, but since all she would be doing was cleaning, washing and cooking, there could be no real harm, and it would prove to be a challenge for her.

Lisa did not waste any time and started cleaning first of all the kitchen area and then the room she was to share with Rosa. She wondered what her roommate would be like but hoped that at least she would be friendly. When Lisa felt that she had made some improvements in the cleanliness of the place, she returned to her room and lay down on the floor wrapped in her blanket. It was after eight in the evening, and she had still not seen Rosa.

Lisa felt quite tired, as it was at least two hours after dusk and at home most people would be asleep before eight. Her family kept passing through her mind, making her feel homesick already. However, she was determined now to show her mother that she could live and work away from home, as she had suffered constant derision after running back home from her previous employer. She was determined not to repeat her earlier mistake.

It was after nine when the door to her room opened. Lisa was still awake and saw the figure of a woman enter. The light was on, and since Lisa was not yet asleep, she greeted the woman she assumed to be Rosa. "Hello, I'm Lisa. You must be Rosa."

The reply was not quite as friendly as she had hoped. "Yes. And I'm very tired. I need to sleep." Rosa was wearing a somewhat faded red dress, which she quickly unzipped and, stepping out of it, dropped the dress untidily on the floor. She took a pair of jeans and jumper off one of the shelves and after putting them on wrapped herself in a blanket and lay on the floor, ready for sleep.

Lisa had always washed herself and cleaned her teeth before bed, but Rosa was obviously not as concerned with such important matters of hygiene. Lisa was disappointed at this air of indifference and hoped it was purely because of tiredness.

She felt that Rosa must be in her late twenties, but somehow, she looked much older. Her face was lined and lacked expression, while her shoulder-length black hair looked as though it needed a good wash and brushing. It took quite a while before Lisa managed to fall into an uneasy sleep, but she woke with a start when she heard a sudden noise. It was well after midnight.

Rosa had obviously needed to relieve herself. Instead of going to the toilet, she crouched over the sink, urinating into the drain. Her standards of hygiene were inferior to Lisa's, whose mother had taught her how to conduct herself, particularly when staying with strangers. Rosa did not even bother to turn the tap on, resulting in the air smelling strongly of her urine. Lisa buried her head in the blanket and did her best to return to her sleep.

When Lisa awoke at six-thirty, Rosa was fast asleep and snoring gently. She did her best not to disturb her roommate and quickly left, closing the door gently behind her. After a visit to the toilet and now feeling quite hungry, she found rice in the kitchen cupboard and soon had some boiling in a pan. Even the pans and all the dishes needed a thorough cleaning before they could be used. It surprised her that Juan had tolerated such conditions. This was probably why he ate at Jose's restaurant so frequently. In addition to the rice, Lisa had found some dried fish, and soon the air smelled of the fish cooking in oil and garlic.

The inviting smell of fish cooking must have attracted Juan, who appeared, still looking a little sleepy, in the kitchen. "Good morning, Lisa. That smells great. Is there enough for both of us?"

"Why, yes. There is enough for all three of us. I expect Rosa will be hungry as well."

"Oh, she usually sleeps until late morning, so I wouldn't bother about her. She doesn't seem to have much of an appetite." Juan enjoyed his breakfast, even helping himself to a second portion of rice and fish. "I think that maybe Jose will be seeing a bit less of me if that is a sample of your cooking, Lisa."

Lisa laughed at his compliment. "I've always enjoyed cooking, thanks to my mother's guidance, but I'm afraid there's not much food in here. Do you mind if I buy some from the market? I could go this afternoon while the bar is open if that's all right?"

"Yes, of course, that's fine." He pulled a wad of notes out of his pocket and peeled off some, handing them to Lisa. "There are two hundred pesos. You buy whatever we need to fill the cupboards."

This really pleased Lisa. To be given free reign for shopping would help to make the job that bit more interesting. "I think I also need to buy some cleaning liquid and cloths if you don't mind."

"No, that's okay. You get whatever we need. Is that enough money?"

"Oh, I'm certain that will be enough. I will be very careful with your money, Juan."

"I'm sure you will. I feel I can trust you. I was very lucky to find you yesterday, walking along that dusty road. This place is looking better already."

Lisa was proud that her efforts had already been noticed by her new employer. She was determined to do her very best in this job. After clearing the breakfast dishes, she decided it was time to clean the bar area while it was closed. As she entered the large room, she looked for the mirror through which she had observed the customers. It amazed her that she could not distinguish it from an ordinary mirror. Making a start, she soon realised that this room would by far be her biggest challenge. It would probably take a few days before she would be satisfied with the results, but after three hours of hard work she could see and feel a significant improvement. There were many beer stains both on the carpet and seating, which would take a lot to remove, but she would do her very best to make the room cleaner and more presentable. Lisa made certain that she had finished her work in the bar before it was due to open at two o'clock.

When Juan looked at the results of her work, he was pleased with her efforts. She felt a sense of achievement as she returned to her room. To her surprise, Rosa was not there. Lisa had hoped to make friends with Rosa but as yet had not been given an opportunity. There would be many other chances, so Lisa thought nothing more about it as she left the bar to go shopping.

Lisa headed generally in the direction of the shopping area, and although she did not yet know much about Toledo, she soon found the market area without any difficulty. Her mother's training over many years, in knowing what to look for when shopping, was now proving invaluable. Lisa bought rice, fish and cheap cuts of meat, cooking oil and spices, and by the time she had added cleaning liquid and cloths, there were several heavy bags for her to carry back to the bar.

She felt very fortunate to have come across Juan and as a consequence now had responsible employment. Even with all her purchases, she still had nearly forty pesos remaining. It was a relief to unload the heavy bags when she returned to the bar. The kitchen cupboards were now stocked with enough food to last for several days. Again, Lisa spent the rest of the day by herself while Juan and Rosa were working in the bar.

Once she had finished her duties, Lisa sat at the table in her room and wrote a letter to her mother. She was eager to let her family know about her new job and responsibilities. She promised to send some money as soon as she had been paid.

Over the next few days, there was never any chance for any discussion, as Rosa constantly avoided verbal contact with her new roommate. Lisa found this a little disappointing. She posed absolutely no threat to Rosa's job and could think of no other reason why Rosa should be jealous.

Lisa did not see a great deal of Juan either, except for meals together, when he would show great enthusiasm over her culinary skills. Rosa never joined them, preferring to eat by herself when Lisa was not in the kitchen area. During one meal, Lisa asked Juan, "Is there any reason Rosa doesn't want to talk to me?"

"Oh, I would not worry about her. She can be very moody, reserved and shy at times."

"She's not worried about me wanting her job, is she?"

Juan laughed at this question. "No, I'm certain she isn't. Don't worry about her. Give her time and I'm sure she'll become more friendly."

Lisa was not convinced by his answer yet did not pursue the matter any further. Instead, she asked, "One of the rooms off the bar area is locked. I'll need the key if I am to keep it clean."

"Don't bother about that room. It doesn't matter."

His short reply made her even more curious. She wondered what could be in there that he did not want her to see. Still, without a key, there would be no way of finding out.

Next day, when she was cleaning the bar area, she again tried the door, but it was still firmly locked. She tried to peer through the keyhole, but with the room in darkness nothing could be seen. Still curious, she tried to work out what size the room would be by checking which rooms bordered it. It must have been about ten by twelve feet, which to her mind was quite a large room to just forget. One of the walls formed the passage wall at the side of the building, but frustratingly there were no windows through which she could have looked. There was a mesh-covered ventilation opening, but this was at too high a level to prove of any use.

Although she did not like mysteries, Lisa resigned herself to ignorance of this room's contents and true purpose. Not wanting to upset her employer, she put it to the back of her mind and concentrated on the task of cleaning, cooking and washing.

It did not take very long to work out the real purpose of the room. On several occasions, noises could be heard coming from what Lisa assumed to be the secret room. Even to the naive Lisa, it was the unmistakable sound of a couple having sexual intercourse. She was shocked to realise that Rosa was providing much more than just drinks for Juan's customers.

This must be where Rosa disappeared to for much of the time and why she was always tired late in the evenings. Although it amused her initially, Lisa was shocked to discover that the woman with whom she shared a room was a prostitute. It also explained why Juan had wanted to keep her from entering the room. Her mother would certainly not approve of her working in a place where men who were probably married came to have sex with Rosa.

This discovery intrigued Lisa even more, and one day she found the room was unlocked. Rosa was asleep in her room and Juan was out, making it impossible to resist the temptation to look inside.

Cautiously, she pushed the door open and peered into the previously hidden space. It was sparsely furnished with just a large bed, a small cabinet and a chair. Lisa sat on the bed, imagining what crude acts this room had witnessed. The bed felt quite soft, and several cushions lay scattered around the room. A drawer in the cabinet contained many small paper packets like little envelopes, which Lisa studied with curiosity. One was open, and inside she found a pink, rubber-smelling shape a bit like a balloon—something she had never seen before. Not wanting to be discovered, she quickly returned the items to the drawer and closed it. Although traces of perfume could be smelled in the room, it had not been sufficient to cover the strong odour of sweat and other body fluids soaked into the bedding. Lisa shuddered at the thought of drunken customers using Rosa to satisfy themselves. The place could have done with a thorough cleaning, but Lisa thought better of it, carefully pulled the door closed and continued with her normal work.

Chapter Twenty-One

BY KEEPING HERSELF busy, for Lisa, time passed quickly, and soon two months had passed since that first day she had accepted a lift from Juan. As she spent very little money on herself, she already had six hundred and fifty pesos saved up to give to her mother. She thought that after another month she would visit her family and take the money with her.

It came as quite a shock when she looked in her bag and could not find the bundle of notes she had been saving. Frantically, she emptied everything out of her bag, to no avail. Her bag had never left the room in which she slept, which meant that only one person could have stolen her hard-earned savings.

Rosa, who still kept herself very aloof and private, was the only possible perpetrator. Lisa could not imagine why, when Rosa must have been paid so much more, especially considering the extra services she provided for their clients, she should find it necessary to steal what to her must be a fairly small amount.

With the entire savings from her labours lost, Lisa felt so miserable and depressed. She wondered what she should do. She certainly had no intention of forgetting about it. If Rosa was confronted with the allegation, she would probably deny it. The only course of action was to let Juan know of her loss and at the earliest opportunity. Lisa decided that it would be more sensible to tell him during breakfast next day rather than when he was tired after closing the bar late in the evening.

Lisa had become quite accustomed to Rosa's sullen silence when she entered the room, and on this sad day made no attempt at conversation with the older woman. Instead, she buried her

163

head in her blanket and tried to sleep. This proved difficult, as she kept thinking of how her money had been stolen by the woman who now slept just a few feet away in the same room with her.

Next morning at breakfast, her lack of sleep had resulted in Lisa looking tired enough for Juan to comment on her appearance. "What's wrong, Lisa?"

"I…I didn't sleep very well last night." Before she could stop herself, Lisa burst into tears.

Juan seemed genuinely concerned. "What's happened? You're usually such a happy young woman. Whatever it is it must be bad to have upset you so much. Tell me."

"I was saving money to send to my family. I kept it in the bag in my room. There were six hundred and fifty pesos. And now it's gone. Stolen!"

Juan's normally calm features showed surprise and anger on hearing the cause of Lisa's distress. "Rosa," he said. "It has to be Rosa. Leave it with me. I'll deal with her."

The way he expressed the word 'deal' worried Lisa. "I don't want to get her into any trouble. Please don't be too hard on her, Juan."

Juan smiled at her request. "You are a good woman, Lisa. I will deduct the money from her wages and make her understand that she must never do it again. Just don't worry yourself." He pulled some notes from his back pocket and put them in Lisa's hand.

"That is far too much! It was only six hundred and fifty pesos."

"Let's say this is compensation for the trouble she has caused you. Come on now, dry your eyes and enjoy this great breakfast." When Lisa checked later, she found that Juan had given her eight hundred pesos—almost two weeks' wage as compensation— which she appreciated greatly.

She decided to keep the money in the back pocket of her jeans for now and would buy a strong bag for her few valuable possessions when she was next shopping. One with a lock. From now on, she knew she must not place too much trust in other people. Why had she not thought earlier about the security of her earnings?

After this traumatic incident, Lisa put the matter well behind her and kept herself busy with cleaning for the rest of the day. That evening, Lisa was lying on the floor wrapped in her blanket and ready for sleep when she heard raised voices. It could only be Juan and Rosa. He must have told her that he knew what she had done. It was a very heated argument, although Lisa could not hear what was being said because of the walls between them. Even so, it was clear that Rosa was verbally retaliating, which surprised Lisa. She had assumed Rosa would be too afraid of losing her job to argue with Juan. The biggest surprise, however, was when Rosa came into her room. Lisa had assumed that she would be too ashamed to say anything, but she was wrong.

"You bitch!" The look of pure hatred in Rosa's eyes shocked Lisa to the core. "I hope you enjoyed getting me in trouble with Juan!"

"No, I didn't enjoy getting you in trouble, but if you hadn't taken all my savings, nothing would have been said!" Lisa sat upright as she angrily retorted. "That money was for my family. You had no right to steal it!"

Rosa did not answer and showed no sign of regret as she prepared herself for bed. She flung her clothes down in an untidy heap as if directing her contempt at anything she could lay her hands on. Lisa was glad that this violence had not been directed towards her.

With no apology and not even a hint of remorse from Rosa, Lisa was sad and puzzled as she lay down and once again wrapped herself in her blankets. It took quite a while before she was able to fall asleep, but at about two in the morning, something disturbed her. She listened and soon realised what the noise was. Rosa was lying on the floor wrapped in her blankets and shaking convulsively. Lisa was worried and wondered what she should do. No matter what her feelings were towards the older woman, she did not want any harm to come to her. But then the convulsions stopped as quickly as they had started and Rosa appeared to be fast asleep. This happened several times during the night, resulting in a very uneasy, disturbed sleep for Lisa.

When it was time for her to get up the following morning, she still felt very tired. Lisa washed, dressed and prepared breakfast, ready for a new day. Juan seemed just the same as usual when he appeared for breakfast. He noticed Lisa's heavy eyes. "I hope Rosa didn't give you a hard time last night?"

"She appeared to be very angry with me." Lisa was not going to pretend that nothing had happened. "Juan, does Rosa have something wrong with her? She was shaking a lot during the night."

"I wouldn't worry. There's nothing physically wrong with her, but she sometimes has a very hot, uncontrollable temper. She'll soon get over it."

"I can't understand why she still doesn't talk to me. It's as though she really hates me, but I don't know what I've done to deserve it."

Juan patiently replied, "I'm certain that you have done nothing at all to deserve it, but I'm afraid it's a problem with Rosa and nothing you do will change her mind. How about you? Are you happy here?"

"Oh, yes, thanks, Juan. The work keeps me busy, and I'm happy I can earn something to help my family back home." Lisa realised this was probably a good opportunity to ask a question. "Do you think I could have a day off next weekend to visit my family?"

"Yes, of course you can," Juan replied without hesitation. "You deserve it after making such a fantastic difference here. The place has never been so clean!" His eyes twinkled in amusement as he said, "Jose is not very pleased with you, though."

"Why? What have I done?" Her worried expression seemed to amuse Juan further.

"You've lost him a good paying customer, now that I'm eating here a lot more, thanks to your excellent cooking." The two of them laughed, and Lisa felt relieved that at least her employer was pleased with her efforts.

When weekend arrived, Lisa used a jeepney bus for the journey to her family home. It had been nearly three months since she had seen her family, and she was excited at the prospect of seeing them all again. When she jumped down from the jeepney, she ran the short distance to the house. Dolores was sitting outside under the shade of a tree reading a book.

Lisa had no doubt that it would be the bible, as Dolores spent many long hours studying its contents. Dolores raised her eyes from the book as her daughter came into view. "Lisa!" She quickly put the bible down and stood, opening her arms to greet her daughter. The two of them hugged for several minutes as if their separation had been for a period of many years instead of just three months.

"I've missed you so much, Nanay." Lisa put her hand into her pocket and pulled out the money she had been saving. She kept only fifty pesos for herself, giving her mother seven hundred and fifty pesos. "This is for you." She pushed the money into her mother's hand, pleased that at last she was able to contribute towards the family finances.

"Thanks a lot, Lisa. Are you certain that you have enough left for yourself?"

"Oh, yes. I don't need much." As the two women walked together into the house, Lisa started talking about her new job, about Juan and how Rosa had stolen her savings.

When Dolores heard of Rosa, she said in a concerned voice, "Be very careful with that woman. It sounds as if she may be jealous of you and could be dangerous."

Lisa's father was in the house, sitting quietly and seeming more withdrawn than ever. He showed no sign of enthusiasm on seeing his youngest daughter. She gave him a hug but felt no warmth towards him, the memories of her childhood still preventing her from any such feelings. The rest of the family were far more enthusiastic, giving Lisa a heart-warming welcome. The house was filled with the chatter of happy voices as all except Pedro joined in the many conversations.

Dolores was, as expected, apprehensive about Lisa working in a bar but was pleased at the level of responsibility she had so quickly attained. Everybody ate well that evening, celebrating Lisa's success in her search for useful employment.

The only two members of the family not there were Antonio and Diding. Lisa was worried when Dolores told her that she had not heard anything from them for over two months.

"What's happening in Cotabato now?" Lisa enquired.

"From what I've heard, life there is very uncomfortable. The military are everywhere, trying anything to get people to inform on NPA members. I know there have been many arrests, deaths and houses being burnt down. We were right to move out when we did."

"I do wish that Antonio, Diding and their families would move here as well. I worry about them so much." Lisa felt a heavy burden of responsibility for the dangerous situation her family and all her friends in Cotabato were in. She wondered how much her killing Captain Rodriguez had inflamed the already sensitive situation. Lisa would have to live with the burden for the rest of her life, but she put these thoughts to the back of her mind and talked happily with her family and enjoyed their company for the evening.

Lisa slept at home that night, and after a little breakfast the following morning, she was ready to return to her job in Toledo. Dolores walked the short distance with her to wait for the bus. After a few minutes, the lumbering single-decker came into view, and Lisa signalled to the driver to halt. She gave her mother a final hug, not knowing when she would be able to see her again.

"Take care, Lisa. And be very careful with Rosa. She could cause you a lot of trouble." Dolores waved as her daughter boarded the crowded bus for Toledo. Lisa quickly found a vacant seat as the bus picked up speed to continue on its long journey.

As soon as she returned to the bar, Lisa concentrated on her duties, cleaning the place as thoroughly as was possible. Rosa, as usual, avoided any contact with Lisa, while Juan seemed genuinely pleased to see her back again.

It proved to be quite a lonely job for Lisa, as she only saw Juan for a few brief periods every day. She had, however, made friends with a few other young women whom she had met while out shopping in the market. Like her, they were housemaids at shops, businesses and houses in the area. It was not a very exciting time of her life, but at least Lisa now had some form of stability and was earning a living.

After another month had passed, Juan spoke at length to Lisa while they were having breakfast one morning. "You have made such a difference here, Lisa. This place has never been as clean as it is now."

Lisa wondered where this conversation would lead. She desperately hoped that she was not about to lose her job.

"The problem is that the furnishings in the bar are many years old and are in need of replacement. I wondered if you would like to assist me in choosing new furniture and fabrics?"

A big smile lit up her face. "Yes, of course! I'd love to!" Lisa was so pleased that he trusted her enough to make this important request. The only worry she had was Rosa. "Are you certain you want me to do this instead of Rosa? I don't want to cause even more problems between the two of us."

"Don't worry about Rosa. She has absolutely no interest in such matters. And to be quite honest, I don't think her sense of colour coordination is good enough for the task."

"As long as you're certain then I'm happy to try my very best. How do you want me to start?"

"There is nowhere here in Toledo for decent furniture. Next week, I'll leave my cousin and Rosa in charge here while you and I go to Cebu together. There are plenty of stores with a good choice in Cebu."

Lisa was excited at the prospect of shopping for furniture in the city. For her, it was a bit like a holiday. She hoped that she would be able to look around Cebu, as the only time she had seen it was when they had arrived on the ferry from Cotabato, and that had been a very fleeting glimpse.

"Before we go, Lisa, I'd like you to make a note of what furniture we have in the bar now and the size of the room."

Lisa did not waste any time, and later that day began an inventory of everything in the bar. She meticulously recorded every detail, taking great care to make the information legible. Apart from writing the occasional letter, she had little experience of clerical work and was afraid of making spelling errors. At times, she wished that she had made a greater effort in school, which could have resulted in some form of qualification, instead of staying as a semi-literate housemaid. For this reason, she was determined to show Juan that she was capable and worthy of his trust. He was really pleased with her efforts and praised her methodical approach to the task. She looked forward with each passing day to their journey into the city. Rosa showed no sign of interest at all and continued her silent hostility towards Lisa.

Chapter Twenty-Two

THE DAY BEFORE their departure, Lisa was excited, and as she lay in her blanket that night, she found she had great difficulty falling asleep. When she eventually succumbed, she had one of the most vivid, erotic dreams in her life. She was completely naked and climbing high into the canopy of a large tree. Snakes gliding silently along the branches slid over her, but instead of revulsion or fear, she experienced great sensual pleasure from the touch of their smooth skin. They gently caressed her thighs, gliding so effortlessly over her pubic area, her stomach and teasing her nipples until they stood proud and erect.

As she lay sighing in ecstasy, the snakes disappeared in an instant, and she felt herself falling out of the tree but falling very slowly as though floating. It seemed an eternity before she landed, finding that she was sitting on the back of Juan's motorbike as it sped along a wide highway. Juan was also naked, and together, they raced along the road. She held on closely to him as the bike seemed to travel ever faster and faster. Then the inevitable happened. The bike crashed into a large truck, throwing the couple high into the air. Again, the two naked bodies appeared to float downwards very slowly. Juan landed softly on his back in a huge bed of orchid petals and smiled as Lisa fell on top of him, enveloping his erect penis in her warm, receptive body. The only sound was that of birds singing happily as the couple made beautiful, satisfying, ecstatic love.

As Lisa awoke from this fantasy, she realised that for the first time in her life she had experienced a 'wet dream', which embarrassed her intensely. She hurriedly washed and dressed ready for her big day. She found herself wondering about her explicitly erotic dream. While she did find Juan attractive, she really could not imagine that she would ever have such a physical relationship with him. Juan, who was fit and quite good-looking, probably already had a girlfriend, yet so far Lisa had not seen her if she existed. The crash in the dream worried her a little. Could this be purely symbolic of their passionate encounter or could it be a warning of what was going to happen?

As a good Catholic, Lisa said her prayers regularly, but on that day she prayed both for a safe journey and the strength to resist and overcome the sexual feelings created by her unusually erotic and powerful dream.

Lisa and Juan left early that day, as soon as they had finished a good breakfast of rice with pork. She was wearing stretch black jeans with a white long-sleeved jumper, both of which she had recently bought for herself in Toledo's market. Taking her seat behind Juan, she waved farewell to his cousin. Predictably, Rosa was nowhere to be seen. The memory of her dream came back to Lisa with a tingle of excitement as she placed her hands around Juan's firm, slim waist and he opened up the throttle, accelerating along the busy highway in the direction of Cebu.

Lisa enjoyed looking at the scenery on both sides of the road as they passed the slower-moving larger vehicles. She tried in vain to remember what the truck looked like from her dream, aware that it was unlikely to appear in real life. The road surface was in places uneven and littered with potholes, but Juan manoeuvred skilfully around these obstacles. Although it was a hot, sunny day, the breeze from their speed kept them at a comfortable temperature.

Within two hours, they had reached the outskirts of Cebu, and Lisa watched with interest as the tall, white, concrete city buildings replaced the lush, green vegetation of the countryside.

Once they entered the city, the traffic became much heavier and slower. It was obvious that Juan knew the city well, as he turned from one street to another, weaving his way through the mass of cars, trucks and jeepneys. Eventually, he pulled up in a narrow street and asked Lisa to dismount before he pushed his bike across the raised pavement, through an opening in heavy, sliding metal doors and into a gloomy store. Lisa followed and looked with curiosity at the many machine parts spread out over the floor in a somewhat disorganised display.

A large, well-built man emerged from an office at the rear and with a beaming smile shouted, "Juan, you old rogue! It seems like ages since you last came here. And who's this lovely young woman with you?"

"Hi, Frankie. This place never seems to change!" The two men gave each other a brief, playful hug. "This is Lisa. She works for me. We are in Cebu looking for new furniture for the bar. Can I leave my bike here while we look around the stores?"

"Of course you can. It certainly would not be safe to leave it on the road. Too many criminals eager to get their hands on any easy pickings. And when you've finished your shopping, you both must have dinner with me. Okay?"

"That sounds good to me." Juan leaned his bike against the rear wall. "We should be back around six."

Lisa took an immediate liking towards Frankie. He seemed a very happy, jovial character. She looked forward to their meal together. It was going to be very late before they returned to the bar in Toledo, but she was not concerned, as it should be a refreshing break from the usual daily routines.

She and Juan walked out of the dimly lit store into the bright sunshine baking the narrow Cebu streets. Juan instructed her to keep close to him, as there would be masses of people crowding the pavements and it would be very easy for Lisa to get lost if separated. She found this to be true as soon as they left Sanciangko Street heading towards the main shopping area. Juan walked much faster than Lisa's usual pace, and she had difficulty keeping up with him so was relieved when he turned into the entrance of a large furnishing store. Familiar with the shop's layout, he went directly to the second floor, Lisa breathlessly following. She was amazed to see such a wide selection of fine furniture.

"Right, Lisa. I want you to take a good look around this place and see what you feel would be best for the bar. We need twelve four-seater tables with chairs. They have to be strong to withstand the occasional brawl, but most of all they must look good."

Charged with such a responsible task, Lisa took immense care as she closely inspected every available choice.

Juan did not rush her, leaving her while he looked at the hi-fi display in a different department within the same store. This was his only opportunity to learn about the latest technologies imported from Japan and America. Such offerings would have been wasted on his clients, as the noise level from conversations in the bar would inevitably overpower the background music. Still, he was more interested in adding high-quality music for his own benefit within his living space.

After a while, he wandered back to the area where Lisa was still busily inspecting each table and chair in every minute detail. "Any luck yet, Lisa? Is it good enough for our bar?"

Lisa emerged from under a table where she had been checking its construction. Her beaming smile revealed her enjoyment of the task she had been given. "Yes, I think so." She led him to an area of the display and pointed to one particular item of furniture. "Take a look at this table, Juan. It's very strong, a good colour and should be easy to keep clean. The chairs look good and should be comfortable and strong enough for the bar."

Juan smiled at her eagerness and looked as directed. "Yes, I like your choice. It should look good in the bar area. Now, remember which ones you have chosen while we find curtains to match."

Lisa had a good sense of colour balance and very soon had picked material for the curtains. This new responsibility had boosted her self-esteem and confidence, which Juan found pleasing.

Once the selections had been made, Juan used his business acumen with the store salesman to buy at the best possible prices, sometimes haggling quite excitedly. Satisfied with the price, he arranged delivery of his purchases, and after paying a deposit, he and Lisa left the vast department store. The heat hit them as they stepped out of the comfortable, air-conditioned building to emerge into the street filled with masses of noisy, sweating people.

Lisa was still surprised by the sheer number of people filling every available space on the noticeably uneven footpath and in many places spilling out into the busy road where drivers sounded their horns incessantly at the unconcerned jay-walkers.

She hurried along trying her best to keep up with Juan. A few minutes later, they arrived once again at his friend's store.

Frankie spotted them as they entered. "Take a seat in the office. It's a bit cooler in there." He shouted to one of his assistants to clear the piles of books and folders, leaving two dusty yet comfortable seats. "Just give me a few minutes to finish this paperwork and then we'll go for a meal."

It was closer to twenty minutes before he was ready, during which time Lisa looked around the office. Several pictures stuck on the walls were of young women wearing not much more than a smile. Lisa was a little taken aback by the nudity and felt certain that Frankie must not be married to be interested in such posters.

Realising that Lisa had seen the pin-ups, Frankie laughed. "I'm sorry, Lisa. I hope that my pictures of naked women don't offend you. It's a little hobby of mine." He quickly clarified this by saying, "In my spare time, my interest is photography. I like to feel that it is artistic, although Juan will probably say that I am just a dirty old man."

Juan laughed. "I wouldn't say that you were old, Frankie."

Lisa joined in with the laughter and somehow did not feel shocked, which, considering her puritanical upbringing, surprised even herself.

"Come on, let's go. I'm hungry." Frankie led the way back through the still-busy streets. It was nearly six o'clock, and the afternoon sun had practically disappeared, but the temperature was still high, the air heavy with sweat-inducing moisture. The restaurant, 'Pete's', was very close, and as they entered, it was obvious that Frankie was a regular and valued customer. A waiter led them through the noisy, busy ground-floor area and upstairs to a more comfortable, quieter air-conditioned room.

Frankie took charge, enjoying the attention afforded by his patronage. "Lisa, is there any food that you don't like?"

She shook her head. "No. I enjoy most foods, especially seafood."

"Good. In that case, let me recommend the mackerel for you. This is one of the best restaurants for seafood in Cebu. How about you, Juan? What would you like?"

Juan was noncommittal. "I'll leave it up to you, Frankie. You know my likes and what's best."

Frankie was pleased that he could make the selection for his friends. He gave his order to the waiter and ended by requesting two bottles of wine.

Lisa heard this and when the waiter had gone said, "Could I have a soft drink, please, Frankie? I don't drink alcohol."

Frankie laughed. "Don't worry, Lisa. I guessed that you didn't drink. One of the bottles is a very low-alcohol wine. It's very pleasant, especially with seafood. Try it for me."

How could she refuse such a request? Lisa nodded, hopeful that she could manage a little of the drink so alien to her taste to appease her host. Her strict Catholic upbringing had not prepared her for this moment. Politely, she joined in the conversation when she could, but her mind was far away, thinking of her mother. There were many times when she felt like a little girl in an unfamiliar world, longing to be comforted by her mother's loving arms.

Two waiters brought many dishes and plates, which practically filled the whole of the table. Lisa was quite hungry and enjoyed the fried mackerel mixed with chunks of tender fresh crab meat all on a bed of steaming rice. Bravely, she sipped the wine, finding it tasted better than she had expected. Frankie would occasionally top up her glass without waiting to be asked, especially since he knew she would never request more. Lisa kept thinking that she would refuse to have any further wine, but in the event she lost count of how many times her glass had been topped up.

The meal seemed to last ages, with so much food to enjoy.

Lisa listened with interest as Juan and Frankie remembered their days at school, where apparently they were in the same class. From what they were saying, the two were not particularly academic, preferring instead to play tricks on other children and teachers. After leaving school, they had joined the navy, where Frankie had developed his interest in engineering.

After four years in the navy, their paths had diverged, Juan moving out to Toledo, where he had been left a large piece of land by a relative. Frankie preferred the city and opened his business selling and maintaining engines and generators.

When Frankie asked Lisa about her own life, she described a very simple, unexciting life, carefully omitting any mention of her role in the Philippine Liberation Army. The wine had relaxed her into a false sense of security. Before she knew what was happening, her head was swimming, her speech was slightly slurred and her legs seemed to resemble jelly. She found herself giggling at anything said that was slightly amusing, which was quite a contrast for the usually reserved Lisa.

Seeing that his plan had worked even better than expected, Juan said, "I think it's about time we went now, Lisa. It's getting late."

Frankie looked concerned. "I think you have had too much wine to drive safely, Juan. Why don't you stay overnight?"

"Where? Do you know anywhere local?" Lisa was too innocent to realise that this situation was being orchestrated and engineered by the two friends and listened to their conversation unconcerned.

"The Mercedes Hotel is just around the corner from here." Frankie stood up. "Come on. I'll take both of you there. The hotel manager is a good friend of mine." He quickly settled the bill, stuffing a wad of pesos into the hands of the eager waiter.

The little man ran to open the door for his apparently wealthy client, saying an excited, "Salamat" to each of them as they passed through the doorway.

Chapter Twenty-Three

THE HOT NIGHT air hit Lisa as she left the restaurant, her head swimming even more from the effects of the wine. In an attempt to avoid falling over, she leaned against Juan for support as they walked along the narrow street. It was quite dark and there were now only a few people on the previously crowded pavements. Within minutes, they were at the reception desk of the Mercedes Hotel.

Frankie asked for the manager, who quickly appeared. He was smartly dressed in a dark suit, white shirt and a red patterned tie. "Frankie! What can I do for you, my friend?" he enquired, smiling broadly.

"These are my good friends from Toledo. Do you have a room for them just for the one night?"

"Of course." He turned to his assistant, giving him a key. "Take these good people up to room two hundred and seventeen."

"I'll leave you two now. It's been great seeing you both. Take good care of her, Juan." He turned to Lisa and took hold of her hand in a friendly gesture. "I hope to see you again, Lisa. You'll always be very welcome here."

Through an intoxicated haze, she smiled. "Thanks for a great meal and a lovely evening, Frankie. I've really enjoyed myself." She did not seem aware how much her speech had been affected by the wine.

The couple followed the porter to the lift and were shown to their room. The fact that they were going to share a room for a night did not unduly worry Lisa, as she expected to sleep on the floor fully clothed while her employer would take the bed.

It came as quite a surprise, therefore, when as soon as the porter had disappeared and the door closed behind him, Juan took hold of Lisa and kissed her gently on the lips. Something within her wanted to resist, yet the sensation was so tender, so unexpected and so passionately exciting that she could not help but to pull him closer, enjoying his embrace.

The feelings she had experienced in her dream seemed to be coming true, or could all this perhaps be yet another dream?

Juan lifted her jumper and gently caressed her small, proud breasts. Her breathing became heavier with every touch, her longing for him becoming increasingly apparent. Pausing from his embraces, she pulled her white jumper over her head and dropped it to the floor. She then unzipped her jeans and slid them down over her slender thighs. Juan watched, entranced, while unfastening his shirt and trousers. Very soon, both were completely naked, their bodies locked tightly together with a passion that took Lisa's breath away. Juan's kisses were deep and tender, progressing from her lips towards her neck. A shivering tingle of excitement rippled through her body as he kissed her on this super-sensitive area. When his mouth moved downwards between her nipples, her feelings of desire and ecstasy rose further, her breathing becoming faster by the second.

After a few minutes of ever-increasing passion, Juan's strong arms lifted Lisa's submissive body and laid her gently on the bed. She was ready to receive his erect penis and opened her legs invitingly. As a virgin, and a pretty naive one at that, her response was an instinctive one. She had never even seen a man's erection before and was amazed by the size of it, hoping that it would not be too big to fit into her vagina.

Juan felt quite certain that she was sexually inexperienced and eased his penis towards her inviting vulva. She winced as he pressed gently, deflowering the young woman as tenderly as he

181

could. Tears ran down her cheeks, partly from the pain and partly the symbolic significance of losing her very precious virginity.

Slowly, he began to move inside her, her excitement overcoming the initial pain of penetration. Juan's arms locked straight, supporting his body and allowing him to find the most arousing position for intercourse. She locked her legs around the back of his thighs, pulling him closer to her for maximum contact.

Juan took his time, keeping his movements steady yet slow, as he wanted to achieve a climax at the same time as Lisa. Occasionally, he would pause to dip his head down to hers and kiss her with a passion that took Lisa's breath away. He teased her hard nipples with his tongue then engulfed each in his mouth, raising her desire to an even higher level.

When he felt that she was ready, his body accelerated to a supreme climax, her pelvic thrusts indicating the strength of her orgasmic response.

Juan let out a gasp of extreme satisfaction as the semen laden with hundreds of millions of sperm escaped from his penis into Lisa's welcoming body. The two collapsed in an embrace of ecstasy, the beads of sweat collecting into rivulets of moisture and dripping off their glistening bodies onto the bed. Lisa's heart was pounding faster than she had ever experienced, and a blush of colour temporarily turned her pale, golden skin to a darker hue.

A strange yet supreme feeling swept over her in waves of ecstasy. Very soon, the couple, still locked in their intimate embrace, were fast asleep. Lisa slept a newer, deeper sleep, her gentle breathing echoing Juan's slow, deep breaths.

The rays of light from the early morning sun streaming through the thin bedroom curtains awoke her. To her surprise, even here in the city, cockerels sounded their wake-up calls.

She looked around the room, trying to remember how she came to be where she was. The naked figure of Juan, still sound asleep and snoring quite loudly, brought back floods of memories of the previous evening. The food, the drink and her seduction brought the reality of the situation very clearly to her.

She slipped out of the bed, trying not to disturb the man who just a few hours earlier had been her employer and was now significantly more. In the bathroom, she showered quickly yet thoroughly as if in a vain attempt to remove the psychological stain from her mind. Panic overtook her as she realised that the act of the previous evening may result in conception and hoped desperately that this would not be the case. To give birth at her age was the very last thing she wanted. She knew exactly what her mother would say if she became pregnant, tears filling her eyes at the thought.

Quickly, she pulled on her clothes and left the room, quietly closing the door behind her without disturbing Juan. Outside, the streets were still relatively quiet, as it was only just after six o'clock.

Lisa was a stranger in this city without any knowledge of the area. Stopping an elderly woman, she asked, "Could you tell me where to find the local church, please?"

The woman paused and looked thoughtfully at Lisa. "That would be Santo Nino." Lisa nodded appreciatively. "I am going there myself. You can walk with me if you like."

The two women walked much more slowly than Lisa would have liked, yet she was grateful for the company.

"Where are you from, my dear?"

"I work in Toledo. I'm in Cebu…on business." Lisa blushed at what the business had turned into. She felt certain that the old woman knew her guilty secret. She might even think that she was a prostitute.

183

"You were not born in Toledo, though, were you?"

"No, you are right, but how...?"

"I have been around long enough to recognise many of the different Philippine dialects. Now, let me see. I would guess Davao or somewhere in that region."

"You are nearly right. I was born in Marbel, in southern Cotabato. We moved to Cebu a few years ago to avoid all the troubles."

The woman nodded, understanding Lisa's situation. After a few minutes, they arrived at the ancient church.

Even at this early time of day, there were hundreds of people attending Mass. Lisa thanked the old woman for her help, and soon the two were separated by the crowds of noisy worshippers filling both the pews and the aisles.

Lisa waited patiently until the Mass had finished and then found herself a quiet place to pray. She fell to her knees, her head bowed in solemn prayer as tears of anguish ran down her cheeks. "Oh, Mother Mary, please forgive me for I have sinned. I have tasted the fruits of carnal desire with a man for whom I have no love. Oh, Mother Mary, what can I do?"

As Lisa wept openly with guilt, a figure approached her. It was the old woman who had walked with her to the church.

"What is wrong, my dear? Can I help?"

Lisa looked up through a misty veil of tears. "No, thanks. This is something I must deal with myself." Lisa realised that she would have difficulty finding the hotel again. "Would you walk back with me to the place where I met you, please? I'm still not familiar with Cebu."

"Yes, of course." The old woman smiled fondly, realising that Lisa was very troubled by something, but she did not intrude upon her privacy. She handed Lisa a handkerchief to dry her eyes.

"Thank you. You are very kind." Lisa stood up and walked with the old woman out of the magnificent church that was Santa Nino. Slowly, they made their way back through the streets towards Sanciangko Street and the Mercedes Hotel. "Thank you for being there when I needed someone."

Seeing the depth of Lisa's gratitude, the old woman took hold of her hand, clasped it warmly and said, "Take good care of yourself, my dear. I'm certain that God will forgive you. From the little time I have known you, I can tell that you are a truly genuine person and hope that you will find great happiness in your life."

Lisa smiled and waved goodbye. She turned into the doorway of the Mercedes Hotel, paused and turned back. To her surprise, the old woman had already disappeared. There were a few more people around now but no sign at all of the person who had shown her such kindness. Could she have been a messenger from God? Perhaps even the Virgin Mary? Lisa made the sign of the cross.

For some unknown reason, Lisa felt uneasy about entering the hotel to confront Juan and instead went back into the street. With a sudden idea, she walked along Sanciangko Street towards Frankie's store. Juan would have to go there for his bike, ensuring that she would not be stranded in Cebu.

Frankie seemed surprised to see her without her employer. "Hello, Lisa. Where's Juan on this fine morning?"

"I think he will be here shortly." Lisa was deliberately evasive. "Do you mind if I wait here for him, Frankie?" She was relieved to see Juan's bike still leaning against the wall.

"No, not at all. Make yourself comfortable." Frankie scooped up a pile of catalogues from one of the more comfortable chairs, dumped them heavily on the floor and wiped off some of the dust with his large hand. Lisa sat demurely on the offered seat, hoping that the accumulated layers of dust would not dirty her jeans. The phone rang. While Frankie answered it, Lisa wondered what Juan's reaction would be upon finding she was not in the hotel room. She desperately hoped he would not be angry with her. It would not be very long before she would find out.

The surprise on Juan's face as he entered the store said it all. Strangely, he made no mention of her absence, and Lisa could only assume that he did not want to make a scene in front of his friend.

"Come on, Lisa. It's time we were heading back to Toledo."

Frankie quickly finished his telephone conversation. "It's been great seeing you two. Don't leave it too long before you come back here again." Lisa gave him a friendly hug. "Take good care of this fine young lady, Juan. She's very welcome here anytime."

Chapter Twenty-Four

JUAN PUSHED HIS bike out of the store and into the now busy road. Sitting astride the machine, he started the engine and, without speaking, motioned to Lisa to take her place on the pillion. Obediently, she sat behind her sullen employer and waved a farewell to Frankie as they accelerated along the road.

Juan said nothing for the whole of their return journey, making Lisa feel very uncomfortable and anxious as to what he may say or do on reaching his bar in Toledo. It seemed strange that only a few hours earlier they had been making hot, passionate love, yet now it was as if there was a huge block of ice between them.

Lisa watched the scenery as they sped along the busy highway, yet nothing really registered in her troubled mind, her thoughts taken up with her precarious situation. She found it hard to believe when they reached Toledo that the journey had passed so quickly, especially since she had been dreading the event. Lisa dismounted from the motorbike and watched Juan as he put the machine out of the way of would-be thieves. He showed no sign of any emotion and acted almost as though Lisa was not even there. She walked in sadness to her room. She had hoped that perhaps Juan was in love with her after their night of passion, but judging from his actions and cold indifference towards her, that didn't seem likely.

Rosa was in the bedroom sitting at the table and reading a magazine. She glanced up at Lisa and seemed to sense the young woman's sadness.

"What's wrong, Lisa? You look upset."

187

Lisa was astonished Rosa was actually bothering to talk to her.

"Oh, it's nothing," she lied. "The ride on the motorbike has given me a headache."

"I don't believe you. I think I know exactly why you're unhappy."

Taken aback by Rosa's sudden change in attitude and her refusal to accept her explanation, she asked quietly, "Oh? What would that be?"

"Well, now, let me see." Rosa looked up as though she were trying to solve some difficult mathematical problem. "Juan took you to the shops in Cebu. He appeared to give you plenty of responsibility in selecting furniture for the bar. Afterwards, you met up with Frankie and had a meal together." Lisa listened, spellbound, as Rosa continued. "You had a lovely meal and too much wine. Afterwards, Juan and Frankie decided that it was too late to ride back here, and Frankie took you both to the Mercedes Hotel where you spent the night together. While you were subdued by the effects of the drink, Juan raped you."

It was the final words of Rosa's description that shocked her. Had she been raped? The thought of the dreadful truth made her burst into tears.

"How do you know this?" she sobbed.

"Because, Lisa, that is exactly what happened to me eight years ago. When Juan told me that the two of you were going to Cebu, I knew exactly what he had in mind."

Lisa stared in amazement at Rosa. "You mean that this was all set up just to take advantage of me?"

The older woman nodded. "Of course. It's a way of breaking you in for the next stage of his plan."

The more Lisa heard the more frightened she became. "And what is his plan?" She feared Rosa's answer.

A smile appeared on the older woman's face as she continued. "He will expect you to sleep with his better-paying clients. To put it crudely, he was breaking you in as a prostitute."

"Oh God, no!" she wailed. Unexpectedly, the usually reserved Rosa put her arm around her.

"The worst part of it is that when you're getting a bit older, he'll look for someone new, younger and prettier to replace you."

Lisa was inconsolable. She sobbed, thankful that Rosa had been so open and honest with her.

"Come on now, Lisa. I have to go. Believe me, I really hate what I do but it is all I can do to support my family."

In those few short minutes, Lisa understood Rosa fully. She could now appreciate why Rosa had seemed so resentful when she realised that a fresh, younger replacement had arrived on the scene. Rosa had never mentioned her family before, but now it all made so much sense. But what should Lisa do?

Deep in thought about her situation, she changed her clothes and began to clean the floors, ready for the lunchtime customers. For now, she had no choice but to rely on Juan for her employment, however uncomfortable she may feel. Of one thing, she was certain. In no way would she sell her body should Juan request this. Lisa made herself busy in an attempt to bury the events of the past two days.

She did not see Juan until mealtime that night. He was cool towards her, yet she tried to be pleasant, acting as though nothing had happened. This situation continued for several days, each avoiding the other as much as possible.

When the tables, chairs and curtains were delivered from Juan's supplier in Cebu a week later, Lisa found it very difficult to be excited about the new purchases. It did make a huge difference to the bar area, but it also reminded Lisa of what else had happened during their excursion to Cebu. From what Rosa had said, the furniture now being replaced was only eight years old, yet with all the heavy drinkers filling the bar every day, the tables and chairs looked quite old and worn, and the curtains were faded.

One evening when the bar was busy, a customer not looking what he was doing spilled his drink over the floor and Juan called for Lisa's assistance. Her face flushed as she felt the eyes of several men watching her diligently clean up the mess. They even cheered as she completed her task.

She scurried away, trying to avoid their lascivious stares. Lisa intensely disliked large groups of men, especially when their attention was drawn towards her body. Safe back in the confines of her room, she prepared for bed and was relieved as she pulled the blanket around her, closing her eyes. Everything had been different since the excursion to Cebu and Juan's methodically organised plan to destroy her virginity. She had lost the one thing that could never be regained, and it made her feel so ashamed. It was like a stain that could never be removed, no matter how hard she prayed for forgiveness. She imagined her mother's disgust if Lisa ever had the courage to reveal her sordid secret.

Chapter Twenty-Five

A FEW DAYS LATER, before the bar was due to open, Juan asked Lisa to sit down while he spoke to her. This was the first time since their visit to Cebu nearly two weeks earlier that he had spoken more than the slightest utterances. She wondered what he was going to say, expecting some critical barbed comment about her leaving him in the hotel. She imagined his reaction on finding no sign of her in the room. His contemptuous, stern look on seeing her at Frankie's was one she would always remember.

"I have an opportunity for you to increase your earnings considerably, Lisa." Juan seemed a little uncomfortable at broaching the subject. "One of my most regular customers noticed you the other day when you were in the bar cleaning that spillage. He took a liking to you and would pay well for you to take care of his needs, perhaps about three times a week."

Lisa swallowed. She could not believe what she was hearing. "Needs? What do you mean?" She would make Juan spell out the meaning of this curious little word 'needs' even though she knew precisely what he was referring to.

"Well, his wife has deserted him recently, and he is missing the physical side of the marriage. All you have to do is go to bed with him, and for each time you will get an extra one hundred pesos."

The coldness of the proposal still shocked Lisa, even though she had expected such a request. Her body would be just another physical commodity like beer or cigarettes. "What do you think I am, Juan? I'm not a prostitute!"

Juan could see the fire of anger in her eyes yet persisted. "Just think about it, Lisa. Think about the money you could earn for you and your family." He realised that he was not going to persuade her straight away. "I will give you time to think about what a difference it could make to your life." Juan walked off, giving her chance to slowly calm down.

Although Lisa continued with her cleaning chores, she was stunned by Juan's disgusting suggestion and worked almost in a daze for the rest of that day. Her hope was that he would accept her decision and let her continue her life as before. The only person she could now confide in was Rosa, who later in the evening, when the bar had closed, listened to Lisa.

On hearing her story, Rosa sympathised with her. "Nobody can tell you what to do. It is your body and your life."

"But do you not find it repulsive to be used by men?"

Rosa laughed, yet there was a serious tone in her voice when she said, "Of course I do. The only way I can handle it is to detach myself from what they're doing. I lie there, open my legs and think about my childhood while they get themselves worked up. The worst is when you get someone who is fat or has bad breath or worse still both."

Lisa found herself laughing at Rosa's unusual way of handling such a repulsive job. "What about hygiene? Aren't there many diseases you can catch through having sex with many men?"

"Yes there are, but I always insist that they wear a condom. There are many who want to do it without and offer me much more money, but I'll not give in to them. It's the only way to keep your health."

Lisa remembered the curious little paper packets she had discovered in the hidden room and realised that these must have contained condoms. The Catholic faith and priests had always condemned all types of contraception, but in Rosa's case, they were a necessary and wise precaution to safeguard her health.

Lisa could not help but admire her newfound friend. "I could never handle it the way you do, Rosa. It is just too much to expect of anybody."

"Well, to be honest, Lisa, I hope you don't agree to do what Juan is asking. I know exactly what would happen. With your good looks and slender body, in no time you would be the favourite, and I would be left out of a job without any money."

This final comment made Lisa even more determined. "You don't need to worry, Rosa. I won't take your job. I just want to remain a cleaner, earn money honestly for my family and do my best to keep my dignity."

Rosa looked very concerned. "You will have to be really careful with Juan. You've not seen him when he is at his worst. He can be charming one minute and then change immediately into a really nasty, bad-tempered, violent person."

"Thanks for the warning, Rosa. There's no way that I could do what he is asking. Somehow, I will have to convince him to forget the idea." She pulled the blanket up around her, and the two women settled down to what was to be a troubled night's sleep. Juan's possible reaction really worried Lisa. She may lose her job and with that her small income and somewhere to live. Frightened about what would become of her, tears filled her eyes.

When she awoke the next morning, Lisa tried to dispel her fears by concentrating on her work and began to prepare breakfast.

This was successful until, after breakfast, Juan stopped her. "I want to discuss what we were talking about yesterday."

Lisa felt uncomfortable, already afraid of what was to come.

"My client finds you very attractive and is keen to make a start. He would guarantee you a bonus of one hundred and fifty pesos each time you go to bed with him."

"It doesn't matter even if it were one thousand five hundred pesos each time! I'm not selling my body to satisfy the drunken wants of one of your customers! What right do you have to ask me to prostitute myself?"

"You seemed to enjoy it when we were in Cebu."

Lisa had thought he might bring this up. "That's unfair. You and Frankie gave me too much to drink, and then you took advantage of me by raping me!" Lisa shook with emotion as she declared her feelings. "I'm not the sort of woman who would have done that willingly."

This retort sparked the anger in Juan which Rosa had mentioned. "Don't you dare talk like that! Nobody would ever believe you!"

It dawned on Lisa then, that Juan was worried about the possibility of her contacting the police and claiming he had raped her. She had never even considered it, yet this was a serious crime, which in the Philippines could result in Juan facing the death penalty. Suddenly, Lisa realised she had some control over Juan, which she must use to avoid the life of prostitution he wanted for her.

"I won't say anything to the police as long as you forget about this 'job' of sleeping with your customers."

She had seriously miscalculated his reaction. What she said inflamed him to the extent that with one powerful swing of his arm, he hit her full in the face, knocking her off balance. As she fell, her head came into sharp contact with the corner of the nearby table, and she crashed heavily to the floor where she lay, unconscious, a thin trickle of blood running from an ugly, open head wound.

The loud noise had attracted Rosa's attention. She ran through to the bar and found Juan, seemingly unconcerned, looking down at the body on the floor. She stared, horrified, at him.

"Juan! What the hell have you done? Oh, no! Lisa!" She lifted Lisa's head but found that there was no sign of any response from her newly found friend. "Don't just stand there, Juan! Give me a hand! I can't move her on my own."

Without saying a word, he lifted the young woman's body and carried her to her room, where he placed her on the blankets. A thin trail of blood had followed their route from the bar area. "We need to get her to the hospital, Juan. She may die if we do nothing, and you would be facing a murder charge!"

"No!" His response was unequivocal. "No hospital. You patch her up as well as you can and then get rid of her. She's finished here. Understand?" He pulled a wad of pesos out of his pocket and handed them to Rosa. "Here. Give this to her."

"You bastard! You really don't care about anyone except yourself, do you?"

Juan's open hostility was obvious. "Just get rid of her. If you say anything about this, I'll kill you! *Understand*?" He stormed out, leaving Rosa to care for the still-unconscious Lisa.

Quickly, she found a clean cloth, dampened it with surgical spirit and dabbed at the still-leaking wound. Once she was assured that Lisa still had a pulse and was breathing properly, she rushed out and ran to a nearby house.

She hammered frantically on the door, desperately hoping that a man she knew would be at home. It came as a relief when the door opened, and a middle-aged man appeared. "Rosa! What's wrong?"

"It's my friend at the bar. She's hurt her head badly. Do you know anybody with medical knowledge who could help?"

He looked thoughtful.

"Please hurry, Pepe. She may die if we don't act quickly."

"The hospital is the obvious place to take her."

"That's not an option. Juan made it very clear that she must not be taken to a hospital."

Hearing this, Pepe understood the situation clearly. "There is Romayla, about six miles towards Cebu. She used to be a nurse at the hospital. Yes, I think she's probably the best person to help."

"Good!" She practically pulled Pepe out of his house. "Please help me to get her there. We can take a taxi."

Pepe just managed to lock his door before running back towards the bar with Rosa. Pepe called out to a friend, asking him to get a taxi to the bar as quickly as possible. He and Rosa rushed into the tiny room where Lisa was still lying unconscious.

When Pepe saw the cuts and bruises on the young woman's swollen face, he knew this was no accident. "What did Juan do to her, Rosa? How—"

"Please don't ask, Pepe. Just help me to get her to safety."

Rosa threw Lisa's few possessions into her bag and carried it out while Pepe cradled Lisa in his strong arms and carried her out of the bar. Thankfully, a taxi was already outside in the road. It was not easy to put the recumbent woman in the passenger seat, yet somehow Pepe managed it. Rosa sat next to her, holding her head to avoid it hitting against the metal frame of the taxi. Pepe jumped on the pillion and shouted directions to the driver. The vehicle lurched forward, making it very difficult for Rosa to cushion the effects of this rough type of transport for Lisa. Every bump, twist and turn made Rosa flinch as she worried about her friend's health. Eventually, they came to a halt outside a large, concrete house set well back from the road.

Pepe jumped off the back of the motorbike and ran up to the door. After what seemed an eternity, he returned, saying,

"It's okay, Rosa. Romayla will help your friend. Just hold her head while I lift her out of here."

Together, they carefully lifted the limp body of Lisa out of the tricycle taxi and carried her into the house.

Romayla, a middle-aged woman, directed them into a bedroom, where Lisa was placed onto a comfortable bed. "Why didn't you take her to a hospital? She looks to be in quite a bad way."

Rosa answered this probing question. "I'm sorry to ask you to help us, but I'm afraid hospital was not a possible option. Will you take care of her? Please?"

Seeing the pleading look on Rosa's face, she nodded. "Of course. Leave her with me."

"Do you think I could stay until she comes round?" Rosa felt that she could not leave Lisa until she was certain of her recovery.

"Yes, of course. As long as you keep well out of my way."

"Thank you so much." Turning to Pepe, Rosa said, "You don't need to stay. I'll make my own way back." She gave him some money for the taxi fare and went to the door with him.

"Be very careful, Rosa. I did know that Juan had a temper, but he must have hit her very hard to hurt her so badly. If you have any trouble with him, just let me know." He gave her hand a squeeze of reassurance as he left her.

Shutting the door, Rosa returned to the bedroom where Romayla was tending Lisa's head wounds. Her medical knowledge was obvious as she treated the bruising after ensuring that there was no further blood loss.

"What's your friend's name?" Romayla asked as she continued with her work.

"Lisa Tiguelo. Is she going to be all right?"

"I think so, but we will know better when she regains consciousness. It will be best if Lisa sees a familiar face when she comes round. She'll probably be suffering from shock, which could cause complications."

For the first time that Rosa could remember, she bowed her head in prayer. Asking the Lord to help with a full recovery for Lisa, she made the sign of the cross. Rosa was aware that she had missed the midday opening of the bar, though hopefully she would be back for the evening. But how could she think of going back when the person she worked for had nearly killed Lisa? She hated herself for even considering it, but if she did not, where would she go and how could she earn any money?

In the space of just a few short hours, her whole life had been turned upside down. Tears ran slowly down her cheeks as she realised the full impact of what had happened on this fateful day. For now, Lisa's recovery was the most important thing on her mind. Rosa sat at the side of the bed and squeezed Lisa's apparently lifeless hand, watching the once-beautiful face of Lisa, which had initially created such jealousy and resentment, now swollen with dark blue bruises and disfigured with scarring where her head had hit the table. Ironically, it was one of the new tables Lisa had helped to select. Rosa would have given anything to restore Lisa's beauty and desperately hoped that she would not be scarred for life.

"I'm so sorry for the way I treated you, and I know it was very wrong of me to steal your money." She bent her head in shame. "Please forgive me, Lisa."

After what seemed to be an eternity but was only about thirty minutes, Lisa began to stir. Her eyes flickered open and looked up at an unfamiliar ceiling. She tried to lift her head off the pillow but sank back as the intense pain made its impact felt. Rosa spoke gently, trying to reassure the young woman. "It's all right, Lisa. Don't try to move. You are safe now."

Lisa's voice was quite weak and trembling as she asked, "Where am I?"

"You are far away from Juan. You're in the house of Romayla. She's a nurse who is doing her best to help you. Now, please don't try to move."

At this point, Romayla entered the room. "Hello, Lisa. You've been very badly hurt, and I will do my best for you. If it wasn't for your friend, you may well have died." Romayla's voice was calm and reassuring. "For now, rest is going to be the best cure. The bruising will improve after a few days, and I will have to keep a check on that head wound to make sure there is no chance of any infection."

"Can she stay here?" Rosa sounded anxious. "She has nowhere else to go now."

"She needs proper attention. After what she has been through, it's the least I can do. I take it that a man did this to her?"

Rosa nodded. "I'm afraid so. He was her employer. He has a very strong, violent temper. Thank you so much for helping Lisa. You're very kind." Turning to Lisa, Rosa said, "I've brought your belongings in your bag. Juan gave me this money for you." She had no idea how many pesos were in the bundle of notes she handed to Lisa. "I'll come back and see you in a couple of days. I'd better go now before Juan sacks me as well."

Lisa put the money in her jeans pocket and then held Rosa's hand in a gesture of gratitude. "Thanks, Rosa. You're a very special friend. I'll never forget what you have done for me. Are you really going back to Juan?"

"I don't know. I don't really want to." Rosa thought about Pepe. "I may ask a friend if I can stay with him. I'm sick and tired of my life at the bar. It's just not been anything I could ever be proud of."

Lisa felt happier that Rosa may not be going back to Juan. "Please be careful, Rosa. We both know his temper and just what he is capable of."

"I'll take good care of myself. You get better now, and don't worry about me. Okay?"

Lisa closed her eyes as Rosa left the room. Her head was still throbbing with such intense pain that she wondered if she would ever recover from Juan's brutal assault.

Chapter Twenty-Six

ROMAYLA RETURNED, CARRYING a small cup. "Try and take this, Lisa. It should help relieve the pain, but it will make you very drowsy." She supported Lisa's head as she sipped slowly from the cup. The liquid tasted awful, but Lisa did not care as long as it helped to relieve the pain. The medicine soon began to take effect, helping her to fall into a deep restful sleep.

It was several hours later before she awoke once again. Initially, she kept her eyes closed, but after a few minutes, she opened them. The sight that confronted her gave her such a shock that she screamed loudly.

"Please don't kill me!"

The man flinched at her reaction.

"Nobody is going to harm you, Lisa," Romayla tried to reassure the frantic young woman. "This is my husband."

What had shocked Lisa was the man's features. He was Japanese, and Lisa's mind had flashed back to what her grandfather had told her just before his death three years earlier. Lisa sank back into a troubled sleep, her dreams revisiting her last contact with the one man who had meant anything in her life.

Her grandfather's ashen face had caused her so much anxiety about the state of his health as he recounted the story of Monalisa—his wife and Lisa's grandmother—who had died long before Lisa was born.

***

201

"When your father Pedro was about four years old, the Japanese invaded the Philippines. We fought them, with the help of American forces, but we were poorly trained and supplied by our allies. Many of the Americans were killed, either by disease or the better armed Japanese, and when the Americans surrendered on 6th May 1942, it marked the end for us. The Japanese took complete control of the whole of our country. They set up camps for their soldiers all over the place. One of these was in Davao, not far from where we lived."

The old man paused to catch his breath while Lisa listened spellbound.

"The Japanese soldiers were very cruel people and treated Filipinos as slaves. Men who were reasonably fit, like me, were forced to work long hard hours with little food or rest. Anyone who could not work because of weakness was kicked and hit with rifle butts. Many died, but the Japanese could not have cared less."

Another pause, this time as he chose his words carefully.

"Lisa, do you know what a prostitute is?"

Lisa's face had flushed with embarrassment at this strange question, but she had nodded silently.

"The Japanese soldiers took many young Filipinas and used them as unpaid prostitutes. Strangely, these women were called 'comfort women.'"

Lisa had a terrible realisation as to where this talk was leading.

"Was Lola a 'comfort woman', Lolo?"

Tears filled the old man's eyes. "Yes, I'm afraid so. Because of her unusual beauty, Monalisa was reserved for one of the higher-ranking officers, a Captain Yakamoto." The bitterness and resentment were obvious in his voice as he pronounced the name of the Japanese soldier. "Your father was looked after by your great-grandmother. It was the worst time of my life."

Tears flowed down her grandfather's cheeks.

"I missed her so much. When the Americans liberated the Philippines in 1945, I thought the nightmare would be behind us, but I could not have been more wrong. Before the Japanese fled, they killed as many Filipinas as they could." His voice shook with emotion. "Including my Monalisa, my beautiful little wife."

"Oh, Lolo, I'm so, so sorry." Lisa squeezed her grandfather's hand gently and kissed him on the cheek. "Does anybody else know of this awful tragedy?"

He shook his head. "I was too ashamed to say anything, so I told everybody that she had died in an accident."

Lisa realised what a terrible burden this secret must have been for her grandfather over all those years.

"Life was unbearable without my Monalisa. I felt like killing myself so I could be with her. Many times, I nearly shot myself. But I still had a responsibility to your father, the only fruit of our marriage. To have only one parent is bad enough, but to have none is too much for any child to have to bear." He smiled and looked straight into Lisa's eyes. "I could not believe when you were born just how much you were like your grandmother. That is why you, especially, have meant so much to me. It's uncanny how closely you resemble my Monalisa, both in looks and character. I believe God sent you to make up for the loss I suffered all those years ago."

Tears ran freely down Lisa's face as the full impact of this awful account hit her. She buried her head in her grandfather's chest. "I love you so much, Lolo. I would do anything for you."

"I know. You are a truly wonderful person." He hesitated. "There is one thing you could do for me, but I am too afraid to ask you."

"It's all right, Lolo. If I can, I will be happy to do it just for you."

"You might change your mind when I tell you what it is. I am not a bitter person, but my hatred for Yakamoto still burns deep within my heart. May God forgive me for asking this of you! I don't care how long it may take, but if he is still alive and you are able to seek revenge against him, I would rest easier in my grave a happier soul."

Lisa was stunned by his unusual request but understood how much it meant to him. "If there is any way I can do what you ask, I promise to do it just for you, Lolo."

His expression became less troubled, the burden of his terrible secret, now shared, easing. "His full name was Captain Hokashi Yakamoto, and I am certain that he survived the American takeover. I think he'll be in his late sixties by now. Thank you so much, Lisa. I can rest in peace now." He closed his eyes, his body visibly relaxing.

Lisa realised that he had been holding on to what little was left of his life until he had told his sad, awful story to his adoring granddaughter.

"Oh, Lolo, please don't die! I need you so much," she pleaded, but there were no further signs of life as she hugged the man who had filled her world with so much love and affection. Knowing that her mother must be allowed to say her last farewell, she left the room, sobbing, and told Dolores about her grandfather's deterioration.

***

All these terrible memories had flooded back on seeing the Japanese man's face looking down at her. She wondered how much fate had played a hand in delivering her to this house. Could this be the link to fulfil her grandfather's dying request?

Over the next few days, Romayla nursed Lisa back to reasonable health. The scars on her face would take longer to heal,

204

but at least she had recovered sufficiently well to help around the house. Apparently, Romayla's husband Kioshi worked for a Japanese engine manufacturer. He was the service manager at a repair base on the outskirts of Cebu. The couple had just one child, an eleven-year-old daughter called Suzy. Romayla told Lisa that she was enjoying her company, as her husband worked very long hours, starting quite early and not returning home until seven each evening.

Rosa had also visited Lisa a couple of times and was happy with her friend's speed of recovery.

The first question Lisa had asked Rosa was, "Are you still working for Juan?"

Rosa smiled and shook her head. "No, thank goodness. I should have left him a long time ago, but I never had the courage. When he nearly killed you, that was the final blow for me. I told him I'd had enough."

"How did he react? I was worried about what he might do to you." Lisa was genuinely concerned for her friend.

"He was very angry. He threatened to do to me what he'd done to you."

"Oh God, no! Were you scared?"

"Yes, of course. I was terrified. I could not have done it without Pepe's help and support. Juan only picks on those who are smaller than him. Thankfully, Pepe is a big strong guy who would not stand any nonsense from Juan."

"So where are you living now?"

Rosa blushed slightly. "I'm living with Pepe. He promised to take care of me, and I think he really loves me."

Lisa gave Rosa an affectionate hug. "I'm so pleased for you. Do you love him?"

"It's early days yet. But I think I will come to love him in time. After being used by so many men for such a long time, for me, true love is quite a difficult concept. I don't think much of most men, especially those in Juan's bar, but I do feel Pepe is a genuine guy."

"Well, I hope you and he can make a good life together. This experience has certainly taught me a lesson. I don't think I will ever trust a man again."

Rosa laughed at this comment. "You are still young, Lisa. Just make sure that your eyes are wide open before you start any relationship. Don't be too trusting. It's a good part of your character, but one that could let you down if you don't question a man's motives."

Lisa knew that this advice was based on a lifetime of experience and it was accepted gratefully.

Chapter Twenty-Seven

LISA WAS WORRIED about what would happen to her once Romayla was satisfied that she was fully recovered. She did not want to live with her parents again, for although she really missed her mother, her independence was now far too important to lose. The thought of being practically homeless depressed her, and with such an uncertain future, she became increasingly morose as her health steadily improved.

Noticing this, Romayla asked, "What's wrong, Lisa? Even though you're getting better, I sense a great deal of sadness in your heart."

Lisa burst into tears. "I'm so sorry, Romayla. You've been so good to me, but I'm afraid of the future. I have no friends and nowhere to live. What is to become of me?"

Romayla put a reassuring arm around the teenager. "You have Rosa and me as friends, and..." She paused, thinking. "I could really do with a housekeeper. I'm sure my husband will have no problem with you staying here and making this your home, but I must ask him first."

This idea instantly lifted Lisa's spirits. "Oh, Romayla! It would make me so happy to stay here with you and your family."

"I can't make a promise just yet, but I will definitely ask Kioshi tonight."

For the rest of the day, Lisa prayed that Kioshi would agree with his wife's idea. He was a quiet, studious man, and Lisa had great difficulty in determining whether he was a sincere person. She stayed in her room that evening, giving Romayla plenty of opportunity to discuss the matter with her husband. It was ironic that her future rested on a man whose race was so despised by her grandfather.

When Romayla came into Lisa's room late that night, she had a big smile on her face. "I have some good news for you. Kioshi has agreed to you staying here as a housekeeper."

It was as if a great weight had been lifted from Lisa's shoulders, and her smile returned once more. "Thank you so much, Romayla. You don't know how much this means to me."

Romayla gave the grateful teenager a hug. "I'm very happy for you, and I will enjoy your company. You can use this room for your personal space. We will provide all food and drink and a salary of five hundred and fifty pesos a month. How does that sound?"

"Wonderful! I promise to work very hard for you and your family."

"I know you will do your best, Lisa. You're a good, hard worker, and I really feel that you will become a close member of our little family."

Lisa was curious to know why they only had one child, which was uncommon in the Philippines where anything between six and ten children would be considered typical. "Suzy is your only child, Romayla?"

"Yes, I'm afraid so. There were complications after her birth, which meant I was unable to have any more children."

Lisa felt guilty for asking such a personal question. "I'm so sorry."

"Don't worry about it. It would have been nice to have more, but at least I was able to continue with nursing, for which I am truly grateful. I used to work at the hospital until a couple of years ago."

"Why did you leave?"

"Politics." Lisa could tell from the tone in Romayla's voice that she had touched a raw nerve. "I hated the fact that patients would only be treated if they had the ability to pay the hospital fees. I've seen wealthy people with the slightest complaint treated while countless others have died painfully because they have nothing. It broke my heart to see such hypocrisy. Now I do what I can for anyone, irrespective of their means."

To Lisa's mind, this further confirmed how genuine and kind a person Romayla was, and she was tremendously grateful that Rosa's friend Pepe had known of her existence. She marvelled at the strange sequence of events which had brought them together and believed divine intervention had played an important part at this stage of her life. Lisa slept a more settled sleep that night, reassured about the immediate future.

***

True to her word, Lisa worked hard for Romayla and her family and kept the house in meticulous order.

Suzy was the only flaw in what seemed to be perfect happiness. Unlike her parents, she treated Lisa as a slave and on many occasions deliberately made a mess just to have the satisfaction of ordering her to deal with it. This irritated Lisa, but she could not tell Romayla for fear of upsetting her precarious situation.

Suzy knew this and took full advantage. She had commented on one occasion, when Lisa was clearing one of her deliberate spillages, "Who do you think my parents would believe? A servant or their adored daughter?" It was true that many parents could not accept that their offspring would ever be spiteful and calculating in the way Suzy was. Lisa had no option but to swallow her pride and accept her tormentor's demands.

The family had a small black-and white-television, and one evening, Kioshi called everybody urgently. Puzzled as to what could be so important, Lisa followed the others into the room, and they sat, spellbound, as some disturbing news was breaking.

It was 21st August 1983, and an emotional newsreader was relating what had happened to past president and exiled Liberal leader Benigno Aquino.

"At the age of fifty, leader of the Liberal Party since 1968, Benigno Aquino was today assassinated at Manila International Airport. He had been living in exile in the United States since 1980 and had returned to help coordinate current election campaigns, despite threats to his life. He was being escorted off the China Airlines aircraft by military personnel when a lone assassin was able to shoot Aquino.

"He died instantly from a single bullet from a Magnum .357 fired into the back of his head, according to the police chief General Prospero Olivas. His alleged assassin, who managed to evade a tight military cordon around the airport, was killed in a volley of bullets from the soldiers. Aquino was about to board a van when a man darted out, and the security was caught flat-footed at that point, only noticing the man when they heard the shots.

"Journalists were shown the body of the alleged gunman, which, four hours after the assassination, still lay in a pool of blood surrounded by 22 spent cartridges.

He was dressed in jeans and a blue-and-white shirt. Foreign correspondents who travelled with Mr. Aquino from Taipei said that the moment the aircraft came to a halt, three soldiers and a number of plain-clothes security men came on board and escorted Mr. Aquino down the stairs from a side exit. Other soldiers with guns prevented the dozen reporters from accompanying Mr. Aquino. Shots were heard, then a pause, then more shots.

"Mr. Bill Stewart, an American radio correspondent said, 'Immediately I heard shots, I looked out of one window and saw this man dressed in blue firing. He was standing upright, and when he fired, he sort of did a little dance... a little jig... as though he was maybe deranged.

"The president of the United Nationalist Democratic Organisation, Mr. Salvador Laurel, walked out to a huge roar from three thousand

Aquino supporters waiting outside the airport arrival gate to be told that their leader had been shot."

The tearful woman reporter continued.

"President Marcos issued a statement on the killing of his chief rival, which said, 'It was a heinous and outrageous crime, and the perpetrators will be brought to justice in the quickest possible time. I join the nation in condemning in the strongest possible terms the perpetrators of the slaying of Mr. Aquino, although he had been warned repeatedly and strenuously that certain elements had plotted against his life on the event of his return.'"

Kioshi was noticeably enraged by this terrible news. "It's that hypocrite, Marcos! He knew Aquino would beat him at the next election, so he made certain that there would be no opposition!"

It was the first time Lisa had seen any sign of emotion from Romayla's normally reserved husband. From her knowledge of Ferdinand Marcos, what Kioshi had said was probably true, especially considering her own treatment by government forces. The need for a democratically elected government and the end of corruption in the Philippines was long overdue, and she prayed for the end of Marcos and his heinous regime.

***

When Romayla had enquired about Lisa's family, she'd told her where they lived and how much she missed seeing her mother. Romayla did not hesitate in allowing her time off to visit her family. Lisa had written to her mother, telling her of her new employment but carefully omitting any mention of Juan's assault. Her mother had never been happy about her working at the bar and would be very critical of her if she learnt of the near-fatal outcome. For the same reason, Lisa waited until her scars had healed sufficiently before visiting her family. Some scarring would probably take years to heal properly, but fortunately, these were under her hairline and, with careful combing of her fringe, would hopefully be hidden.

When the day came, she took a tricycle taxi and during the journey felt quite nervous and apprehensive, yet at the same time she was excited at the prospect of a family reunion.

Her mother burst into tears on seeing her daughter. "Oh, Lisa! You seem to have grown up so quickly since we last saw you. You can't imagine how much we've all missed you."

This open show of emotion upset Lisa, and tears began to roll down her beautifully sculpted cheeks. "I love you, Nanay. I've really missed you and Tatay." Lisa gave both her mother and father an affectionate hug. "Look, Nanay. I've something for you." Lisa pulled a bundle of banknotes out of her pocket and handed them to her mother. "There are three thousand pesos to help towards paying all the bills."

Dolores' eyes widened in amazement. "So much? Are you sure you have enough for yourself?"

"Yes, I'm certain. I don't need much. My employers are very kind and generous people and look after me well."

Satisfied with this answer, Dolores pocketed the pesos, saying, "Your tatay will kill a couple of chickens to have for our meal together. We must celebrate seeing you again after such a long time. I'm so pleased that you finished working at that bar. I always worried about you when you worked there."

Lisa's thoughts returned to that terrible day when she nearly lost her life at the hands of Juan. Her mother had good reason to be concerned.

"How did you manage to find your new employer?"

"Oh, it was a friend of Rosa's. Rosa knew Romayla needed a housekeeper, and she and I both thought it might be a more secure job." Lisa was trying carefully not to say anything that might arouse her mother's suspicions.

"I thought that you and Rosa did not get on very well?"

212

"She was much nicer once I got to know her better. In fact, she's also given up her job at the bar now."

"Really? So poor Juan has to find two new employees?"

The word 'poor' was not what Lisa would have used to describe Juan. "He won't have much difficulty in finding replacements for us both." Feeling very bitter after her experience, Lisa wondered if some other unsuspecting young woman had already fallen for Juan's outer charms. She wished she had some way of warning others before they fell into the same trap she had, but it was impossible and would only serve to put her in even more danger. At least Juan could not use the excuse of needing to replace the tables, chairs and curtains anymore, although he was devious enough to think of an alternative way of seducing another young woman. Lisa hoped and prayed that would not happen. She also thought about Frankie's part in her seduction and felt the same hatred for him as she did for Juan.

That morning, Lisa went with her mother, grandmother, brothers and sisters to the local church while her father stayed behind looking after his beloved chickens. During Mass, she once again felt the guilt of her sexual relationship with Juan and, bowing her head in silent prayer, asked for God's forgiveness. It had been many months since she had seen her family, and during the rest of that day she made the most of her visit by finding out what had been happening to all of her relatives.

Her mother showed her a letter from Ricky, the man who had taken over her grandfather's mango plantation after his death. Ricky had, as requested, continued to send money to Dolores, and his business had been doing well. He had also managed to purchase the pineapple plantation off Allan's friend Francisco, who had died recently. Lisa had fond memories of Ricky, on whom her grandfather had placed so much trust and responsibility. She hoped to one day return to her homeland in Davao and visit the plantation. Perhaps when she had carried out her grandfather's wishes, she would make the journey to see him. Lisa did not like keeping secrets from her mother, yet Allan's dying request and her short-lived intimate relationship with Juan had to remain secret.

After several hours of talking with her family, the time came when she had to leave to return to her employer. She gave each member of her family a comforting, parting hug, not knowing when she would see them again.

When her mother gave her a kiss on her cheek, she stroked Lisa's hair back in an affectionate gesture and gasped when she noticed the scar on Lisa's forehead. "Lisa! What's happened to you?"

"Oh that." Lisa blushed and tried to dismiss it as though it was nothing. "I slipped on a wet floor and caught my head on a kitchen cupboard." She hoped this explanation would satisfy her mother's curiosity.

Dolores held Lisa's hair back to look more closely at the wound. "It looks very nasty. I hope you had it treated properly."

"Yes, of course, Nanay. Romayla cleaned and dressed it for me. She's a very good nurse, you know." Lisa's cheeks were hot with embarrassment that her scar had been discovered.

"She seems to be very kind to you. I would like to meet her someday."

Lisa smiled at her mother. "You may well meet her yet. She is a wonderful, caring person. I'm so happy working for her and the family."

"What about her husband? What is he like?"

"I don't see much of him. He's always busy with his work but he seems okay. He's a very quiet man. Anyway, I'd better go and find a taxi back now."

"I'll walk to the road with you." Slowly, the two picked their way down the steep, rough track that led to the busy highway.

It was nearly dusk and the lights from the continuous flow of traffic lit up the night sky. The two women chatted happily as they stood on the rough ground at the side of the road, the noise of the traffic making it necessary for them to shout. Lisa kept looking for a tricycle taxi that was not already crammed full of passengers. Eventually, she spotted one with sufficient space for her and signalled to the driver to stop.

Knowing it could be quite some time before she would see her daughter again, Dolores gave her a final hug. "Please take good care of yourself, especially that cut on your head. Don't let it become infected."

Lisa had to sit on the pillion along with another passenger while the driver, eager to maximise his earnings, sat astride the petrol tank. The vehicle bumped along, straining under the heavy load of six passengers, its tiny engine complaining noisily, with Lisa holding on to the metal frame of the sidecar for support. It was a relief when she reached the point on the highway close to Romayla's house. She called to the driver to stop, which he did with a screeching of poorly maintained brakes. After paying him the few pesos, she walked along the tiny road leading back to the rambling house, which she had now accepted as her home. Somehow, she had a feeling of calmness and security since she had moved in with Romayla and her husband.

Lisa's employer greeted her warmly and asked about her family.

"They were all fine. It was so good to see them again. Thanks for letting me visit them, Romayla."

"That's okay. You are a hard worker and deserve time off occasionally."

"Nanay noticed the scar on my forehead. I told her that it had been an accident. I don't want her to know what happened to me."

Romayla looked thoughtful. "Lisa I've been thinking about an idea."

Lisa wondered what this could be, hoping that it was not going to damage their friendship.

"You seem quite bright and capable of more than just housekeeping. How would you like to assist me with my medical work?"

Lisa's eyes lit up at this suggestion. "Do you think I could do it? I must admit, I was not very bright at school."

Romayla laughed. "What you were like at school makes absolutely no difference. With the right training, you would make a good medical assistant. You'd work closely with me and I'd teach you everything you need to know."

"Oh, Romayla, I would love to help you. You're so very good to me." She paused for a moment, a thought crossing her mind. "But what about the housekeeping?"

Romayla smiled. "For the time being, I would like you to continue with the basic cleaning, and if everything works out, I can take on another helper to keep the place clean."

This sounded fine to Lisa. It was not a difficult house to keep clean, and she did prefer to be kept busy. Her parents could never have afforded to send her to college to study nursing, but now, thanks to a twist of fate, she had been offered the perfect opportunity on a plate. Could this be assisted by her dead grandfather, or was it God's helping hand? Either way, it did not matter, yet she was thankful for her faith and her Catholic upbringing.

She did not realise at the time the true significance of this change in direction and how it would also help her achieve her ultimate goal.

Chapter Twenty-Eight

LISA WAS A quick learner, and over the next few months she worked extremely hard. She listened to everything Romayla taught her, read many medical textbooks, and steadily, her medical competence improved. Romayla's daughter Suzy appeared jealous of Lisa's newfound knowledge and the attention her mother was showing the former servant. Her taunts were less frequent, but the obvious feelings of hatred and antagonism remained. Suzy enjoyed giving orders to the subservient Lisa whenever she could, usually when her mother was out of earshot.

One day, Suzy picked up a half-full plate of rice and meats and deliberately emptied it onto one of the best dining chairs. "Oh dear, how clumsy of me. Lisa, be a good girl and clear up this mess."

Suzy did not realise her mother had entered the room behind her until she noticed Lisa looking despondently beyond her, and she spun around only to be faced by her angry mother. She blushed, stammering, "It ... it was an accident, Nanay."

"Don't you dare tell lies to me, you little bitch. I saw you with my own eyes. Lisa will certainly not clear that mess up, but you definitely will!"

Lisa held back a smile of satisfaction, relieved that Romayla finally knew what her scheming offspring was capable of.

"In fact, you can clean this room as well. I need Lisa to assist me with an emergency. Come quickly, Lisa."

Obediently, Lisa followed Romayla, helping her to pack a bag of medical equipment and drugs, leaving the shaken Suzy shamed and speechless.

Hurriedly, they left the house and jumped into a waiting tricycle taxi. No sooner had they sat down than the taxi lurched forward, its tyres slipping on the concrete road with the over-zealous use of the throttle.

"Where are we going?" Lisa asked. Most treatment was carried out at Romayla's house.

"Toledo. Some poor girl is in a bad way. I just had a phone call a few minutes ago."

Lisa felt a shudder of fear ripple through her body as she guessed where they may be heading. Her worst fears were realised when the taxi pulled up outside Juan's bar.

"Oh God, no!"

"What's wrong, Lisa? This isn't where you used to work, is it?"

Lisa nodded, tears welling up in her eyes. "He's done it again, hasn't he?"

"I understand what you must be feeling. Stay out here if you prefer."

"No, I must do what I can to help. I could have avoided this happening if I'd reported his assault on me to the police."

The two women hurried into the bar and found a girl who was probably no more than fifteen years old lying unconscious in a pool of blood on the floor. Standing nearby, Juan was taking a great effort to appear concerned, although as Lisa knew all too well, it was just an act to impress.

When he noticed Lisa, complete with medical tunic, his jaw visibly dropped. She said nothing and ignored his incredulous stare while she assisted Romayla with medical care for the injured girl. Romayla checked for signs of life and was relieved to feel the weak pulse in the girl's wrist.

"What happened to this young girl?" Romayla looked up at Juan.

He shifted uncomfortably. "She was standing on a chair, cleaning around the top of the window. I think she must have missed her footing and slipped off the chair, catching her head."

"You expect us to believe that pack of lies?" Lisa shouted angrily. "You're up to your old tricks again. Just like you did to me!"

"No, I never—"

Romayla interrupted. "Never mind about that just now! What's her name?"

"Zenaida." Juan looked sheepish, faced with these two hostile women. "Look, if there is anything I can do to help, I ..."

Romayla was checking the girl's torso and limbs for any breakages. "Yes, there is. I think Zenaida has some fractured ribs and must be moved very carefully. You can order and pay for an ambulance to take her to my surgery."

"Yes, of course." Juan obediently left the room to use his telephone.

When he was out of earshot, Lisa whispered, "She did not fall. I *know* he attacked her."

Romayla smiled kindly at Lisa. "I know it too. It's quite obvious he's lying." Looking down at the still-unconscious girl, she said, "We'll know the full story when she's conscious and able to tell us what happened. Our job now is to get her better, as quickly as possible." Romayla cleaned the open wounds with antiseptic lotion and ointment.

Juan returned. "An ambulance will be here in a few minutes."

"I take it she doesn't have the money for full hospital treatment?" Romayla enquired.

As expected, Juan shook his head.

"I'll do what I can as a voluntary medical worker, but the medicines are not cheap. A contribution from you would be appreciated and very helpful."

Forced into a corner by her direct question, Juan dug his hands into his pockets and brought out a handful of crumpled notes. "Here. That should help and also cover the cost of the ambulance."

Lisa was relieved when the aging ambulance arrived and the unconscious girl was lifted into it. She felt distinctly uncomfortable in Juan's presence after everything he had done to her.

Romayla and Lisa clambered into the vehicle, Lisa turning to give Juan one final hostile look. She wanted him to feel the hatred in her heart for what he had done to her and others. Noisily, the ambulance picked up speed, the driver receiving directions from Romayla. The journey was rough but better than by using a tricycle taxi as had been the case when Lisa had suffered her own injuries at Juan's hands.

When they reached Romayla's house, the driver and his assistant carried Zenaida into a spare room, where Romayla directed them to lay her gently on the bed. Having completed their task, the two men stood grinning, an indication that they required payment before they would leave. Lisa could not help but think how much they looked like a couple of monkeys eagerly awaiting their reward. They had little or no concern for the injured girl, their motives being purely financial. Lisa intensely disliked this mercenary approach, so common in the Philippines, from Marcos at the top to the lowest of the low. If only people would care for others with true devotion to the welfare of all individuals, the country would be a much better place.

While Lisa had been daydreaming, Romayla had been haggling with the men, making certain that they did not receive one peso more than they deserved. Not surprisingly, the grins quickly disappeared only to be replaced by anger at Romayla's persistence. Many would have been intimidated by their angry threats, but Romayla stood her ground, threatening to use other medical services in the future.

Frustrated, the two men left, mouthing obscenities as they climbed into their vehicle and sped off into the distance.

With relief, Romayla said, "Right, Lisa. Let's try and make Zenaida a little more comfortable." To avoid movement and possible further injury, Romayla cut through the girl's dress. When her clothes had been removed, the full extent of her injuries became apparent. There was a lot of bruising, but Lisa was more worried by the bleeding from her genital area.

"Don't worry, Lisa," Romayla said. "It's only regla. Ideally, she should go to hospital for an X-ray to check for fractures, but I think her main problem is bruising, which we can handle here."

Lisa was relieved at the older woman's diagnosis and that the blood was nothing more sinister than the girl's menstrual cycle. "Good! Just tell me what I must do, and I'll take special care of her." Lisa still felt guilty that she had allowed Juan to repeat his assault on yet another innocent victim. "I'll stay by her bedside until she regains consciousness."

Over the next few hours, Lisa waited anxiously yet patiently for any sign of movement by the young girl and noticed her temperature was rising. Zenaida began to mumble incoherently as the fever took hold of her. It was a good sign and at least indicated that she had started on the long road to recovery. Lisa vigilantly mopped the beads of sweat from the girl's forehead and talked quietly to her.

Romayla looked in occasionally to check on Zenaida's progress and was quite happy that she was receiving the best attention. If the girl had been taken to hospital, she would not have had the same level of care, as overstretched hospital staff simply would not have had the time to attend to her the way Lisa was doing so patiently.

It was a great relief when, after four long hours, Zenaida's eyes fluttered open. Ever-watchful Lisa moved closer to hear her first words. "Who are you? What am I doing here?" She tried to move but winced as the pain struck her.

Lisa asked her to keep as still as she could before quickly explaining what had happened, and as the memories of her ordeal returned, large tears ran down the girl's pale cheeks.

"How could he try to do that to me? I'm a good girl and work hard for my family. Why did he want my body?" She began to sob, the memories of her ordeal overwhelming her.

Lisa put a comforting arm around the young girl. "I know exactly what you are feeling." Lisa bowed her head, the shame of her own assault still tormenting her.

"How can you possibly know? You've no idea what it is like to have someone you trust try to take your virginity and then beat you up because you would not agree!"

"I'm afraid I do. Juan *did* take my virginity after getting me drunk, then he wanted me to work as a prostitute. When I refused, he beat me just as he beat you."

Zenaida stared wide-eyed at Lisa. Seeing the tears in Lisa's eyes, she knew what had been said must have been the truth. "So he's done this before? The bastard!"

"Yes. And he'll do it again if we don't do something about it. If it hadn't been for Romayla, I could have bled to death."

At this point, the older woman entered the room, pleased to see that Zenaida had regained consciousness. "Don't worry. You're in good hands here."

"But I … I don't have any money to pay for medical treatment! How am I going to afford it now that I am out of a job?"

Romayla put a reassuring hand on the girl's shoulder. "There's no need to worry about the expense. Before we left that pig Juan, I made him give us some money for your treatment."

Hearing that, a smile of satisfaction lit Zenaida's face.

"Are you hungry?" Romayla asked.

"Yes, I'm starving."

"Lisa, would you make some soup for Zenaida?

Lisa obediently left the room and went to the kitchen to prepare some chicken soup.

"We'll soon have you well again, Zenaida, but you're going to need a good, long rest."

On her return, Lisa helped Zenaida sit up a little, making it easier to drink the soup from a large cup. Every movement Zenaida made caused a lot of pain, and it came as a great relief when she was able to lie down again.

Lisa carefully cleaned and wrapped new dressings around Zenaida's open wounds. As she had experienced herself, sleep was the best medicine, and it would be several days before Zenaida could stand up properly. The sprained ankle did not help, but when she was sufficiently recovered, Lisa patiently supported the young girl as she bravely tried to become more mobile.

Not surprisingly, they had a lot to talk about. Zenaida listened without interruption as Lisa recounted how Juan had taken her to Cebu on the pretext of selecting furniture for the bar, tricked her into becoming intoxicated, assaulted her sexually and had beaten her senseless when she refused to sleep with his clients.

In turn, Zenaida told Lisa how she had only wanted to help her family and had worked hard for the few pesos she managed to earn by cleaning.

In addition to caring for Zenaida, Lisa still had to assist Romayla with the endless stream of patients seeking remedies for sickness, constipation and many other typical family ailments.

Her life was so busy, yet she couldn't have been happier, helping Romayla provide medical care to those in need.

Chapter Twenty-Nine

THE TWO YOUNG women had spoken many times about Juan and how much they despised him for what he had done to them. One day, when the surgery was not too busy, they spoke to Romayla, expressing their anger at their ex-employer.

"Shouldn't we tell the police what he has done?" Lisa asked. "After all, he has committed a criminal offence."

Zenaida nodded in agreement.

The older woman looked thoughtful. "Technically, you're correct. But I think you probably don't know much about the police here in the Philippines." She went to the door, making sure it was closed and they could not be overheard before she continued. "What I'm going to tell you must not go beyond these walls. Agreed?"

The two teenagers nodded, wondering what they were about to learn.

"When I was fourteen, my uncle raped me." Romayla lowered her head, the shame of it still affecting her even after all the years. Her voice was quiet and trembled with emotion. "He had always been good to me when I was a child, and I admired him. One day when I went to his house, my aunt was out. I think they must have had an argument. He seemed different, somehow. He started kissing me, and when I tried to get away, he threatened what he would do to me if I screamed." She paused, the memories of the nightmare overcoming her. "He removed my clothes and then raped me. I was very small, and the pain it caused still haunts me."

Lisa and Zenaida were visibly shocked by these revelations.

224

"Did you tell your parents?" asked Lisa.

"He warned me of what he would do if I told anyone, but when I returned home, it was obvious to Nanay just what had happened. She was furious and made Tatay call the police. When they arrived, they questioned me and wanted to know every embarrassing little detail. The uncle I had known for all those years, Tatay's brother, was arrested and sent to prison."

"Good!" exclaimed Zenaida. "That's what he deserved."

"But it was not that simple," Romayla continued. "My uncle owned a lot of land. He sold some of it and with the money bribed the corrupt police and was set free. The irony of it! He was a free man again, and I was made to feel as though it was all my fault. I was pregnant and had a lot of problems. When the baby was born, it was dead, and the delivery had damaged me internally. At such a young age, my pelvic bones had not developed sufficiently to give birth to a child. The doctors told me that because of the damage, I would never be able to have any children of my own."

"But what about Suzy?" Lisa looked puzzled. "At least you proved the doctors were wrong?"

Romayla shook her head. "My husband knew of my condition before we married. Japanese families tend to have only one or two children, so we decided to adopt Suzy, just to have someone we could call our own child."

Lisa was stunned by this revelation. "Does she know?"

"No! And you must not tell her. Please promise me you won't say anything to her."

"Don't worry, Romayla. Your secret is quite safe with us."

Zenaida nodded in agreement.

"I'm sorry I didn't tell you the truth about Suzy, but I hope you can understand my reasons."

"Of course. What happened to your uncle?"

"Oh, he's still around. Always showing how wealthy he is and probably still bribing the police. He's very overweight from eating and drinking too much and hopefully building himself up to an early death." For a person dedicated so much to the welfare of others, this sounded cruel but was perfectly understandable under the circumstances.

"His wife left him a long time ago. In fact, it was shortly after the police released him."

Zenaida, left out of the conversation for so long, sighed. "So all three of us know what pigs some men are, but what can we do about it?"

"We must do something about Juan or else some other unsuspecting woman is going to end up the same way as us," Lisa said, frustrated by the lack of any state-organised punishment against such people. "There doesn't seem to be any justice in this world."

Romayla looked quite thoughtful. "Perhaps there is something we can do."

"I'd like to see the man hang!" exclaimed Zenaida. "He doesn't deserve to live after what he's done to both of us."

"No." Romayla was adamant. "As a devout Catholic, I can't condone the taking of human life. It's against everything I believe in, and we would be coming down to his level."

This statement reminded Lisa that she had already taken a life when she slit the throat of the military commander two years earlier. She still intended to take the life of the Japanese soldier responsible for her grandmother's ordeal and subsequent death, providing she ever had the opportunity. Understandably, she did not mention any of this to either of the two women.

"I have an idea for revenge that could have a much more dramatic impact on Juan's life," Romayla said.

226

Lisa and Zenaida listened intently as she outlined part of her idea. "What we need first of all are two young, strong men to help us."

"I have two older brothers," Zenaida said excitedly.

Romayla smiled. "Good! Yes I'm certain we could do this, and we must take the opportunity now, while my husband is visiting his family in Japan. He would not approve of what I have in mind."

Chapter Thirty

A FEW DAYS LATER in Juan's bar, the smoke-filled air was punctuated by the raucous laughter and chatter of heavily intoxicated men happily spending their pesos on drink rather than providing for the needs of their families.

Two men sitting at a table in a corner of the room were sipping their drinks quietly, watching the spectacle of the others making fools of themselves. These men were strangers, seemingly content to stay apart from the crowd.

When it was approaching closing time, they requested another beer and stood at the bar, chatting happily with other customers.

"Have a drink for yourself," one of them said to Juan.

"Thanks very much." He was unused to such offers from his customers but poured himself a beer. "I've not seen you in here before. Are you from this area?"

"No. Today, we're doing some work in Toledo for a change."

"What sort of work do you do?"

One of the men answered with a smile, "We're carriers. Moving difficult items around for our clients."

"Really? It must be interesting to travel. I don't get far from here. The bar keeps me busy." Another customer beckoned to Juan, requesting a drink. "Excuse me."

Nobody noticed as one of the men emptied a sachet of fine powder into Juan's beer. Juan returned after serving and continued his conversation with the strangers.

"It's very busy in here," one of the men said when Juan returned. "How do you manage on your own?"

Juan gulped a mouthful of beer before replying. "It's not easy. I did have a girl working for me, but she let me down. You don't know of any reliable young woman who could work for me, do you?"

"No, sorry. Why don't you hire a man instead? You might find a man to be more reliable."

Juan smiled. "Look around you. This is a man's bar." Juan laughed. "And what does every man like? He likes to be served and waited on by a pretty young thing. A man just wouldn't do it for them."

The conversation continued as the drug took effect. Juan put it down to being tired and decided it was time to close the bar. There were mumbles of discontent as the customers were asked to finish their drinks, but slowly, the room began to clear. The two strangers hung around, sipping their drinks.

By the time everyone else had left, Juan was visibly drowsy and stumbled around, trying unsuccessfully to shake off the effects of the powerful drug.

"Here, let us help you."

As Juan collapsed, the two men caught him. With one on each side of him, they walked him to the doorway.

"I think you need some fresh air, my friend."

The two laughed as they half carried him to where they had a tricycle taxi. It was difficult getting him into the cramped space of the cab, but eventually, Juan was shut in, and the two mounted the motorbike. The driver kicked the engine into life and opened up the throttle as they manoeuvred the aging vehicle through the narrow passages until they reached the main highway. Completely oblivious to what was happening, Juan lay in a crumpled heap.

In less than fifteen minutes, they reached Romayla's house. If it had been difficult getting Juan into the taxi, it would prove to be even more so to extricate him from the confined space.

After much pulling and pushing, they somehow managed to move him onto the operating couch in Romayla's surgery.

"Thanks, boys."

The 'boys' were Zenaida's brothers, Paulo and Enrico.

"You can relax in the other room while we operate on Juan. Help yourselves to a drink if you like."

Zenaida had told her brothers what Juan had done to her, after which they were very willing to help in any way.

"Right, girls. Let's get started. I'll give him an anaesthetic first. We don't want him coming round in the middle of our operation."

Zenaida had to turn away as the hypodermic syringe was skilfully used to inject the drug into Juan's wrist.

"Can you two help me take off his shoes, trousers and any underwear?"

It was not easy, removing the clothes from the heavy unconscious figure, but with one of the girls on each side of him lifting his buttocks, Romayla managed to pull his jeans off. Juan did not look very dignified now and was even less so when the three women slid his underpants down and threw them on the floor. Lisa unbuttoned his shirt and shoved it up to his armpits, revealing his naked torso. The three women looked at his penis. In its relaxed state, it seemed quite small and not at all threatening. Lisa remembered the night Juan had seduced her. At that time, Juan had been so charming and exciting. She blushed at the thought of their night of passion when she had lost her virginity. It would be a long time before she could ever trust a man again.

Lisa was still not certain what Romayla intended to do to Juan, but she was soon to find out.

Romayla took a piece of string and tied it tightly around the base of Juan's penis. "This is to restrict the flow of blood to his otin." Satisfied that the string was tight enough, she picked one of her sharpest scalpels and without any hesitation sliced

230

straight through the outer skin and the spongy tissue of the male sex organ.

Lisa and Zenaida gasped with surprise as Romayla held the penis aloft. "There!" she said in an excited tone. "He won't be raping anyone else from now on."

Zenaida laughed. "I'd love to see his face when he discovers what has happened to him."

Lisa had very mixed emotions as she looked at the fairly insignificant piece of tissue, relieved that Juan would never be able to sexually threaten any woman ever again and yet sorrow that he could never be a real man in the fullest sense of the word.

"This is what should be done to all rapists!" Proud of her work, Romayla placed the organ in a dish. "This is one small snip for man and one giant leap for womankind!" She smiled with satisfaction and continued thinking about her variation of Neil Armstrong's declaration as he became the first person to step on the moon.

"The next thing we must do is ensure that the urinary tract is maintained. To do this, I'm going to insert a catheter into the stump of the otin." Romayla inserted a small plastic tube into the remaining tissue. "We must also cauterise the exposed surface of the otin to prevent bleeding." The experienced nurse, utilising her clinical expertise, picked up an instrument and switched it on. The tiny element in the tip began to glow red hot. Skilfully, she touched the cauteriser around the exposed flesh. There was a smell of burning as the hot element seared the tissue, sealing the incision to prevent any blood leakage.

"There! We're all done now." She unfastened the cord. "Lisa, can you clean him up a bit while I get myself tidied? Don't forget to remove the catheter."

Lisa carefully eased out the plastic tube and began to wash around Juan's genital area with warm water. She never imagined that she would one day be doing this to the man who had seduced her before assaulting her so brutally when she refused to provide sex for his clients.

After he had been patted dry with a towel, the three women began the task of dressing Juan once again. It proved to be even more difficult than undressing him, but after much pushing and pulling, Juan's modesty was once again restored.

"Will you ask your brothers to come here, Zenaida? We need to get Juan back to his place before the effects of the drug wear off."

Obediently, the girl disappeared, returning with the two men. It was difficult to imagine that they were from the same family; Zenaida's tiny figure looked even smaller against the two much bigger muscular men.

"Thanks for all your help tonight. You'll be pleased to know that this…" Romayla paused as she looked with contempt at the still figure of Juan. "…this sorry excuse for a man will not be able to rape any woman ever again." Romayla showed them the dish containing the severed gland.

Both men winced and squirmed at the thought of having such a vital organ removed but were relieved that justice had been carried out against the man who had injured their young, vulnerable sister.

They lifted Juan off the bed and carried him out of the house, bundling him unceremoniously into the cab of the tricycle taxi. Soon they were on their way back to Toledo, glad that this would be the last time they would have to extricate Juan from the cramped cab of the taxi. Pushing the door of the bar open, they carried Juan into the room and laid him on the floor in front of the bar. Their task finished, the two young men left the bar and headed back home.

***

It was some two hours later before Juan began to return to his senses. Puzzled at finding himself lying on the floor, he scrambled to his feet. It was then that the pain hit him. Walking was unbearable and reminded him of what it had felt like after circumcision as a small boy.

Once he had reached the privacy of his own room, he dropped his trousers to find out what had happened to him. The awful truth dawned on him as he looked at what was left of his penis, and he let out a wail of anguish. He knew only too well that the woman who had helped Zenaida was the only person who could have carried out such an operation. He remembered the look of disgust on the faces of Lisa and Romayla on that day when they came to his bar after his attack on the young girl. It was their form of justice, and nothing he could do would restore his lost organ.

Juan buried his head in his hands and wept openly as the full truth dawned on him. Never again could he enjoy a deeply sexual experience, which for him was a far greater punishment than having to spend any length of time behind bars in prison.

The bar did not open that day nor the next. It would take a while before he would recover physically, though never mentally, from this painful experience.

Romayla and the two girls, meanwhile, were happy that they had achieved something no judicial system could match. Lisa felt as though a cloud had been lifted and proudly proclaimed that if she was ever in a strong political position, she would make such operations compulsory for all convicted rapists.

Chapter Thirty-One

WHEN ROMAYLA'S HUSBAND returned from Japan, he seemed very concerned about something and had a fairly lengthy private discussion with Romayla. Lisa and Zenaida wondered what all the hushed conversation was about but were sure Romayla would let them know as soon as she was ready.

On the next evening, Romayla called the two girls together, and it was clear from her manner that they were about to hear something of particular importance.

"My mother-in-law is quite ill and could really do with having more nursing support. Kioshi wants me to go with him to Japan."

This was far more serious than Lisa had anticipated. She so enjoyed being with Romayla that she did not want anything to spoil her now-comfortable and varied life.

Romayla noticed the intense disappointment on Lisa's face. "Kioshi is also worried about the level of unrest here in the Philippines, especially after Benigno Aquino's assassination. There seems to be a great deal of unrest, particularly against foreigners. Some of his colleagues have already left to go back to Japan, and he wants us to do the same."

Tears were running down Lisa's cheeks as her world crumbled around her.

Romayla continued, "But if I left the Philippines, who would look after the poor people here who need medical attention and cannot afford the expense of normal medical care?

"You see, Kioshi's mother doesn't really need specialised medical attention. She just needs someone to look after her.

So..." She paused looking at Lisa. "Lisa, what I think would be best for everybody is for you to go to Japan with my husband while I continue to look after the local community from here. How do you feel about that idea?"

Lisa was stunned. She had never thought it possible that she would leave the Philippines. Thoughts were racing through her mind. Could this be God's way of putting her closer to her grandmother's killer?

Still shocked at the proposal, she answered, "Yes, I think I would like that. But how can I manage when I don't understand the Japanese language?"

Romayla smiled. "Japanese is quite a difficult language to learn, but many people in Japan have English as their second language in just the same way as we do in the Philippines. Kioshi will teach you some Japanese, but I'm certain that you'll manage. You are more capable and intelligent than you realise."

Zenaida had been left out of the conversation so far but could hold back no longer. "What about me?"

Romayla smiled at the girl, who was understandably concerned about her future. "Don't worry, Zenaida. I would like you to replace Lisa as my medical assistant here. Would you like that?"

A beaming smile lit up the young girl's face. "Oh, yes, please, Romayla. I'd love to help you. I will be very happy to learn how to care for your patients."

"Good! Now everybody is happy." Romayla was satisfied that everybody's future welfare had been decided, thankfully satisfying every person's needs.

A sudden thought crossed Lisa's mind. "What about Suzy? Where will she live?"

"She will be going with you to Japan. Suzy will be safer there. While she is here, there is always the danger that she might be kidnapped."

For Lisa, this was the only drawback to Romayla's plan.

Seeing the disappointment on Lisa's face, Romayla added, "Kioshi knows how Suzy has treated you badly and will make sure she behaves properly towards you."

Chapter Thirty-Two

THE NEXT TWO weeks were hectic. Foremost in Lisa's mind was the need to see her parents and let them know where she was going.

Her mother was surprised to see her as she walked along the track leading to the tiny house and called out to her family, "Lisa's here!" then shook her husband, who was slumbering peacefully on a bamboo seat. "Wake up, Pedro! Lisa is here!"

Lisa ran in and threw her arms around her mother, and the two wept in happiness.

"Oh, Lisa, it seems such a long time since we've seen you."

Her brothers were equally pleased to see her, yet there was still the same remoteness between Lisa and her father.

"Nanay, I have some important news to tell you," Lisa said after the initial welcome. "I'm going away for a while."

"Where to? Manila? You must be very careful there. It's such a dangerous place."

"No, Nanay, a bit further than Manila. I will be going to Tokyo in Japan next week."

Dolores was stunned by this news. She did not even know of anybody who had left the Philippines, and now her own daughter was going far out of her own country. "Japan? But why? It's such a long way to Japan." Understandably, she was worried that she might never see her daughter again.

"Don't worry, Nanay. I won't be staying forever. I'll just be looking after Kioshi's mother. She's sixty-five, so she's already quite old." In the Philippines, people were very lucky to even reach the age of sixty, and it was very unusual to find anyone older than seventy-five. "I'll write to you as often as I can."

Dolores was deeply saddened by the prospect of not seeing her youngest daughter for what could be quite a long time, yet she put on a brave face, saying, "Right. We must make the most of the time you have with us. Tatay will kill a chicken or two, and we'll feast as a celebration of being together."

Dutifully, Pedro lifted his bony frame out of the seat and went outside to carry out his wife's request without speaking or showing any signs of happiness for his youngest child.

"Now, Lisa, how's that wound on your head?"

"Oh, it's fine now." Lisa brushed her hair aside, allowing her mother to inspect the skin. There was still a small scar, but it was no cause for concern. "Before I forget, Nanay, here is something for you." Lisa took a bundle of notes out of her bag and handed them to her mother. "There's three thousand pesos. I will still send you money from Japan, so there's no need for you to worry. I'll take care of you as long as I can."

Shyly, her mother took the money and gave Lisa a hug of gratitude. "You're so good to us."

The two women chatted happily, Lisa telling her mother as much as she could without saying anything about the small operation they had carried out on Juan. Lisa did wonder from time to time how Juan was managing with his shortened penis. She smiled to herself at these intimate thoughts.

News of Lisa's impending departure quickly spread, and friends and family joined them for dinner, making the occasion like that of a fiesta. The noisy chatter of a Filipina celebration filled the air, and by the time Lisa was ready to leave, she had had her fill of chicken, rice and papaya.

Her brothers were happy for her but also a little envious about her impending visit to Japan. Unless their fortunes changed dramatically, they were unlikely ever to be able to leave their island, let alone the Philippines.

Both Lisa and her mother shed tears as they gave each other a parting hug. What surprised Dolores most of all was that as a child, it was Lisa who had always clung to her, never wanting to be very far away. Soon, they would be separated by thousands of miles. Dolores stood there for a while, watching the tricycle taxi disappear into the distance, carrying her daughter away into an uncertain future.

***

Before Lisa could be allowed out of the Philippines, it was necessary for her to obtain a passport and visa, which Kioshi managed to organise quite quickly and without too much hassle. Lisa felt very proud of the small booklet containing her name and photograph. She was completely ignorant of this necessity and had assumed that anyone could travel anywhere in the world without the need for documentation.

When the day arrived for her departure for Japan, there were again more tears shed as Lisa was parting from Romayla and Zenaida. It must have been even more difficult for Romayla and Kioshi.

Kioshi wished Romayla would change her mind and go with him, yet she remained quite adamant. Until the Philippine Government accepted responsibility for its people, she felt that it was her duty to provide medical care for the needy and poor. Kioshi promised to return to the Philippines as often as he could as he bade an emotional farewell to his wife.

Suzy seemed reluctant to give her mother a parting hug. She was a child who showed little to no affection for anyone, which must have been very difficult and hurtful for Romayla. Suzy also had more luggage than Lisa and Kioshi put together.

A single canvas bag held all of Lisa's clothes and possessions, and she did not think it necessary to put it in the boot of the taxi together with the rest of the luggage.

For the first time in her life, Lisa was sitting in a car taxi instead of the usual motor tricycle. Sitting like a queen next to the driver, she looked with interest at everything they passed.

The taxi's passengers were silent as they drove towards Mactan Island, eventually crossing the huge bridge spanning the waters between the islands. Mactan Airport was a busy, bustling, noisy place with hundreds of people either coming out, going in or simply standing around. Suzy and Kioshi had travelled through there many times and were completely unfazed by the hectic atmosphere. As the taxi pulled up, dozens of eager porters descended on them like ants on a tasty scrap of food, each one trying to be the first to get the business.

Kioshi in his usual calm manner pointed to one of the porters, making it plain to the others that they were not wanted. Thankful for being chosen, the porter beamed and quickly pulled a trolley over to the boot of the car. With the trolley full of their luggage, he followed the trio into the check-in area.

When the bags had been unloaded from his trolley, the still-smiling porter hung around until Kioshi had paid him a tip. From the man's expression, it was clear he had expected much more from this rich-looking foreigner, but Kioshi ignored the porter's complaints. Lisa felt that he should have been more grateful, as his job seemed an easy one requiring very little skill.

Again, Lisa had assumed that one could board the aircraft straight away and was disappointed at the waiting around and queuing up to pass through all the security checks.

Many tired-looking people were sitting in rows of hard, plastic seating, waiting anxiously for boarding instructions over the speakers. At last, they emerged from the buildings and walked out to the waiting aircraft. Climbing up the steps, they were greeted by a stewardess who directed them to their seats.

Seeing inside the plane for the first time, Lisa exclaimed, "Wow! It's so big in here, and all these rows of seats!"

"If you think this is big, just wait until we board the next plane at Singapore."

Suzy was used to travelling to Kioshi's homeland and was completely unenthusiastic about the journey, treating it more like a ride on a jeepney along the Philippines local roads. Lisa, on the other hand, was like a small child, over-awed by the occasion, and pleaded to be allowed to sit next to the window.

Realising the extent of Lisa's excitement, Kioshi was happy to let her have her way and allowed her first into the row of three joined seats. Unlike all the other passengers, familiar with air travel, she watched and listened intently to the safety presentations demonstrated by the cabin crew. The possibility of air accidents and ending up in the sea wearing a life-jacket had never crossed her mind and tempered her excitement with a certain nervousness. She prayed silently for a safe journey.

When the time came for take-off, Lisa's eyes were glued to the window, ready to experience the wonders of modern flight. She was surprised by the sudden burst of acceleration necessary to achieve sufficient velocity to lift the huge craft off the ground. As they gained height, she was fascinated to see her homeland as she had never seen it before, with the browns and greens of the land punctuated by the deep blue of the sea. In that instant, she was reminded of how, as a five-year-old girl, her grandfather had first shown her an atlas of the world. At that time, Lisa had found difficulty in imagining that there were other lands beyond the Philippines. In fact, she remembered how he had said that one day she would probably travel abroad. Now his predictions were coming true, it confirmed for her that it was God's way of helping her to carry out her grandfather's dying request.

That day, the sky was quite clear and cloudless, allowing Lisa to keep sight of the land for several minutes before their increasing altitude made it impossible. As they flew westwards over the open sea, her eyes were still transfixed by the spectacle. She could not understand how such a heavy monster as an aircraft could fly through the air; to the impressionable young woman, it was nothing short of a miracle. Now she understood how birds must feel as they sped through the sky.

She was also surprised when the stewardesses brought refreshments. The food, although basic and quite simple, was appreciated, yet it did not stop her gazing through the window.

After a little over three hours' flight, the plane began its descent into Singapore. Suzy and her father had been reading for the whole journey but now put their books away and began to prepare for landing. Lisa noticed that the landscape was very different from her own country, being much more densely populated. She was surprised at the huge number of buildings of heights she never even imagined to be possible.

As the wheels bumped down onto the runway and the engines were put into reverse to assist in braking, Lisa marvelled at the wonders of modern flight and then at the beauty and spaciousness of Changi Airport. It was very different from Mactan Airport in the Philippines. Somehow, even with the thousands of travellers, the airport had a feeling of calmness and efficient organisation. There would be a four-hour wait before their connection to Japan, giving them time to look around the airport but not long enough to leave it. Kioshi knew the place well and was happy to show Lisa all the interesting places. She, in turn, was grateful her employer did not treat her as a servant but more as an intelligent adult and friend. Suzy was indifferent but, presumably following her parents' instruction, refrained from the intimidation she had enjoyed in the past.

Lisa was delighted to see the many beautiful orchids on sale but amazed at the prices. "That would be enough to pay for the family's food for a whole week!" she exclaimed. She was further amazed when Kioshi explained about the Singapore dollar and how it related to the peso. She had just assumed that the peso was the currency for all countries around the world, not just Spain and some South American countries. There was still a lot to learn, and she was eager to absorb as much information as she could.

Chapter Thirty-Three

WHEN THE TIME came for them to board the Singapore Airlines flight to Japan, Lisa was staggered at the size of the aircraft. Suzy had been quite correct to claim that this was far bigger than the plane from the Philippines. There were two aisles with five seats separating them, and the length was equally impressive, with row after row stretching far away to the rear of the aircraft. They were directed to their seats by smartly dressed stewardesses, and once again Lisa was lucky enough to have a window seat.

It took quite a while for all the passengers to embark, but at last, the huge monster began lumbering along the runway. Lisa was worried that it would be unable to lift itself off the ground but relaxed when she felt it become airborne. She still had to get used to the effect on her ears, as the pressure changed with increasing height, and followed Kioshi's advice to keep swallowing to equalise the pressure.

Everything fascinated the young woman, and when she needed to use the toilet, she was amazed at how luxurious the fittings were compared to toilet facilities in the Philippines.

She tried all the scented soaps and perfumes available. One of the stewardesses, concerned by the length of time Lisa had been in the cubicle, knocked on the door and enquired if she was all right. She opened the door and apologised to the beautiful young stewardess.

Realising that this was Lisa's first major flight, the stewardess said in a warm friendly voice, "Please don't apologise. I was just worried that you may have been unwell."

244

Lisa took an instant liking to the young woman. She was particularly interested in the full-length, brightly coloured garment she wore. "I love your dress. It's so beautiful."

"It's called a sarong kebeya, and it's very comfortable. Singapore Airlines stewardesses have been wearing these since 1974." Seeing how interested Lisa was, the stewardess said, "I have some spare time now. Would you like me to show you around the aircraft?"

"Yes, please! I would love that."

Lisa was truly fascinated by everything that Wendy the Malaysian-born stewardess showed her and found it incredible that there were even stairs up to a higher level within the aircraft. She was only allowed a brief glimpse, as this was the bar area for first-class passengers. The highlight, though, was the visit to the flight deck. It was quite dark there, but Lisa was able to make out the numerous dials and instruments necessary for controlling the huge aircraft. The captain and his flight crew seemed very relaxed, considering the tremendous responsibility they had for the safety of over three hundred passengers.

Lisa thought of how her sisters and brothers would be so envious of her experience and would have loved to be where she was right then, exploring a whole new world so remote from their mundane life in the Philippines.

When she eventually returned to her seat, Kioshi enquired where she had been and was surprised to hear of her guided tour. Lisa noted a sense of jealousy from Suzy, who would probably have liked to have been the one offered the treat even though she was not really interested.

For Lisa, everything was a new experience to be appreciated and absorbed. When dinner was served, she felt even more pampered by the variety and quality of food on offer. Her appetite was always good, and soon she had tried and devoured everything edible on her tray. Her hunger satisfied, she wrapped herself in the blanket and settled down to a relaxing sleep.

The eight-hour journey passed quickly, and she awoke to hear the captain telling the passengers that they were approaching Narita International Airport, about thirty-five miles east of Tokyo. She sat upright, checked that her seat belt was fastened and then looked with great interest at this new land which was to be her home for the immediate future. She wondered how long it would be before she was able to return to the Philippines.

When the captain announced the time in Tokyo, Lisa had great difficulty in understanding why the time would be any different from that on her watch as set in the Philippines. Kioshi tried to explain the principles of time zones, but as a new concept, it took Lisa quite a while to grasp. With great reluctance, she adjusted her watch in line with Japanese time.

It was now late afternoon, and as she peered through the window, a light mist shrouded this foreign land. The huge craft bumped gently on the runway as it touched down. After waiting in a very long queue to stand in front of an immigration officer while he checked their passports, they were allowed to collect their cases and leave the airport. Within an hour, they were travelling on the smooth rail network link to the centre of Tokyo.

From there, a taxi took them through the busy streets to the tidy suburb where Kioshi's mother lived. Lisa was struck by the smart, modern buildings and efficient road organisation; it was a far cry from the shambles that typified Philippine towns and cities.

When they eventually arrived at Kioshi's family home, Lisa was surprised to find a small but neat and tidy two-storey house. Land prices in Japan were at a premium, and as a consequence, houses tended to be economical in size, but for many people there was no option but to live in high-rise apartments.

Kioshi's mother Honako was a frail, tiny, elderly lady. She was sitting, quietly reading a book as they entered the apartment, but a smile lit up her tired face at the sight of her son and granddaughter.

Kioshi introduced Lisa, saying, "Lisa is going to help you, Mother. She has worked with Romayla for quite a while now, and she has good medical knowledge."

Lisa took hold of the old lady's hand in a friendly gesture. It was tiny, very cold and lacked strength. Honako gave her a weak smile of gratitude, but Lisa could not decide whether it was genuine or purely politeness. She still remembered her grandfather's advice to 'look beyond the smile to see the true person'. Nevertheless, it was to be her job to look after the elderly lady, and she would do it to the best of her ability.

Apparently, Honako's husband had died three years earlier, and Kioshi was her only child. Lisa was confident she had enough siblings to ensure her parents would have plenty of family care and support as they grew older, but unlike the Philippines, where families typically had between eight and twelve children, Japan had a low birth rate where one or two children was considered quite normal.

Medical care in Japan was good, but understandably, Kioshi wanted to care for his mother as long as possible. Honako had some help, in the form of a middle-aged woman who did a little cleaning and preparing meals, but this lady had her own family and did not have the time or knowledge necessary to provide adequate medical care.

Lisa soon settled into her new role and took over the job of cleaner, cook and nurse. Honako had suffered from a stroke and had to take a lot of medication every day. Her memory was poor, making it difficult to remember which drugs to take and when, but Lisa, in her usual methodical way, soon had the routine organised. She put her own labels on all the medication to ensure she administered the appropriate levels.

The small house had just two bedrooms, one for Honako and the other for Kioshi and Suzy, while Lisa had to make her bed with blankets in the living area. This was no hardship, as it was quite normal in the Philippines for a family to live and sleep in the same room.

Lisa quickly became accustomed to her new way of life although she did miss her homeland and, more especially, her family. She also missed Romayla a great deal but at least was able to speak to her on the telephone once a week when Kioshi phoned his wife.

Kioshi offered to show Lisa some of the sights of Tokyo, and astonishingly, Suzy willingly agreed to look after her grandmother in Lisa's absence. Lisa particularly enjoyed Ueno Park. It was opened to the public in 1873 and was famous for its many museums, especially the National Art, Science and Shitamachi Museums.

Lisa was fascinated by such places, as she had never seen anything similar in the Philippines. With dictators such as Marcos, it was unlikely that money would ever be spent on public buildings dedicated to the history of the Philippines when he was more interested in plundering the country's riches for himself. Lisa also enjoyed her visit to Japan's oldest zoo in Ueno Park, in particular the giant panda which had been a gift from China in 1972.

On one of her weekend trips, she had an exhilarating experience when they visited Tokyo Tower, a huge, steel structure nearly eleven hundred feet in height. From an observation platform eight hundred feet above the ground, Lisa could see the city of Tokyo spread out beneath her and was truly amazed at Japan's technological achievements.

Kioshi pointed out Mount Fuji, which could be seen in the distance. "You're very lucky, Lisa. The weather is good today, allowing us to see everything perfectly."

She could have spent ages just looking at the beautiful panorama lying beneath her but eventually had to leave the spectacle with a promise from Kioshi that they would come again. He was true to his word, and many weekends were spent touring Tokyo's places of interest. There was an aquarium at the foot of the tower, and Lisa was truly fascinated to see the colourful tropical fish, as she had never seen them before. She found it difficult to tear herself away, almost hypnotised by their grace and beauty.

She wished that one day the Philippines could move into a new era where corruption was a thing of the past and everyone could be proud enough to attract tourists to visit their country just like in Japan.

Honako took quite a liking to Lisa, and in very broken English they had many long conversations. Kioshi paid Lisa well for her work, and Honako slipped an occasional bonus to the appreciative young woman. The Japanese yen was very different from the Philippine peso, yet Lisa soon knew how to convert between the two currencies. She had no need to spend any money and was able to build up a tidy nest egg.

Kioshi had quite a good job working for the same engineering company that he had worked for over the past few years in the Philippines. With Suzy attending the local school, it meant Lisa had a great deal of spare time, even though some of her time was spent looking after the old lady. She used this time to good effect, learning as much about Japanese life, culture and the language as possible.

Lisa slowly began to appreciate the cultural differences between Japan and the Philippines. She had assumed that the Catholic faith was practised by people in all countries throughout the world, and it came as a great shock for her to find that Buddhism was the dominant religion in Japan.

She was also surprised to learn that unlike the Philippines, Japan had a democratically elected government but without a president. There was a royal family, and at that time, Emperor Akihito was the ruler of the fast-developing country.

By reading all she could, Lisa hoped that she would be more equipped to carry out her grandfather's wishes when it became necessary. At that time, she had no idea how she would find and execute Yakamoto. She knew, of course, that he may already be dead. By 1984, he would have been about seventy-two years old, which, by Japanese standards, was still quite young, as many people lived well into their nineties. It could be the diet, way of life or a combination of the two which somehow managed to produce the longest living people in the world.

If Yakamoto was dead, true justice would never be possible. For this reason, Lisa hoped he was alive and not too far away from where they were living.

Chapter Thirty-Four

IN DECEMBER 1984, Lisa was to have quite an unexpected surprise. It was her nineteenth birthday. As a young girl, she had been used to feasting on such occasions with all members of the family. There had never been any money to buy gifts, but just being together had been enough to make the occasion something very special for her.

In Japan, thousands of miles away from her family, she had resigned herself to a day without celebrations. It came as a pleasant surprise, therefore, when Kioshi gave Lisa some parcels and several cards. She was amazed to find that her family had sent a birthday greeting. There were also cards from Romayla, Zenaida, Kioshi and Suzy.

The presents were from Kioshi, presumably assisted by Suzy. Lisa could not believe her eyes when she ripped a parcel open to discover a beautiful red silk kimono. Another contained a black leather shoulder bag. Apparently, Honako had suggested the dress as a traditional Japanese souvenir to remind her of her time in Japan. Lisa was overjoyed that her birthday had been remembered and gave each of them a warm yet polite hug of gratitude.

There were still more surprises to come. Since it was a Sunday, Kioshi was not working and had organised several treats for his hard working employee. First of all, he took her to a house where Lisa had her hair cut, shampooed and styled. The woman was a professional hairdresser, and a close friend of Honako's, who was quite willing to work on a Sunday. It was the first time in her life that Lisa had experienced professional hair styling.

251

Normally, she would let her hair grow long and then would trim it herself. Washing and combing was the only attention it normally received.

The hairdresser was also a specialist in cosmetics and took great care in applying make-up to the young woman's face. Early in the afternoon, Lisa put on the kimono, which fitted her slim figure perfectly. She looked absolutely stunning with the style of her long black hair complementing the brightly coloured dress.

Kioshi had also organised someone to look after Honako while he, Suzy and Lisa went to a restaurant for a birthday meal. It reminded her of the time when Juan and Frankie had treated her to a meal in Cebu, but thankfully on this occasion, there would be no hidden agenda, no obligation, and Kioshi did not try to talk her into drinking any alcohol.

Lisa did notice a young man looking at her throughout the meal, though, and his were not the only admiring glances. Her stunning beauty caused quite a few heads to turn, but this man kept giving her an occasional smile. Lisa knew instinctively that he was interested in her but felt that starting a friendship with a Japanese man would get in the way of her mission and could cause complications when the time came for her to escape the country.

She was grateful for the attention he was showing yet did not return his glances in the hope that it would deter him from approaching her.

In a way, it came as a relief when they finished the superb meal and left the restaurant, although Lisa noticed the man looking a bit despondent as they were leaving. From there, the three travelled to the Kabuki theatre, where Lisa watched, enraptured, as the figures on stage danced in traditional Japanese dress accompanied by the haunting musical sounds so typical of Japan. The complete performance could last for up to five hours, yet Kioshi had booked just one act lasting about an hour and a half, as he felt this would be long enough for Lisa.

The whole day was an experience she would never forget, and when they arrived back home, she thanked Kioshi profusely. She wrote letters back to the Philippines, telling her family and Romayla of the memorable events of her nineteenth birthday. Aware that her brothers and sisters would be even more envious of her experiences, she emphasised how much she was missing them all.

Late one evening, the three of them were watching television and Lisa was deep in thought, wondering how she was going to find her grandmother's killer, when to her surprise the name Yakamoto came from the television. She tried to listen intently, but her grasp of the Japanese language was not sufficient to understand what was being said. Careful not to reveal her true level of interest, she asked, "Who is that?"

"He is the agriculture minister," Kioshi answered.

"Why is he on television?"

"He's refusing to increase the subsidy paid to farmers. They'll never win. He's a very stubborn minister, and once he has made up his mind, he is unlikely to change. It must be his military background that makes him so tough."

This sounded very promising, Lisa thought. "He looks quite old."

"I think he is in his early seventies."

It had to be the man she was looking for. The name, age and military background all pointed to him being the person she had promised her grandfather that she would assassinate. But how could she get close enough to this government minister to carry out her task? She needed to find out much more about the man for whom she felt such hatred. A good grasp of the Japanese language was going to be crucial to the success of her mission, encouraging her to study as hard as she could. Kioshi was surprised at her eagerness to learn Japanese but was willing to help her as much as possible.

Her attempts at this strange language were the source of a great deal of amusement with Kioshi and Suzy, but gradually, Lisa gained more confidence and before long managed to speak not fluently but in simple sentences. She even found it possible to understand a little of what was being said on television, yet it was very difficult, as the speech tended to be too fast for her to follow.

Lisa was still responsible for looking after Kioshi's mother, whose health was slowly deteriorating. The old lady needed help with toilet functions, bathing, dressing and feeding and now took a great deal of Lisa's time. She was rewarded well by a grateful Kioshi.

During the daytimes, she would take Honako out in her wheelchair, providing the weather was good enough. The climate in Japan seemed to be cooler and wetter than that of the Philippines, but one bright, sunny day, Lisa was pushing the wheelchair through the streets of the city when a noisy commotion could be heard not far away. Curious to find the source of the noise, Lisa hurried along, wondering what she would discover. As they rounded a corner, crowds of hostile people were shouting at some public official. Lisa's understanding of the language was sufficient for her to realise that these were farm workers, which meant that the object of their anger was probably Yakamoto, a fact reinforced by many shouting the minister's name with a great deal of hostility.

Lisa kept her distance, not wishing to get caught up in the melee. A group of police was busy keeping the agriculture minister safe from the angry crowds, and Honako was beginning to show some signs of distress, encouraging Lisa to push her back towards their home, but not before she had managed to get a good look at Yakamoto struggling to keep on his feet in the swaying crush of bodies. There must have been many farm workers who would willingly have killed Yakamoto, but that would not have satisfied Lisa. She knew that the time was approaching when she would have to carry out her task, but she still had no idea how she could do so.

On their return, Honako rebuked Lisa for taking her so close to the riots. The strokes Honako had suffered were taking their toll on her brain and frail body, and she was growing noticeably weaker by the day. It was only a matter of time before her body gave up the fight. Until then, Lisa would take the utmost care of the frail old lady.

The riots were shown on television that evening, giving Lisa the opportunity to mention Yakamoto to Kioshi. "He doesn't seem to be a very popular minister."

"That's true," Kioshi agreed. "I don't know how he ever managed to become a member of the government. I can only assume that he used his money. He's very wealthy."

Lisa thought this sounded more like the Philippines, where the money of rich politicians was used to gain political power. "I suppose he has a fantastic house if he has so much money?"

"I believe so. He has a house in the smart residential area in the affluent southern Tokyo region."

"Really? Is he married?" Lisa was thankful for any information that might help her complete her mission.

Kioshi laughed. "He was married about thirty years ago, but his wife died in suspicious circumstances after only a few years together. There was quite a scandal at the time, but as ever, he managed to escape from it." Kioshi seemed almost embarrassed and lowered his head as he continued. "He is what you might call a man of doubtful morals. I understand that he still has..."

He paused choosing his words carefully. "Young ladies of the night are said to frequently visit his house."

This just had to be the right person. His character fitted exactly with what Allan had told Lisa as he had lain dying. Even in his seventies, Yakamoto still sought the 'comfort' that Monalisa had been forced to provide over forty years earlier. All this information would hopefully assist Lisa when the time was right.

After some discreet enquiries, Lisa managed to find Yakamoto's home address, which she carefully noted and hid away from prying eyes. Occasionally, she made the excuse of needing some fresh air to take a walk around the select residences, the objective being to observe any visitors to Yakamoto's place. Her efforts were not in vain, as she noticed several young women including, surprisingly, some Filipinas calling at the minister's front door.

There was a small park nearby where Lisa was able to sit and observe without making her interest too obvious. One night, a man approached her, probably assuming she too was a prostitute. She had realised that this might happen and had always dressed modestly to avoid giving the wrong impression. She quickly left the park, merging into the bustling crowds and hoping to lose any followers.

Lisa had, by now, a good working knowledge of the area and knew of many different ways to return home. Tokyo had a strong police presence, helping her to feel even more secure than in the Philippines. Of course, this could work to her disadvantage when she was ready to carry out her murderous task.

＊

Even with Lisa's meticulous nursing, Honako's health continued to deteriorate, and it came as no surprise when the life finally ebbed away from the old lady's frail, tiny body. The medication which Lisa so carefully administered had helped to ease the pain, and her passing was a quiet, dignified end to a very long life.

Kioshi was understandably upset by his mother's passing but was relieved that her long suffering had finally come to an end. Arrangements were made for the funeral, and Lisa realised that once everything had been sorted out, they would probably be returning to the Philippines.

Her timing had to be perfect: she would have to execute Yakamoto the night before her departure. She felt extreme anxiety at what was to be the most dangerous action of her life. When she had killed the military captain at the age of sixteen, it had been an impulsive act, giving her no time to think about the consequences of her actions, but this was very different. Her love for Allan would keep her to her word; there was no way that she was going to back out of the task so passionately requested by her grandfather.

While arrangements were being made for the funeral, Lisa was meticulously planning the assassination. There were still many troublesome thoughts, especially through her Catholic upbringing. Would God ever forgive her for carrying out such a deed? Would she be confined to spend the rest of eternity in hell?

She remembered all the details of Allan's funeral four years earlier, but the Japanese dealt with death in a very different manner. Both Buddhist and Shinto traditions had to be observed during the funeral service. There seemed to be endless prayers and speeches until eventually the casket disappeared for later cremation.

The thought of bodies of loved ones being burnt into ashes appalled Lisa, as this practice was unusual for the Philippines.

Kioshi had to make arrangements for the sale of his mother's home, and each night after dinner, while he sorted through Honako's belongings, Lisa excused herself, giving her time to walk close to Yakamoto's residence where she could observe who was going in or coming out of his house.

The pattern was fairly regular, with young women visiting him every Monday, Wednesday and Friday evening. They would arrive around seven o'clock and stay for about an hour. Lisa even began to recognise the women, as there seemed to be just three, each being allocated the same night every week. Lisa felt only a little guilt knowing that with her actions, their income from Yakamoto would cease. Presumably, they had other clients to rely on.

After a few weeks, Kioshi told Lisa that very soon all the loose ends would be tidied, making it possible for them to return home to the Philippines.

Nervously, Lisa asked, "Do you have a date booked for the flight?"

"Yes. The first Saturday in October. It's an early flight, at nine-forty, so we'll need to be ready early that day."

That was perfect timing, giving her the Friday night to carry out her task. "Good! I'm looking forward to getting back home to the Philippines."

On edge, Kioshi closed the door so that Suzy could not overhear their conversation. "Lisa, I have something to tell you. But first, you need to understand that Suzy must never know about this."

Lisa nodded in agreement. She could not imagine what could be so sensitive to preclude Kioshi's own daughter.

"You know that my mother had become very fond of you, especially for all the care and attention you showed her through her illness? Well... although she did not change her will to include you as a beneficiary, she asked me to ensure that you benefit from her estate after her death."

Lisa's eyes widened in amazement at this news.

Kioshi continued in even quieter tones, "I want you to have this." He took an envelope out of a cabinet and handed it to her. "There are three and a half million yen in the envelope. I know my mother would be happy for you to have this for all your hard work."

Lisa was staggered by his generous gesture and was almost lost for words. "I...I don't know what to say. Are you certain you want to give me all this?" She knew roughly the exchange rate between the Japanese yen and the Philippine peso, and using her agile brain, she quickly calculated that she was now about two hundred and fifty thousand pesos richer—something she had never even imagined possible.

"It was my mother's wish, and I will honour it. The money is yours to do with as you will."

Together with her savings back home, the money made Lisa quite a wealthy woman. "Thank you so much!" She quickly put it away as Suzy entered the room.

Over the next few days, Lisa ensured that all was packed ready for their departure. As the fateful night approached, she became increasingly anxious about her task but was able to blame it on the excitement of returning home.

Chapter Thirty-Five

I T WAS FRIDAY, the day Lisa had dreaded for so long, and she could only hope she had the nerve to go through with the execution. Even more importantly, she must manage to evade capture by the police. The last thing she wanted was to spend the rest of her life in a Japanese prison. She still had a major conflict between Christian ideals and carrying out her grandfather's dying request. Would she spend the rest of eternity in hell for committing such a serious offence against God?

Many nights had been spent turning this conflict over and over in her mind, and there were many times when she was convinced that she could not carry out her difficult task.

When it was early evening, she excused herself saying that she wanted to have a last look around the area before leaving Tokyo. It did not arouse any suspicion, as her evening walks were accepted as part of her daily routine.

Thankfully, it was a dry, clear night as she walked her now-familiar route. She waited in the park area for Friday's prostitute to appear. It seemed like ages, but eventually, she saw the young woman crossing the square towards Yakamoto's house.

Quickly, Lisa approached her. As they drew close, Lisa smiled at her.

"Komusta?"

This traditional Filipino greeting had the desired effect. The woman stopped and spoke in a soft, friendly voice. They had a brief discussion about their hometowns in the Philippines. It was clear the woman did not want to be delayed and arrive late for her appointment, as she began to walk again, although slowly.

"What is your name?" Lisa asked.

"Rosita. Now if you'll excuse me, I must hurry."

"I wonder if I could take your place at Yakamoto's just for tonight, Rosita?"

The woman stopped abruptly and looked stunned. "You know why I am going there?"

"Yes, and I'm willing to pay you twice what he would pay you. Just for tonight."

Rosita eyed Lisa with suspicion. "But why? Are you trying to steal my client?"

Lisa shook her head. "No. I will not be in Tokyo after this weekend, so you don't need to worry about losing your business." She did not bother to mention that after tonight, Rosita would have one less client to service.

Rosita's natural suspicion grappled with the desire for some extra income. "Okay, just for tonight. I could do with a break anyway."

Lisa heaved a sigh of relief and enquired what her fee was. She suspected that Rosita would probably inflate her usual rate, but Lisa did not worry about the expense.

"I still don't understand why you want to go with Yakamoto. He's old, smells a lot and has quite strange, specific requirements."

"Let's just say that it's been a lifetime ambition for me to meet Yakamoto. Can you very quickly tell me what his likes are?"

Rosita hurriedly described what she usually had to do for Yakamoto, saying, "You had better hurry now. He does not like to be kept waiting."

"Thanks so much, Rosita." Not knowing the intricacies of what a prostitute would do for their clients, Lisa was sickened by what she had heard from the young woman but accepted the information gratefully.

Plucking up all her courage, she approached the door which she had been observing for so long. Her fingers trembled as she pressed the door button, and she prayed to God that she would have the strength to see it through.

The door opened slowly, and the man whom Lisa had seen briefly on television appeared. He was surprised to see a stranger at the door and brusquely asked, "Who are you?"

"My name's Monalisa. Rosita is not well, and she asked me to come instead. She did not want you to be disappointed tonight."

The old man smiled broadly, appearing quite pleased to see this new face. "Please, come in." When he saw her face in the stronger lighting within his house, he stopped in palpable surprise. "Have I met you before? Your face looks familiar."

"No, we've never met. You must be thinking of somebody else." Lisa knew her resemblance to her long-dead grandmother had triggered something in his elderly brain, but for now, she let him puzzle over where he may have seen her.

"You are very beautiful and remind me of someone, but I can't remember who."

In a way, that annoyed Lisa more. Her grandmother had sacrificed her precious life because of this man, yet he did not even have the decency to remember her.

"Come. I'll show you the bedroom. Oh, before I forget, here's your money." He handed over a bundle of notes, and Lisa mumbled her thanks, quickly stuffing them into her pocket. She could well understand why so many women turned to prostitution; it was much easier than working long hours for a living, although the thought of having sex with a stranger was horrifying.

The bedroom was sparsely decorated and smelled musty. Lisa felt weird walking into an old man's bedroom, especially when he expected to have sex with her. "Do you have any special…talents, Monalisa?"

"Oh, yes. I think you will find that I have a few surprises in store for you." She did not intend following Rosita's advice about his personal preferences, especially those more perverse sexual routines Rosita had described in graphic detail. Lisa started to unbutton the old man's clothing. He obviously enjoyed her touch and very soon was completely naked, displaying a strong erection. This surprised the naive Lisa, who thought that a man of his age would not be so easily aroused. She had only seen an erect penis once before, when she and Juan had sexual intercourse in Cebu.

Yakamoto's penis was not as long as Juan's but perhaps a little thicker, and in his excited state, he began to fumble with Lisa's clothing. She knew that if she was to be convincing, she would have to endure the embarrassment of exposing herself to the old man, who was now desperate to get close to her skin. It was something Lisa really did not want to do, but she had no choice.

"It's all right. Here, let me help." She unzipped her dress and let it fall to the floor. Stepping out of it, she seductively removed her bra and pants, standing facing him completely naked.

Oddly, she did feel a little aroused by her closeness to Yakamoto, together with her own nakedness. Lisa thought again about Juan seducing her at the Mercedes Hotel in Cebu. She also remembered her vengeance, when Romayla had cut his penis short. It had been very satisfying. Still, providing her plan worked, she would soon be able to end the old man's life.

Yakamoto's lusting eyes penetrated her embarrassment, and she knew that he was ready to have intercourse with her. She shuddered as he put his hand on her breast, yet her nipples hardened under his touch.

"What a superb body you have. Come, let me enjoy you."

"Not yet. I told you I have a few surprises." Lisa opened the little bag she had been carrying and carefully removed a small vial and syringe.

263

Yakamoto suddenly looked anxious. "What is that for?"

"You don't need to worry about this. In the Philippines, we have developed a harmless drug which makes a man's erection last for at least two hours. You'd like that, wouldn't you?"

She saw the glint of interest in his eyes. "Yes. That sounds a great idea. Okay. Where do you want to inject it?"

"It takes effect quickest when it is injected directly into the main vein in the groin area, but I promise it won't hurt. I'm well practised at using syringes. Now, if you lie on the bed, I can make it easiest for you."

"On just one condition," the old man said.

Worried by this possible diversion, Lisa asked, "What is that?"

He smiled and said, "Give me oral sex first."

Lisa gulped at this request. Rosita had told her oral sex was one of his preferences, but she had hoped she would not have to do it or anything else.

Boldly, she replied, "I'm not used to doing oral sex. Isn't there something else I can do for you?" Her heart was beating fast at this unexpected turn of events.

The old man looked hard at her. "Oral sex is one of the easiest and most pleasurable things to do. If you want me to continue, then it is oral sex or nothing."

Realising that if she did not satisfy this requirement, she may fail in her mission, she plucked up courage and asked, "Okay, how do you like it?" She felt revulsion that after exposing her naked body to his greedy eyes she was going to have to submit to his sick demands.

"It's very easy." He lay down on his bed, still looking at Lisa's firm breasts, and grasped his penis, displaying it proudly. "Take as much of this in your mouth as you can and make me come by sucking." He patted the bed to the side of his body.

"Come on here, Monalisa. This will put you in the best position to satisfy me."

Lisa really did not want to do this degrading act but climbed on the bed by his side and knelt, his sweaty penis entering her open mouth.

"More! Deeper down, and suck hard," he insisted.

She did as he ordered, feeling as though she was about to gag as his thick penis reached the back of her throat. As she sucked, she felt his organ harden even more, and then he was pushing even further into her mouth. She put one hand on his testicles and gently squeezed, caressing him seductively. He seemed to like this and moaned in ecstasy. Lisa was surprised how quickly his movements and her sucking resulted in a sudden squirt of semen into her mouth.

"Swallow it, Monalisa," he instructed in a firm yet dreamy voice.

Lisa had not expected this. She thought that she would be able to spit it out somewhere, but where? With no choice, she did as he requested, finding the taste of his semen a little salty and utterly revolting. Still, she placed a smile on her face to keep the old man happy.

Lisa thought that this would be enough, yet the old man said, "That was good, Monalisa. Now I want you to place your knees on the bed, one on each side of my head, so I can pleasure you."

This was not going as Lisa had planned, and there was no way of avoiding his demands. Moving the pillows to one side, she knelt as instructed with her crotch directly above his mouth. As she looked down at his body, she noticed that his penis was still standing very erect. She felt an involuntary shudder as he pushed his tongue deep into her vagina, moving it about, exploring this sensitive area. She felt her face flush and was surprised to feel hot and excited by this intrusion into the most personal, intimate area of her body, accompanied by convulsions of sexual pleasure, a soft moan escaping her lips. As if this was not enough, she felt a wetness from her, which Yakamoto greedily swallowed. He handed her some tissues to dry herself as she climbed down from the bed, her breathing still faster than she had expected.

Although Lisa felt repulsed at having such strong sexual responses to the old man, she also had a strange feeling of guilty pleasure, which she had certainly not expected.

After wiping between her legs, she tried to compose herself, determined to return to her original plan. "Okay. Now I will show you what I can do for you."

He was still lying on his back, his erect organ pointing straight up. Lisa flipped the cap on the vial and sank the needle into the rubber seal, filling the syringe as she withdrew the handle. Satisfied that she had the correct amount, she located the vein in Yakamoto's groin and without hesitation injected the solution through the skin. After emptying its contents into Yakamoto's blood stream, she removed the syringe and returned it to her bag. From there, she took out a bottle of fragrant oil.

"While that is taking effect, I am going to give you a massage you'll never forget." He did not argue and lay obediently as she spread the relaxing oil over his vast expanse of aging skin. She noticed his eyes closing as he relaxed under the spell of her manipulative fingers. She no longer felt any embarrassment as she knelt naked on the bed, moving around Yakamoto's recumbent body, concentrating on her long-planned mission. She heard him sigh with pleasure as she ran her nimble fingers up and down his inner thighs, letting the back of her hand brush lightly against his testicles.

At last, she calculated the time was right and pinched his skin slightly to waken him from his slumbers. His eyes widened as he looked up at Lisa, who was now standing at the side of his bed. "What is it? Why have you stopped?"

Ignoring his questions, she said coldly, "Do you not recognise me yet, Captain Yakamoto?"

Her use of the word 'Captain' must have at last struck poignantly into his memory.

"I'm Monalisa Tiguelo, granddaughter of the woman you abused and killed over forty years ago."

First a frown and then a sudden look of realisation crossed his broad face. "What are you doing here? What is it you want?"

"What I want is justice for what you did to ruin my grandparents' lives. The only payment is the ultimate sacrifice—your life."

For the first time, Yakamoto looked worried. In an attempt to save himself, he reached towards the head of the bed, and it was then that he realised he had been drugged. His limbs felt so heavy, he found it impossible to make any quick, concerted movement.

Lisa looked where Yakamoto had been trying to reach and noticed a tiny button on one of the panels in his bedhead. Cautiously, she pressed the button and was amazed to see the panel slide smoothly to one side revealing a secret cavity. Concealed within the space was a small revolver and a folded piece of paper. Taking a tissue out of her bag, she placed it over the gun and lifted the weapon onto the bedside table, well out of Yakamoto's reach. She was wise enough to know how to avoid leaving incriminating fingerprints.

In a desperate effort to save his life, Yakamoto said, "Listen, Monalisa, I can make you a very rich woman. Spare my life and I will share a secret that would change your fortune beyond belief."

"I'm not interested in your money. I promised my grandfather when he was near to death that I would kill you, and I intend on keeping my promise. You have only minutes to live, so if you have a god, you had better start praying to him right now."

"No, please listen to me, Monalisa." He pointed to the paper still lying in the compartment. "That is a map showing the location of Yamashita's gold still buried in the Philippines. Spare me and you will never regret it. You will be rich beyond your wildest dreams." Although he probably did not yet realise it, his speech was becoming less distinct from the increasing effects of the drug.

Lisa laughed. "You really don't know anything about me, do you? You think that I have just drugged you so I can suffocate or stab you? The fact is, Captain Yakamoto, that you are already dying. That injection I gave you ten minutes ago was a huge dose of pure morphine. It's working its way around your body, and within another ten minutes, you will die. Nothing can be done to save you now, even if I wanted to!"

With this sudden realisation, Yakamoto sank back and closed his eyes. Tears ran down his cheeks as he was forced to accept defeat. Lisa looked with contempt at this once-feared military commander, whose naked body was finally shedding the last vestiges of life. His erection had now deflated, reminding her of Juan after his minor operation. She began to pull her clothes on, but she was not ready to leave just yet. Lisa kept checking Yakamoto's pulse until at last, she was satisfied that there were absolutely no signs of any remaining life in the old man.

The police would be thoroughly checking the room for forensic evidence once Yakamoto's body was discovered, and Lisa was going to have to be meticulous in removing any signs of her presence. Satisfied that nothing remained to link her with Yakamoto, she was just about to leave when she had a sudden thought. The paper which was supposed to indicate the location of Yamashita's gold was still lying in the secret compartment.

Picking it up out of curiosity, she unfolded it and looked at the ancient map, which at first glance did not indicate any place familiar to her.

As it would no longer be of any use to Yakamoto, she folded it once again and put it into her small bag, along with her few other incriminating possessions. Finally, she replaced the gun in the compartment and closed the panel, amazed by how cleverly the space had been concealed.

Now that she had actually carried out the execution, her heart was beating faster than ever as she prepared to leave the house, hopefully without being spotted, but as she reached the front door, voices of at least two men could be heard approaching Yakamoto's house. Another second and she would have walked straight into them. Standing motionless behind the door, her heart pounding, she prayed that the visitors did not have a key or her discovery would be inevitable.

After what seemed ages, the voices grew quieter as the men walked away. Lisa waited a few minutes longer and then cautiously opened the door. Thankfully, there was nobody in sight, allowing her to slip quietly away from this house of death. She deliberately walked a route that would be difficult for anyone to follow. When well away from Yakamoto's house, she dropped the deadly syringe into a waste bin. There were so many drug addicts in this area, it would be virtually impossible to connect the weapon to the body.

Before she became too confident she had escaped without being followed, a heavy hand landed on her shoulder, and she spun around, startled and expecting to see a policeman ready to arrest her.

Her heart raced as she faced the man, but as soon as he spoke, it was obvious he was drunk and looking for a prostitute.

Turning away, she tried to continue her journey. Yet again, he put his hand on her shoulder, tugging at her. Even in his drunken stupor, he was much stronger than she was and started to paw at her breasts.

Seething with anger at this unwanted attack, she raised her knee and struck her assailant firmly in the testicles. He let out a loud gasp of pain and released his hold of her, clutching his genitals. This gave Lisa the opportunity to escape, and she ran the rest of the way, tumbling through the door to Kioshi's mother's house, breathless from her exertions.

"What's wrong, Lisa?" Kioshi asked as soon as he saw her. "What happened to you?"

"Some drunk thought I was a prostitute and tried to attack me, but I managed to knee him in the groin and escape."

Suzy heard this and laughed at Lisa's bravado, while Kioshi seemed relieved.

"I was worried for your safety. It can be dangerous for a young woman to be out around here this late at night."

"I just had to see Tokyo for one last time."

This experience had temporarily taken Lisa's mind off what her real purpose had been and was useful in concealing her anxiety. Earlier that night, she had not been certain that she could go through with the execution. It was against every religious doctrine she had been taught, and the only consoling thought was that it was what her grandfather had wanted and asked of her on his death bed. She slept uneasily that night, troubled by her conscience but also excited to return to her homeland.

She rose early next morning and helped Kioshi to pack all their belongings. Still nervous that the police would come to arrest her, she jumped when the door bell sounded. It was the taxi arriving to take them all to the airport. Once they had loaded all the luggage and were on their way, she felt a little safer but would not feel completely secure until she was out of Japan and back home in the Philippines.

Chapter Thirty-Six

THE STONY-FACED OFFICIALS dealing with passport control made Lisa extremely apprehensive. Even though she doubted Yakamoto's body had yet been discovered, she was convinced the guilt showed on her face as the official inspected her passport. At last, after all the formalities, they were able to board the aircraft and relax for the seven-hour journey back to Singapore. As the huge wheels lifted off the runway, Lisa gave a sigh of relief. Now the only problem she had to face was her own conscience, which could take quite some time to come to terms with—if she ever did.

Tired after her troubled night, she fell into an uneasy sleep, tormented by vivid dreams of Yakamoto chasing her. He was carrying a huge hypodermic syringe with which he was trying to inject her. She awoke with a start to find a stewardess offering her a meal. Beads of perspiration trickled down her face as she struggled to return to the upright position and take the tray. She had no appetite but ate nevertheless and went back to sleep, only waking up as they approached Singapore.

Changi Airport with its unusually relaxing atmosphere felt very welcoming to her after the contrasting bustle of Japan's busy airport. There was a three-hour wait before their connection, giving them the opportunity to look around the duty-free shopping areas. She bought small gifts for her mother, father and Romayla and was looking forward to seeing all of them after her fifteen-month stay in Japan.

271

Lisa really felt as though she was nearly home when she was able to board the smaller aircraft ready to fly to the Philippines. Even though she admired the grace and beauty of the Singapore Airlines stewardesses, it was still a welcoming sight to see the Filipina flight crew on this three-and-a-half-hour journey. At last the plane touched down on the runway of Mactan Airport and taxied to a halt and everyone gathered their belongings.

Much more relaxed now, Lisa walked behind Kioshi and Suzy as they joined the stream of passengers jostling to leave the plane. It was nearly four in the morning, and the airport lights pierced the blackness, dazzling the weary passengers. The familiar smell and sounds of the Philippines gave Lisa a feeling of security and comfort as she walked down the steps leading from the craft.

As she stepped onto the concrete, a security guard who had been watching the passengers disembark approached Lisa. "Miss Lisa Tiguelo?"

Her heart sank and her mouth suddenly became very dry. "Yes? What is it?"

"Please come with me, Miss. We need to ask you a few questions."

Kioshi intervened, asking, "What's wrong, Officer? Why do you need to question Lisa?"

The guard turned to Kioshi. "And you are, sir?"

"I'm Lisa's employer. What is she supposed to have done?"

"I'm afraid I can't go into detail, but it's in connection with a suspected murder. I suggest you carry on with your journey, and if we need to question you, we will be in touch."

Kioshi and Suzy watched, open-mouthed and motionless, as Lisa was led away.

The guard was armed, making Lisa tremble with fear as she timidly followed his instructions. She could not understand how they had managed to identify her so quickly. She was led to a waiting car and told to sit in the back. Sullen-faced guards sat on either side of her, and for the thirty-minute journey, not a word was spoken. Although Lisa had no idea where she was being taken, it was a safe assumption that it would be the police headquarters in Cebu city.

The car stopped outside a large, anonymous building, and she was told to get out. Obediently and full of sadness, she followed the guard into the building, through several hallways and eventually to a closed door at the end of a long corridor. The guard knocked and waited for a response.

A voice barked, "Enter!"

The guard pushed the door open, and Lisa was motioned to step inside.

She found herself in a large office with just one man sitting behind a huge desk. The man, who was probably in his mid-forties, clean-shaven and wearing a smart police uniform, was reading and did not lift his head as he said, "Take a seat, Miss Tiguelo."

She sat, bowing her head in shame for her awful predicament. The man ignored her while he read a sheaf of papers. After what seemed like an eternity, he lifted his head and leaned back in his chair, putting his hands behind his head in what appeared to be quite a relaxed manner.

"You've given me quite a problem, Miss Tiguelo."

Lisa said nothing.

"The Japanese State Security is requesting an extradition order on you in connection with the suspicious death of one

273

of their government ministers, a Mr. Yakamoto. Do you know of this man?"

Lisa nodded her head.

"Did you kill him?"

"Yes, I did." Her voice was almost a whisper as she confessed her guilt. "I killed Yakamoto." At this point, she burst into tears and buried her head in her hands.

The man showed no sign of concern. "Perhaps you could help me out a little. Why did you feel that you had to kill this man?"

"I had no choice. My grandfather asked me to do this for him four years ago, as he was dying. It was in revenge for my grandmother's death at the hands of Captain Yakamoto during the Japanese occupation of the Philippines in the 1940s. This man used my grandmother as a comfort woman, even though she was married and had a son—my father. I don't want to die, but if it has to be then I will sacrifice my life in honour of my grandparents."

This statement seemed to move the man. "As Chief of Police, I'm aware of Yakamoto's wartime reputation." He pointed to the thick sheaf of papers lying untidily on the desk. "I've been reading of all the crimes he committed against the people of the Philippines over forty years ago. If it is any consolation, I sympathise and understand your position."

"How did they connect me to Yakamoto?" Lisa asked. "I thought I had been careful in avoiding possible detection."

The police chief smiled. "I'm afraid Japanese technology caught you. As a government minister, he was obliged to have a security camera outside his house, recording images of all visitors. When Yakamoto's body was found, the recordings were checked, and you were identified as probably the last person to see him alive. By the time your passport picture was matched with the recording, you were already on the flight from Singapore to Cebu. That is when the Japanese authorities requested that we detain you for questioning and probable deportation to face the authorities in Japan."

Lisa felt foolish and was annoyed with herself for being identified so quickly, especially after all the precautions she had taken. "So what happens to me now?"

"We have to get you on a flight back to Japan. You'll have a police escort and will be handed over to the authorities on arrival in Tokyo."

Lisa hung her head in shame at the thought of being forced to return to face prosecution and probable life imprisonment.

Looking at the sorry figure in front of him, the police chief rubbed his chin and said, "There is one possible alternative."

Lisa lifted her head. "What do you mean?"

"Well, I could say that you resisted arrest and were shot dead trying to escape."

"Why would you do that for me?" Lisa's heart pounded with excitement at this possible reprieve.

"Let's say that as a Filipino, whose family also suffered during the occupation, I have little liking for those Japanese who ruled our country all those years ago. For a young woman such as yourself to have not only found this war criminal but actually had the courage to execute him, you have my greatest thanks and admiration."

Lisa could not believe her ears. "I would be eternally grateful if you would do this for me. I just want to see my family again."

The man looked serious and shook his head. "No. If I use that story, you must literally disappear, even from your own family and friends. Otherwise, you will be caught and I will be in a great deal of trouble for allowing you to evade justice."

Lisa's heart sank once again. She knew he was right. Even though she considered Kioshi a good friend, he would not be able to keep her secret. It would hurt so much not to see her family again, but she reasoned that was preferable to rotting in a Japanese prison or, worse still, being executed. She remembered when, at the age of sixteen, she had joined the New People's Army and had accepted the possibility of separation from her family in order to serve her country.

"Okay, I will agree to that. I don't know how to thank you enough."

He smiled. "It is me who should be thanking you for having the courage to rid the world of this evil monster. Now, we need to work out our plan so that it is believable."

Lisa had a sudden thought. She pulled her wallet out of her handbag and removed some money. "My family are very poor. If you could give this to them, it would make a big difference to their lives."

The policeman looked doubtful.

"Please. If you want them to believe that I'm dead, then passing on the money I'm carrying would be the natural thing to do.

Thoughtfully, he said, "Okay. I promise they will receive this." He took an envelope out of a drawer, inserted the notes and wrote Lisa's mother's name and address on the front. Lisa also gave him a couple of personal mementos to add to the evidence of her demise.

The one item she decided to retain was the chain and locket her grandfather had given her when she was a small child. It meant so much to her that she could never bear to part with it. The money, still in Japanese yen, was equivalent to about fifty thousand pesos and would make a vast difference for her mother while still leaving Lisa with enough to start a new life.

"I want you to stay here while I get something," the police chief said. "The fewer individuals who know about this deception the better."

Lisa waited patiently, and after a few minutes the man returned. He was carrying a woman's police uniform and a pair of scissors. He gave a nervous laugh as he said, "I'm afraid I'm not much of a hairdresser, but we have to shorten that very distinctive long hair of yours."

He placed a waste basket in a suitable position to catch the locks of beautiful long hair that Lisa had spent so many years growing and grooming and snipped gingerly until, with her hair cropped short, she looked like a completely different person.

"I'll spare your modesty by looking away while you change into this uniform." True to his word, he turned away while Lisa removed her dress and replaced it with the regulation uniform. It was a bit too large for her, but it would serve its purpose. She hoped she would not have to wear it for very long.

"Okay. I'm ready now."

He turned back to face her and seemed satisfied with the results.

"I'll take your dress and return it to your family once I've put a few bullet holes through it."

Lisa could see a flaw in his plan. "It won't have any of my blood. I think we need to make it a bit more convincing. Do you have a clean pin?"

"Yes, I think so." He opened a drawer in his desk and searched through all the contents. "Will this do?" He handed Lisa a badge with a pin attached to the rear.

"That should work." She rustled through her bag and brought out a plaster and a small plastic bottle with a screw top. The tough police chief grimaced as Lisa used the pin to penetrate the skin on the inside of her elbow, puncturing the vein. A trickle of blood ran from the wound and dripped into the bottle. When she was satisfied that there was enough, she quickly stopped the flow and placed the plaster over the wound. Once again, she was thankful for Romayla's superb medical training, knowing that her body would soon replenish the missing blood.

Screwing the top onto the bottle, she handed it to the police chief, who for all his training looked shaken by Lisa's brave actions. "What will you say when they ask for my body? They are bound to want a decent burial for me."

"Practically every day we're finding the bodies of young women who have overdosed on heroin. I'm sure we can find one to send them, especially if we put your dress on the corpse."

Lisa shuddered at the thought of another woman's body being sent to her family, but it was the only way for her to escape being sent back to Japan.

She then thought about the Philippine custom of putting the recently deceased in a glass-topped coffin for relatives to mourn and see for nine days. When she mentioned this to the policeman, he thought for a few moments and said, "If we're able to find a woman's body where the face has been disfigured by gunshots, the normal mourning routine may be waived."

Lisa hated the idea of her parents suffering like that. Would it work? Could it work? She felt terrible at this planned deception.

Satisfied that they had covered every possible aspect, the policeman said, "Come with me and we'll get you out of here." Together, they walked along the corridor, the police chief directing her through little-used areas to the closest exit. As they stepped out into the early morning air, he said, "I suggest you adopt a new identity. Remember that Miss Lisa Tiguelo has been killed while trying to escape."

Lisa smiled at the police chief. "I'll be eternally grateful to you for all your help. Will you tell me your name, please?"

The police officer gave her a warm smile. "Alfonso Lopez. Perhaps we will meet again someday, Miss Tiguelo. Good luck with your new life and change of identity."

Saved from a dangerous, uncertain future by the actions of this police chief, Lisa smiled and walked away from the police station. Her freedom felt strange, especially since she was now dressed as a policewoman.

Traffic was already heavy through the streets of Cebu as she caught a jeepney heading towards the quayside. Arriving near the ferry terminal, she sought out a money exchanger. All her currency was still in Japanese yen, and when this was converted, it gave her a total of two hundred and ninety thousand pesos. Out of this, she spent four hundred pesos on a one-way ticket to the island of Mindanao.

After a long, uneventful journey, she arrived at her chosen destination and caught a jeepney to Marbel. It felt like such a long time since she had left the place of her childhood, yet everything still seemed to be exactly the same. Lisa had to use some of her money to buy new clothes and a strong rucksack to carry her few belongings. She felt a little conspicuous in the police uniform and was relieved when she was able to discard it and change into normal, comfortable clothing. A pair of white, close-fitting jeans, pale blue cotton top and a denim jacket made her feel properly dressed again. She was ready to make the journey to the small cemetery where her relatives were buried.

To her disappointment, her grandfather's grave had not been kept tidy and required some clearance work around the stone before she was satisfied. At last, when all the debris had been removed, Lisa stood up, made the sign of the cross and said a silent prayer.

Overwhelmed with emotion, tears ran down her cheeks as she spoke.

"Dearest Lolo, I did as you asked, and I am proud to have avenged my grandmother's death. What I need now is God's forgiveness for what I have done. Lisa Tiguelo no longer exists, and I am reborn as Maria Lopez. From now on, I will do everything in my power to help the ordinary people of the Philippines. Not another mouth to feed but still a child of God's with even greater needs."

Epilogue

Although Lisa Tiguelo has been forced to change her identity to avoid arrest and imprisonment in Japan, this is not the end of her story. There will be at least one more novel, possibly several, following her further adventures—assuming that my mind and body permit me to continue writing in my old age.

J. S. Raynor
December 2022

About the Author

John Stephen Raynor, born in 1944 in Oldham, Lancashire, was diagnosed with a serious progressive eye condition, retinitis pigmentosa.

At fifteen, he began working in architecture, eventually becoming a self-employed software developer and marrying his first wife in 1967. Sadly, the long hours building up his business took their toll, and the couple separated in 1989.

It was in the Philippines he found his soul mate, whom he married in 1993. Her experiences are the inspiration for much of John's fictional work, including his first novel, *A Comfortable Death*.

After twenty years of keeping diaries, John drew on these to publish *A Chronicle of Intimacies*, followed by *Who wants to be British?* – the two autobiographical works describing his most traumatic period.

Registered blind since the age of thirty-five, John relies on his computer with speech synthesis for software development and creative writing.

Also by J. S. Raynor

Fiction

Cocktales & Nibbles

Cocktales and Nibbles is a collection of twelve stories, ranging from the shortest such as 'Lite in the Sky', which was my first story written in 1973, to the lengthy 'A Universal Threat', written in 2017. The title of this book, Cocktales and Nibbles, is meant to signify the short stories as 'Nibbles', while the longer stories are representative of the 'Cocktales'. Please forgive my change to the spelling of  'Cocktails' – this is how my mind works! These stories were written over a period of forty-four years.

The Gaudi Façade

Adam Sheldrake, a young British architect, travels to Barcelona for what should be a fairly ordinary holiday. By chance, he meets beautiful, talented, twenty-seven-year-old Italian artist Caterina Fonteras at the Olympic Stadium, and from this point, the holiday turns into a life-changing experience for both of them.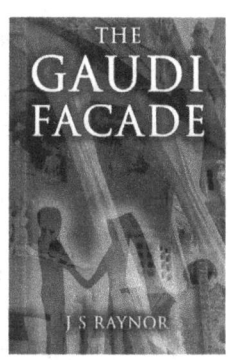

With a common interest in Antoni Gaudi, the famous Spanish architect, they visit the

Sagrada Família and are drawn into a world of violent fanaticism, resulting in their capture and imprisonment. This romantic thriller, set in the year 2012, leads the reader into many twists and turns, a major threat to the Catholic faith and some quite extraordinary revelations.

See All Evil

When British soldier, Alex McCloud is injured and blinded in Afghanistan during 2011, he is offered the chance of sight using bionic implants, developed by Professor Goldman of Moorfields Eye Hospital in London, in conjunction with Augmented Reality specialist, Major Jennifer Sherlock of the CIA.

These implants not only provide him with sight but much, much more, proving to be of great interest both to the MOD and the CIA. His new life as an intelligence officer based in London brings him many challenges utilising his unique abilities.

Autobiographical Works

A Chronicle of Intimacies

It was 1991 and John Raynor's life was in a mess. At forty-six, two years after separating from his wife, he was living on his own and the future seemed very bleak. And then, there was Carol, a divorcee two years younger than him. Suddenly, everything changed, hopefully for the better. The bond was immediate and intense. The problem was that one day, Carol would need John, both physically and emotionally, while the next, she would be secretive, cool and distant.

284

This is the true account of a sixteen-month relationship which turned John's life upside down, with the added complexity of him being registered blind. During this period, he travelled to Paris, Amsterdam and Singapore and made close friends with Wendy, Angeline, Jasmine, Mirz, Amanda and Sarah, but Carol had stolen his heart. Everything is factual, except for Carol's true identity.

Who wants to be British?

Following on from the turbulent events described in A Chronicle of Intimacies, John Raynor's luck seemed, at last, to be turning in his favour. In January, 1993, he flew from Manchester to the Philippines to meet Aleth Ledres, a Filipina twenty-three years younger than him. The two had been writing for several months, and within a short space of time, they fell in love and their marriage was planned for April.

Unfortunately, nothing was ever simple for John and Aleth, as many problems seem to prevent them from enjoying a life together in the UK. Cultural differences, the Catholic Church and British immigration officials all seemed destined to destroy any chance of future happiness. This true account of the couple's romantic adventures echoes the uncanny forecasts of the psychic's predictions.

Find out more about John's previous and upcoming works on his website: www.jsraynor.co.uk

Beaten Track Publishing

For more titles from Beaten Track Publishing,
please visit our website:

https://www.beatentrackpublishing.com

Thanks for reading!